OWEN BAILLIE

THE BATTLE OF HELL RIDGE BOOK ONE

BLACKOUT

aethonbooks.com

ALSO IN SERIES

Blackout
Invasion
Resistance

ACKNOWLEDGMENTS

Thanks to my old mate Trevor Bacon, who again spent a lot of time weeding out silly plot lines and bad character choices. Trev seemed to enjoy this story more than others so hopefully that translates into happy readers. And to Kim Richardson who always gives me a lot of great content to think about. Kim nailed exactly what I was feeling this time, and again, helped strengthen the story with her feedback.

Thanks to Nicholas Sansbury Smith for reaching out and connecting me with Aethon Books, and to Rhett C. Bruno at Aethon for taking a chance on this. To Lauren Carruol, also at Aethon, who edited the story, thanks for your hard work to fix all my mistakes, and the content feedback that surely made it better.

PROLOGUE

November 8, 2022, 07:42.

Shandong (17), Type 002 Aircraft Carrier, South China Sea

Senior Captain Zhu Yao slid out the plush leather chair and sat at the polished wooden table in the main conference room on A deck. A dozen empty seats surrounded him, and he hoped the cold emptiness of the room wasn't a presage of what was about to occur. He adjusted the cuffs of his shirt, brushed the fabric of his dress jacket, ensuring there were no creases or fluff and that he'd meet his superior's expectations.

On the vast wall at the front of the room was a one hundred twenty-inch screen displaying an empty square where Zhu's colleague would soon appear. He'd received a dispatch to attend the O Group at twenty-three hundred hours the night before, with no forewarning as to what the meeting was about or why he had been sought. All he knew was that it was an unofficial meeting with the Assessment Committee Chairman—but not any of the other members. Usually, the committee met every two weeks, but the last meeting had been less than a week ago.

Something was wrong, Zhu thought, as he sipped hot green tea from a ceramic cup on the table. No, not wrong, but something had *changed*. Four of them had been meeting for eighteen months now. Why was he the only one to meet with the General now? Zhu checked his watch again, just to be sure. 0754. He was safe. He had made it his business to be timely all his life and it had played a small part in helping him climb the ranks of the Chinese Navy from lowly Seaman Apprentice, before switching to a commissioned officer position and then eventually to his current position as Senior Captain of the *Shandong* aircraft carrier. Back in his small country village, his parents had drummed punctuality and self-organization into him and it had helped impress the hierarchy along his pathway.

There was movement on the screen and General Yang slid in behind the camera, his clean, serious face filling the screen. He was the highest-ranking officer Zhu had ever dealt with and Chairman of the Assessment Committee. He had a flat face and thick jowls; his neat hair had mostly turned grey.

"Senior Captain."

"Hello, General."

Zhu always kept his comments short. Truth was, the man scared him. He had the power to end his career—his life for that matter—at the push of a button or a spoken word. Whilst Zhu was a Senior Captain and wielded considerable power aboard his ship, he was playing in a bigger pond now, with a very big fish that liked to bite the heads off other fish when it pleased him.

"Apologies for the short notice, Captain. It couldn't be avoided." Zhu nodded. "This is not an official gathering for our South Pacific Strategic Operation, so I won't run through the normal agenda" Now Zhu would learn what had initiated the meeting. "We're bringing forward our D-day. From April to late January." Zhu felt his stomach drop. "Our Superiors feel that the Australia Day celebration at the end of January will provide advantageous timing. It still gives us eight weeks to get ready. Is that going to be a problem, Senior Captain Zhu?"

Zhu shook his head from side to side. "No, sir." It was a problem, but less of a problem than telling General Yang that the new D-day was unachievable. "No problem, sir."

"Good." General Yang gave a stiff smile. "That's it." He began to move, then paused, looked directly through the camera to the conference room on the *Shandong*. "Our job is to *serve the people,*

Captain. We are making history. *Changing history.*" Zhu said nothing. "Don't fail us, Zhu. Failure would be catastrophic. This will be our people's finest moment."

Zhu nodded. "I wont, General."

But Zhu's hands shook as he gripped the chair and waited for the General to leave.

ONE

Sunday, January 22, 2023
Day 0

Heat. Like a blanket, smothering his skin and suffocating his will to breathe. Twenty-something years of Victorian summers through January and February, ninety-five klicks, or almost sixty miles north of Melbourne, Australia's second most populous city, and you think he'd be used to it. Some days it could reach forty-six, or one hundred and twenty in the old scale. It wasn't quite that hot on this day, but there was no end to his perspiration until the sun fell well below the western horizon; relief, usually on a cool breeze, was an absent friend. Sometimes, it would linger at a hundred through the night and anybody lucky enough to sleep soundly would feel like a million bucks the next day.

Parker Richardson sat in the hills of Kinglake on the banks of the King Parrot Creek, a tributary of the mighty Goulburn River, with his fishing rod in the water and a not-so-cold beer at his side. It was peaceful, a contrast to his life for most of the last twelve months that had included his mother's death, the downward spiral of a business with his best mate, and the eventual separation from his long-term girlfriend. He thought about Maise momentarily. They had broken up a little over a month ago after two and a half years of dating. It was still raw for Parker. Not his decision. But he was teaching himself not to dwell on it too much anymore.

His good mate, Sam, would arrive soon and probably jump right into the stream to cool off. Parker had reached the Hell Ridge camping spot earlier that day for a two-week trip. They had been planning it since spring when they'd had their last adventure. Both worked through Christmas, staying on call for their respective companies—Parker as a plumber, Sam as an electrician—and now had finished a number of work commitments in the lead up to the Australia Day holiday so they could enjoy the extended break. Once Sam arrived, Parker would really be able to relax, enjoying the companionship and laughs of his second oldest friend.

Through a cluster of tussocks and blackberries, the tip of Parker's fishing rod quivered. He leant forward from the plastic camping chair, gathered up his beer and took a quick sip, watching with interest. Although the creek was shallow and clear enough to occasionally see the camouflaged shape of a cruising trout, it had produced its fair share of fish over the years. Parker had been driving up the mountain road with his father and friends since he was barely old enough to hold a fishing rod. Back then, they slept in the back of his dad's station wagon on thin layers of foam and cocooned themselves in sleeping bags. The memories were still sharp, but they stung with nostalgia. Somewhere along the road, Parker had progressed to camping with his mates, or alone, purchasing most of his own gear, with a little bit of his father's old equipment that was still more reliable than most of the high tech modern stuff you could buy these days.

The rod tip stopped moving. Parker decided it was probably the current, or a stick. He settled back into his chair and nestled his beer into the pouch in the arm. Even with a stubby holder, the beer was warming quickly. He preferred it ice cold but wouldn't complain. It was the first time he'd had a drink in weeks, and actually felt good about it. Maise would be proud.

His thoughts drifted back to her. This time, Parker didn't push them away. He felt bittersweet about the break up. Maise had been a catch, no question about it. She received plenty of attention from other guys—girls too. At five and a half feet, she had dark, wavy hair, neat, precise features, and made any outfit look stylish. She was clever too, far better at numbers than Parker would ever be. She could total up the groceries without the register and used it as a challenge on the days she was particularly bored. Working at the IGA was not the peak of her career, though, Parker was certain of that, but she did it part time to supplement the accounting degree she was enrolled in at Latrobe University as a mature age student. Parker was proud of her ambition and commitment. Although he had never told her, he wished he were more like her in a number of ways.

The break up had been coming though. In fairness, Parker probably hadn't been the easiest boyfriend to get along with over the past twelve months. His mother had passed away in February after a long battle with breast cancer. He'd never really experienced loss and his mother's death hit him far worse than he had antici-pated, despite its imminent arrival. He had felt himself spiraling, but was helpless to do anything about it. Parker had pushed those close to him away and his already indulgent drinking habit had gotten worse. After a time, and at the tireless insistence of his father, he had spoken with a psychologist. But he had never told Maise or his friends about the sessions. He'd made some bad deci-sions and the business he ran with his best friend—Maise's brother, Mark—had struggled with Parker's lack of effort. Parker had used business money to feed his gambling habit—something he wasn't proud of and felt the sting of shame every day. Parker and Mark had ended up parting ways in business and in friendship. The whole period made him feel sick. Everything he'd worked hard to build had crumbled following his mother's death.

Would Parker and Maise ever get back together? Everyone thought so. But Parker wasn't so sure. It wasn't his choice—Maise had been the one to end it. Well, they had both sort of agreed—Parker saw the relationship ending in a fireball and was smart enough to realize if he didn't agree to the break they would never speak again. Truth was, he still cared deeply about Maise and always would.

A gentle breeze tickled the gum trees and Parker closed his eyes, feeling a welcome coolness on his skin. When he opened them, he saw the rod tip vibrate, what his old man would have classified as a genuine bite, and he felt the familiar pull of excitement. Things were looking up—he was almost out of beer and would have to return to camp and refill soon, but with the breeze, the heavily scented eucalypt gum trees overhead and the stars soon above, he could get very comfortable here catching trout all night long. This is what he needed; recently, his days at work had dragged out, he'd been hitting the snooze button on his alarm more often and arriving on the job sites later each morning. The site supervisor, Nathan Wales, had challenged him and after Parker had confessed to his mindset, Tom had suggested the extended break so Parker could rest and reset himself.

The end of the rod bent over and Parker leapt forward out of his seat, placing his hands loosely around the reel, ready to strike.

"Come on, baby."

He focused on the tip, waiting for the critical moment.

It bounced again and he snatched the rod up, lifting it high, setting the hook. Halfway across the creek, a circle of water exploded, the fish's tail slapping the surface as the trout fought to escape.

"Yes!" Parker shouted. It was nice to know the fish were biting; it would be one of their main food sources for the next two weeks.

The rod curved downward and he began winding as the fish torpedoed upstream and then down, splashing water in a circle. The long arm of a tree branch poked above the surface to Parker's right, so he pulled the rod left to avoid the trout using it to aid its escape.

In a few moments, he had the fish flopping in the shallows; it was too small to keep and he did not need the food yet, so wanted to keep it breathing. It flipped, attempting to dislodge the hook. He wet his hands; a trick his father had taught him many years ago to avoid damaging the fish's protective coating, then took the trout in one hand and the hook in the other. He backed the hook out and kept hold of the fish in his left hand.

Parker pulled his phone from the front pocket of his shorts. A low battery message flashed on the screen and he dismissed it.

Only 1% remained. He was never any good at keeping it charged and he'd be lucky if it lasted another minute.

He dialed Sam's number for a Facetime call and waited. His best mate's troubled expression appeared.

"Hey mate," Sam said. There was an edge in his voice Parker hadn't heard in a while. Parker turned the phone around and showed the fish. "Nice one. Too small to keep, but a good start."

Parker released the fish then turned the phone back on himself. "I'm on 1% so my phone will probably die, but you all good? You sound stressed."

Sam looked around. "Not sure, mate, but it's really strange down in Whittlesea at the moment."

"What do you mean?"

"Some big things have gone down in the US and Europe. They're saying it might be a terror attack, but basically, those countries have gone dark."

"Dark?"

"You know, anything with a microchip isn't working. There's no communication with the US. Most of the Internet has shut down. E-mail servers are down. Networks are down. Most of the websites don't work. The news reckons if you try to call someone in the US, you get nothing. Same with Europe."

Parker switched feet nervously. "How do you know this?"

"It's on the news. They're saying they don't know too much yet, but everyone's on edge about it. Even the news readers sound worried."

"Weird. What's the cause?"

"You know what an EMP is?"

"Yeah. Electro magnetic pulse."

In the distant sky, a brief flash of light shone, causing Parker to look up through the trees. He waited for a repeat, but only the barest crack of thunder sounded. Parker held his gaze, but after several seconds, he lost interest. *Storm must be on the way.*

"That's it. Either from a solar flare or—"

Parker's phone died. The battery had finally given up.

"Shit."

He sighed and sat down in his chair and stared out at the

gurgling water. Europe and the US were under attack of some sort. That was massive, but he couldn't help but be surprised if he really thought about it, given all the challenges the world had faced over the last couple of years. From fires and floods, to riots and looting, and COVID-19—several times over. This was probably just another trial they'd all have to face. It seemed as though it was a yearly thing now—somewhere in the world, masses of people fighting for their lives. He just hoped if Australia was affected, that people wouldn't suffer the way they had through the fluctuations of COVID.

Parker swallowed the last gulp of his beer and tipped the final dregs out into the grass. Maise's brother, Mark, had often teased him about it. If he was honest, Parker missed the banter with Mark. They both gave as good as they got.

With the trout rod lying over a clump of tussock grass on the bank, Parker climbed out of his chair and walked the thirty or so yards through the ferns and bushes back to the campsite. It was a public place; about a hundred and fifty yards from the main road at the bottom of a dirt track at the northern end of Flowerdale, in what would have been Hazeldene before 2014, when the Murrundindi shire joined the two locations.

The campsite had evolved though all the trips—big and small—over the last twenty years and was simple, yet efficient. A four-man tent sat as the centerpiece, where they slept, with a smaller two-man tent beside it for their supplies and the two fridges. Two three meter by three meter Coleman gazebos were erected at the front of both tents to provide extra shade and protection if it rained. They had planted an old generator twenty yards behind the tents, running on low speed, keeping the fridges cool and supplying power to the lights at nighttime. It was rusted and noisy, but Parker and Sam tuned out it's annoying whine, having used it for so long. His father had purchased the thing along with an electric fridge back in the early 1990's and Parker never had the heart to stop using them after his father had ceremoniously handed them over five years ago. Under the gazebos sat two six-foot long trestle tables where they ate and prepared meals. On one table was a small butane gas cooker with two burners that ran on those little cans of inexpensive gas. Parker always had a huge store and had purchased ten packs of four on special. They wouldn't need that many for two weeks, but he could use them for their next trip.

Parker tossed his phone onto one of the airbeds he'd blown up using the electric pump. He'd charge his phone later after Sam arrived; he could do without it for now. Part of the point of camping was to leave technology behind. They had no TV; no laptops or I-pads; his phone was the only connection with the outside world. There was nobody besides his father—who was travelling up north—with whom he regularly spoke now.

From the coldest fridge, Parker took another two beers, now with icicles around their necks, and walked back to the creek. It might rain soon, given he'd heard the thunder and seen a flash of lightning off in the distance, but he didn't mind after a hot spell. He would cool off in the rain, hopefully catch a few more trout, and not allow the stress of the last twelve months to ruin his evening. And when Sammy came, they would shoot the shit, drink a few more beers, and probably wake up with a headache.

TWO

Maise Turner was bored. So goddamn bored she was about to throw a scourer sponge or a bag of donuts at the next customer who complained to her. That's what she'd like to do, although she knew she'd never actually do it. Maise rarely responded to customers complaining with anything other than a smile and a nice word.

The grocery store in Whittlesea was set up like most Independent Grocer of Australia stores in small country towns. Sliding door entrance, barriers that sent you to the fruit and vegetable section, then the delicatessen, fresh meat, a row of frozen foods, then aisle by aisle of other items, finishing with toilet paper and tissues. The store was cozy and only had two registers at the front. For a Sunday afternoon it was quite busy and teenage part-timer, Stef, joined Maise to service customers.

She'd given up trying to tally the value of the items before she'd scanned them through the register. That was too easy. Numbers came to her like some people could carry a nice tune. Whenever they were involved, the answers just appeared in her mind. What she couldn't do easily today was get through the time she had to spend blipping people's items over the scanner and placing them carefully into their bags. Today, the heat and her general feeling of boredom tested her mental strength. Still, it was a job, and she was grateful for that. It allowed her to study full-time and help her brother pay the bills. After the death of their father two years ago, Maise and Mark were essentially parentless. Their mother had walked out on the family when they were toddlers. In the beginning, it had been difficult, neither sibling knowing exactly how to play their part in running the house. Maise had been full of ideas, but getting them out—convincing Mark, had taken time. Expressing her opinion was not her strength, even though Maise knew her ideas were generally better than most. But they had worked it out. Maise had conditioned Mark and eventually he had learned to take equal care and responsibility. They still had their mother's brother, who worked at the local police station, to call on when needed.

Ninety-minutes, Maise thought, checking her I-phone as the last customer passed through the register. Whenever she checked her phone, she couldn't help but expect to see a message from Parker. It was silly, she knew, but old habits took time to die. Even though she had ended things with Parker a month ago, she still cared for his well-being. It was hard to let go and she still worried about him. Through the grapevine, she'd heard he and Sam were going camping. Whenever Parker went camping with his mates, she worried about him. He had a tendency to drink too much and end up falling over and hurting himself or doing something stupid like jumping into the shallow creek from a tree. To top it off, he was after all, out in the bush, and even the locals knew there was danger in that. The snakes alone could turn a person's blood cold, not to mention the spiders, the bats, and the myriad of other things. But they had all grown up trudging through the long grass, over rocks and beside the creeks. They had seen their fair share of snakes and spiders and been lucky many times. She hoped he'd be safe.

A new customer arrived with a trolley load of groceries. "G'day." Maise smiled.

"What's good about it?" the middle aged woman said. She had a bright pink blouse on, with silver blonde hair in a large bun and carried a handbag over her shoulder. Maise's eyes widened. "My husband is stuck on the couch at home watching the cricket. I'm here shopping when I'd rather be on holiday."

Suck it up, Princess, Maise thought. *We'd all like to be doing something else.* "I'm sorry to hear that. Hopefully your afternoon will improve."

The woman rolled her eyes as Maise checked into autopilot and began to swipe her goods. Her mind wandered back to Parker and she felt the familiar seed of sorrow.

It could have been different between them. Maise felt she had given Parker so many chances. But in the end, she wasn't prepared to comprise his selfishness when she was so willing to be unselfish. Parker always found a reason not to spend time with her; always another boys trip away, another post-football match party, or a night at the pub. They just didn't spend enough quality time together. Sure, there was after work in front of the television, which she loved, but at least one night every weekend, Maise was alone. And when they did attend a party or catch up with friends, Parker would end up drunk, unable to get himself into the car, or walk home if they were close by. And then, if he wasn't throwing up in the toilet, he was asleep before his head hit the pillow. The last few months had been the worst. They barely saw each other. He never came to the house because of Mark. It wasn't her fault that he and Mark had fallen out of friendship. It had become her responsibility to drop into his place and she did so several times a week. It hadn't always been that way. Before his mother had died, they had spent every other night together and Parker's behavior had been far more caring. Maise had berated herself long enough for resenting his actions and allowing his behavior to continue because of his mother's death, but in the end, not even that was enough.

Maise scanned the last item into the bag, totaled up the list and set the customer up to pay by credit card. When Maise handed the woman her receipt, the old bat didn't even look at her.

"I hope your afternoon gets better," Maise said, false smiling. *But I doubt it will because complaining is your life's work.*

Maybe Mark was right about Parker. He had persuaded Maise that she could do better. After their friendship broke, he had been in her ear repeatedly about Parker's lack of commitment.

According to Mark, Maise deserved more—someone who *wanted* to spend time with her. It wasn't that her and Parker's time together wasn't fun or enjoyable, there just wasn't enough of it. He was selfish, self-centered, more focused on himself than anyone else. That was the bottom line. All Mark did was reinforce the things she had already identified. Maybe it just wasn't meant to be.

Several people headed toward the register at the same time. One was Keith Whitehead, the other, a smallish blonde woman with sunglasses on the top of her head and a trolley full of goods. Keith took an extra step and pushed in front of the woman.

The lady stopped, mouth open. "Rude?"

"Sorry," Keith said, flashing a smile that revealed unnaturally white teeth. "I've just got a few things. Will only take a sec."

"Hey Maize," Keith said, his smile widening. He placed a handful of items on the belt.

Keith had strong blue eyes and medium length blonde hair suffocated in gel that he tousled to look like he'd just gotten out of bed. He was always at the gym or sucking down one of those protein shakes. He was good looking and charming, and unlike Parker, he *liked* spending time with her. Maise knew because she had dated him for almost six months. There were many aspects to Keith that Maise liked, but she just couldn't hold a serious conversation with him. For Keith, it was all about sports or cars. His whole life revolved around those two things. At least with Parker they could talk about entertainment or the news. It made her sound like a snob, but Maise enjoyed those discussions. With Keith, they simply did not exist and never would. He wasn't a bad guy—though he could be terribly chauvinistic and sometimes had a short fuse—and was devastated when Maise broke it off. He was also a local sports star, and as juniors, had been one of Mark and Parker's biggest rivals, particularly Parker. They hated each other and Keith carried some silly theory that Parker had stolen Maise from him.

"Hi, Keith." They had remained on somewhat friendly terms. Maise hadn't deleted him as a friend on either Facebook or Instagram, probably because she had been the one to end it. She felt a little guilty. There would come a time though when that guilt would pass, and she'd cut him off entirely. Keith on the other hand, still wasn't over the relationship.

"You still wasting your talents on this place?" He looked around, as though offended by the fact that she was working in a supermarket. "My dad's plumbing company is looking for a new receptionist. You know he'd give you that job tomorrow if you wanted it."

She couldn't imagine anything worse than working for Keith Whitehead's father. She had avoided spending time at Keith's house because of him. He was an overweight slob who had no understanding of manners or courtesy. He chewed his food like a pig and spoke to everyone as though they served his existence.

"Thanks, but I'm studying right now, so I need the part-time flexibility. Should have my degree by the end of next year."

"Yeah?" Keith asked, his face washed with surprise. "In what?"

"I'll be a qualified accountant, remember?" she asked proudly. And she was proud; after a couple of early jobs in financial admin roles, she tossed it all in to go back to school on the recommendation of the Financial Controller at the last place she worked.

"For real? Wow. Who'd have thought? You never said anything about doing that when we were dating. " *I did*, Maise thought. "Good on you, though. I always knew you could do anything you wanted."

That struck Maise. "Really?"

Keith put a hand out, touched hers and looked into her eyes. "Maise... I spent half my time when we were together telling you how smart and amazing you were. Don't you remember?"

"Not sure it was half your time," Maise said with a smile, retrieving her hand. He was complimentary though. Sometimes over the top, and she had wondered whether it had been fake.

"Maise, I swear, I always thought it and still do. You're the smartest and most capable woman I've ever met."

She watched his expression for a hint of sarcasm or falsity. She couldn't detect either. "Okay." She shrugged. "Thanks."

Smiling, Keith nodded towards the cigarette counter behind her. "And a pack of Winnie Blue's."

"You're smoking again? I thought you gave up?" Maise reached around the front counter for the cigarettes.

"I'm on and off," Keith grinned.

Maise tossed the cigarettes onto the counter and finished preparing the payment transaction. "That's fifty-three eighty."

Keith fished his wallet out of his back pocket and removed the credit card. "Hey, I heard you weren't going out with Parker anymore."

Maise waited for the sarcastic addition. Normally, Keith couldn't bring up Parker without it. "Yeah. It's true."

"Well, I was kinda thinking then, what about us maybe going out sometime? You know, start off small, grab a coffee or maybe a drink. You can tell me about your degree?"

The distant rumble of thunder sounded. Suddenly, the lights cut and the supermarket fell into darkness. The green text on the register disappeared. Several groans and comments sounded. The big green EXIT sign at the entrance and the soft white globes that lit the coolers near the back of the store had gone dark. The sliding doors had stopped halfway open. Screeching tires rang out from the car park outside followed by the heavy thud of a car crashing into another. Glass shattered, tinkling for a second or two, followed by voices, shouting and calling out. Someone ran away from the entrance in the direction of the crash.

Maise paused in action, catching Keith's eye.

"Might have been a smash," Keith said, noting the same surprise.

"Can I come back to you on that?" She asked, somewhat absently as she glanced around the store.

"Sure," Keith said, his expression reflecting surprise that she hadn't immediately turned him down. "Sure thing."

Keith, along with several other people, stepped away from the counter to look out the door. Several people suggested their phones had died. Maise turned to find Mr. Olsen, the Store Manager, scuttling along the busiest aisle from the direction of the milk, his neatly combed hair unmoved. He wore a red standard issue IGA shirt with black slacks. He must have been hot, Maise thought, and would only get hotter now that the air conditioning was out. She did not particularly like him; he was overbearing, thought he knew everything, and did not listen to other people's opinions. But she respected his position.

"Bloody power's out," Olsen said, hands on hips. "That's all we need. Frozen food will be stuffed in hours if we don't get the generators working."

"Hopefully it doesn't stay off for long. Knowing our power company, though, it might be hours before it's back on."

Several people had put their shopping baskets down and left the store. *Lazy turds,* Maise thought. She knew who was going to have to put the stock back.

"Finish off the customer and then get any of the stuff they leave out put away. We won't be able to process anything but cash until the power comes back on."

"What about the manual credit card machine, I think we still have a couple under the counter."

"Cash only," Olsen said, and scurried away.

Keith returned. "I can't process this on credit now," Maise said. "Well, I could but Mr. Olsen doesn't want us using them."

He sighed, then grinned. "Lucky I'm all cashed up." From his back pocket, Keith took a fat wallet, retrieving a fifty and a five-dollar note.

She gave him a thin smile. "I'll have to write out a manual receipt."

She processed the order and wrote out a receipt for Keith, including the date, time, sale value, and the items, since it was only a handful. Keith waited, smiling, then took the receipt and stuffed it into his pocket like rubbish.

"I'm sure the power won't be out for long," he said.

"Hope not."

"You working late? I can come back and check on you later."

"That's sweet, Keith, but not necessary. I'll be fine."

There was a glint in his eye and a curve in his smile that told her in that instant if she'd asked him to get back together he would have agreed.

"Well," he said as he turned his back and departed the check-out, "I'll keep an eye on things, anyway."

"Thanks, Keith."

He stopped at the doorway and turned back to her. "You know, I've never gotten over you," Maise said nothing. "I know you moved on and went with Parker and all that, but for me, I'm still waiting."

Maise nodded. "I'm sorry for how it ended. But at the time, it just wasn't meant to be."

Keith watched her, waiting for a response, but Maise had said enough. Finally, he smiled, waved, and left. Momentarily, the reasons she had broken up with him seemed distant. He looked out for her, and she never wanted for time with Keith.

The next customer reached the checkout, snatching Maise from her thoughts as more people passed by having abandoned their goods to see what had happened out front of the supermarket. Anybody else might have left the register just for a moment, but not Maise; sticking to her post was important.

"Am I gonna be able to pay for this?" A woman with dark skin and short, curly black hair asked. She was a regular customer; Maise knew she liked diet-Pepsi, cheese balls and mild salami.

"Do you have cash?" The woman shook her head. "I can only do cash right now." The woman shrugged and left her overflowing trolley where she was standing and marched out of the store.

Ass. Maise suppressed the notion to tell the woman to come back and return the stock to every location from where she took it. But she didn't say it. *Couldn't.* For some reason, it just never came out. That was something she was working on; being more honest; telling people what she thought.

The queue was empty. Maise pulled her phone from the front pocket of her black standard issue IGA trousers. It was dead. She held the power button and tried turning it on again, but the empty screen only stared back at her. *Odd.* It had been more than half charged earlier.

She stepped around to the other side of the register and took the woman's trolley, steering it back down the aisle towards the relevant locations so she could return the items to their shelves. After she'd emptied the contents, she collected up four baskets and did the same with them, opening and the closing the refrigerator doors as quickly as possible to maintain the low temperature. Some appeared to be working with the generator power; others were dark. Bags of ice filled the last two fridges and they gave Maise an idea.

Back at the register, she checked her phone again, but it still wasn't working. Mr. Olsen returned, already sweating. The air conditioning had been a savior for him. His forehead was slick, exacerbating the furrows of his brow, and for the first time in her working life at the IGA, his Lego hair had broken its mold.

"I put all the items back," Maise said. "Do you want me to gather all the ice and start filling the refrigerators that aren't working?"

"Some of them aren't working?" Maise shook her head. "Bugger. We paid Henry's hardware big money for those generators just to keep the fridges working. I'll take that up with him tomorrow. How much ice is there?"

"There's about forty or fifty bags in the big freezer."

"Good idea. Spread them around evenly."

"Someone just walked out with their shopping," a slight blonde lady in high heels said. She adjusted her glasses. "Just walked out without paying. You believe that?"

"Damn thief," Olsen said. "Do you know who she was?" The woman shook her head. "Make note of anyone who steals something," Olsen added. "Names, and if you don't know them, take descriptions." She nodded. "Thanks, Maise."

Another round of shouting sounded from the car park beyond the main doorways. As Maise left the register, an elderly man in a blue-checkered shirt, tan colored pants and cropped grey hair stumbled through the entrance.

Adjusting his glasses, he called out in a raspy voice, as though he'd never been able to quick that pack-a-day habit. "It's China and Russia. I read it on Facebook 'fore the power went down. They've set off a bomb in the sky and knocked out all the 'lectricity. America and Europe have been hit too."

Several more people spilled into the supermarket, bumping the old man into a plastic Labrador dog used for collecting money for the Guide Dogs charity. They snatched up baskets and hurried into the aisles.

Olsen had returned, glancing at Stef and then back to Maise. "Jesus, it's the whole COVID thing all over again. Half the township will be down here. We'll be out of stock in an hour." He walked towards the man by the plastic guide dog. "Stop spreading rumors, John. Somebody's probably just knocked over a pole on Plenty Road. Power 'll be back on by 11:00 PM tonight."

Jasmine Taylor, or Jas, as they called her, reached Maise's register. "Hey, babe," Maise said. Jas was Maise's closest friend. She was Sam's girlfriend, too, and not long ago, there had been six of them in their group that were as tight knit as a grass-weaved mat—Maise, Parker, Sam, Jas, Mark, and Raven. Maise and Jas had gone through school together, from kindergarten to high school graduation. Not always in the same class, but always the closest of friends. They texted or chatted every single day, even if the last thing they said to each other was goodnight.

"Can you believe this?" Jas asked. Shorter than average, her height difference with Sam was exacerbated when they stood together. She had thick, brown hair that cascaded below her shoulders, a broad, steely white smile, and lovely olive skin that Maise envied all year round. She'd avoided braces all through her teenage years until she'd almost hit her early twenties and then found out she had to wear them for two years. Her opinions were plentiful; strong and vocal too, and Maise loved her for it.

"Hopefully the bloody power is back on soon," Maise said.

"No way, love. Did you see the news?" Maise shook her head. "Everything died when that thing exploded up in the sky. That's what happened in America." Jas paid cash for her milk and eggs. "You wait, you're gonna get so busy in here. You know what people are like. COVID all over again, babe, remember?"

"How could I forget?"

They chatted momentarily, and then Jas bid Maise farewell—they would talk later—and as she passed through the entrance, others crowded back into the store—two, three, four, seven, then ten. They were noisy and in a hurry. People were sensitive to anything related to a potential disaster now, Maise thought, whether it was COVID, floods, fires or supply chain issues. She recalled the challenges of the previous year when the IGA couldn't receive the normal volume of deliveries because there was a shortage of wooden pallets. People were now very quickly able to recognize a potential disruption to their lives and take immediate action. Maise thought the place was going to be anything but boring from here on out.

THREE

M ark Turner leaned against his Toyota Hilux parked beside the bowser of the United Petroleum service station, peering at his reflection as he held the nozzle to fill his Ute with diesel fuel. He was slightly above average height, maybe six-one, and that lucky combination of lean and muscly from all those years of digging holes and manual labor. He hated the gym and was lucky enough that the physical work he did as a plumber kept him fit. He wiped the sweat from his brow with the back of a tanned arm—he spent a bit of time in the sun and although his sister Maise harassed him about covering up his skin, he liked the rays. His blonde hair went a bit lighter and his half-Scottish skin turned a soft, milky brown. Lately though, he had yielded to her constant reminders, purchasing a floppy hat to keep the sun off his face, and slapping on sunscreen at the beginning of each day. That was about as much as he could commit, and only because his sister hounded him. He would readily do most things Maise asked to keep her happy.

His dog, Mindy, a black kelpie with tan paws and a similar color patch on her face stared at him from the tray of the Ute, as keen as Mark to get home after a long day on the jobsite. Mark was a plumber, running his own business—only two years old— and times were tough. People didn't like paying their accounts on time, despite having the work done at a level on which Mark prided himself. There were plenty of plumbers in Whittlesea that were happy to charge less but couldn't match the quality. Often, he received the calls from people where jobs had been botched and he had to go in and clean up the situation. Mark guaranteed doing it right the first time, even if he wasn't the cheapest going around. Things wouldn't have been so difficult if it hadn't been for his ex-business partner, Parker Richardson—Maise's ex-boyfriend—with whom Mark had worked until halfway through the previous year. He buried the reminder for another time. It was the end of a tough day, and he just wanted to get home and relax, maybe even take a quick swim in the pool. He always tried to refuel his Ute before he headed home so he could get straight to the job first thing.

Mindy gave a light bark. *Hurry up.* "Yeah, yeah. I'm tryin'"

He finished filling the tank, slotted the nozzle back into the bowser, then gave Mindy a scratch behind the ears. She was a fabulous dog, only three years old, but smarter than half the blokes he knew. She followed Mark everywhere and did just about everything he asked. The day just wouldn't be the same without her. After breaking up with his girlfriend Raven, two weeks ago, Mindy was just about all he had left.

"Stay in the car, will you?" Mindy wagged her tail at him.

Mark started across the fuel station towards the door, head down, in his mind, already at home with his feet up on the couch, watching cricket and enjoying a cold beer.

"Mark?" He looked up and spotted a customer outside the shop. "Mark. It's me, Bill Richardson. Parker's Uncle."

Parker's Uncle. Mark stiffened. He'd attended half a dozen family gatherings and barbecues to know Bill quite well. They always talked when they caught up, whether about football or business. Bill was a good guy, but he hadn't seen Bill since he and Parker had parted ways. Mark hesitated, then stuck out his hand. "Hey Bill. How's things?"

"All right, mate. How 'bout you?" Mark nodded. "We're taking the boat out," he waved at a gold Nissan Patrol 4WD with a twenty-foot speedboat parked at the side of the fuel station. "And heading down the beach for a few days over the long weekend."

Mark had once stayed down there with Parker and Maise. "Nice rig. Should be good."

"Yeah. We're looking forward to it." Bill looked Mark up and down. "You well mate?"

Mark tipped his head from side to side. "As can be expected after a pretty crazy year."

"I heard about the thing between you and Parker. Sorry to hear." Mark wondered what *the thing* entailed, whether Bill knew the whole story. "Look, Mark, I know Parker made some mistakes, but he's had a rough trot. His mother—"

"I get it, Bill, but there's more to it than that. It's not just about his mother. That was a tough situation, but Parker did some things that went beyond the effects of that. He can't keep using it as an excuse."

Bill's face changed to one of disbelief. "It's a pretty big motivator for going off track though, don't you think? A fair excuse for making some mistakes?"

"Not the level of mistakes Parker made. I lost my dad too, I didn't steal money from my business partner and gamble it away."

"I get that, mate. It's not a good look, but nobody got hurt. And he's incredibly remorseful. Neither of you have spoken since it happened. Couldn't you just—"

Mark shook his head. "Nuh. I'm done with him. Parker's had his chance. You know he never even had the guts to apologize directly to me? Never once said sorry mate, I stuffed up when I took the money. It cost me my reputation and a whole lot of work. I'm still paying back debt for it. And it's still costing me because the work was so sloppy during the last few months of Parker's time." Bill looked down. He saw there was no argument for the points Mark made. "I'm the one sitting in bed at night wondering how I'm going to pay the mortgage, Bill."

"I hear you, Mark. I do. Parker made some stupid mistakes. But life is about more than this. You guys were great mates. If only there was a way to forgive."

"Yeah, well, I can't see it."

The faint, almost imperceptible sound of distant thunder made them both look up underneath the massive awning towards the sky in the south. Mark crouched a little lower to try and see further. The lights in the store suddenly went out. Mindy began to bark.

"Excuse me, Bill," Mark said, heading towards the dog.

"Yeah, I've got to push on too, Mark, take care," Bill said. He went into the store.

Mark reached the back of the Hilux and put a soothing arm around Mindy. She continued to bark at some unseen menace, even with Mark comforting her. Her tail was stiff and her ears flattened against her head.

"What's up, girl? What is it?"

An overweight man in jeans and a white polo shirt said, "Pumps don't work, man. No fuel coming out. They just stopped halfway through."

From what Mark could see, everybody had the same issue. The digital display on his bowser, the one he had only just used, was blank. Didn't the place have a generator for this sort of thing? Power outages were not uncommon in heavily treed places where lines were sometimes knocked down.

"This is like that thing in America," the white polo shirt guy said.

"What thing?"

"Heard on the news before that something had happened. Their power is out. Internet and phones are gone. They've got nothing working."

Someone from another car shouted that their phone didn't work. Mark opened the driver's door and reached into the center console. He took his I-phone out and found the screen blank. He pressed the home button. When nothing appeared, he held the power button, waiting for the logo to flash up, but the thing wouldn't function. He couldn't recall if it had low charge or not. An uneasy feeling passed over him. *Just a power issue, that's all. Phone towers are down.*

He tossed the phone back into the console and headed into the store. The line to pay had grown. *Bugger.* This is all he needed. Mark just wanted to get home. The discussion with Bill Richardson about Parker had not helped. His head pounded.

Inside, Bill was number three in the queue, while Mark was seventh. Mark caught Bill's attention. "What's up?"

"Power is out. Systems are not working and we can't pay by card."

Mark had cash. He was probably okay. He held up a fifty-dollar note. "I'm safe."

"Good for you," Bill said with a smile.

Mark went forward to the counter and caught the attendant's attention. Three of them were trying to figure out what had happened.

"Pump six, Vikram," Mark said, handing the fifty towards an Indian guy with a beard.

"Ah, thank you, sir. Can you just wait a moment? My colleague will need to check the pump."

"No info on the pump, mate. It's all blank." The men looked at each other.

A guy shouted from the doorway, "My car won't start. Nobody's car will start."

This was new and unexpected. Mark stiffened. A phone was one thing, but cars were a completely new level. The three attendants now looked more confused and began talking to each other in their native language.

"I'm good," Mark said, and started to leave. He wanted to check his Hilux. The idea that it might not be working made him uneasy.

"Good luck," Bill said as Mark passed.

"You too."

Mark crossed the concrete walkway amongst a number of people now standing around talking animatedly about the situation. Others were at their cars trying to start the engines; some leant against the hoods as if they had given up. Mindy wagged her tail as Mark approached. He climbed in behind the wheel, paused momentarily as he set the key into the ignition, then held this breath as he turned it.

Nothing.

The dashboard was dark. There wasn't even a click to indicate the battery was operating.

He sat there thinking. He turned the key to off and tried again. Still nothing. What could it be? The power was out. Phones and cars were not working. What did that guy say about America? Something about them being dark too. The word Terrorist usually meant a bomb or something of that nature, but if this was a terrorist attack, it was completely different to any attack Mark could recall. And usually an attack was isolated to one location, like a subway in a city, or a shop like that guy who took people hostage in Melbourne. They were a long way from the city.

Mark thought of Maise, his sister, who was working a shift over at the IGA store. If the power was out there, people would converge on the supermarket and that would put her under immense pressure. She could handle it, but Mark wanted to check on her.

He climbed out of the car and shut the door, locking it with the key. And while nobody could currently steal the car, he had tools and supplies in the back that he couldn't risk.

"Stay here, all right?" He said to Mindy, patting her neck and face. She wagged her tail again. "I'll be back." He walked away from the Ute and she climbed up onto the edge of the tray. "No." He waved her back. "Stay there, Min." She dropped back down into the tray. "Good girl."

Mark left the gas station and crossed the street, strangely absent of traffic. The IGA was only a block away as he began a slow jog. Along with Mindy, Maise was the most important thing in his life, and ever since their father had died, it had been his job to protect her. While Mark didn't know how the situation would impact the IGA, he wanted to ensure people were behaving themselves around her. There had been times during the COVID shortages where Maise had suffered abuse from customers. He wasn't going to let that happen again.

FOUR

I t was twenty-two minutes past the end of her shift, and Maise wondered if she'd ever felt so damn hot. Maybe the time the asphalt on the road melted and they walked all the way to Funfields Water Park on the outskirts of Whittlesea. She had floated in the shallows of the wave pool for an hour until the bright spots in her vision had disappeared. Now, the sweat trickled down her neck and behind her hair, covered her brow, and she could feel it under her arms, too. Wearing the standard issue IGA slacks hadn't helped. Even at some of her most intense gym sessions or during summer netball games she hadn't sweated this much. The air-conditioning was not working, the store was still full of people, and she felt a huge amount of pressure to serve them as quickly as possible. Some had simply left, other had been vocal about the delay, but nothing could curb their frustration.

"Come on, girly," an older man with bushy grey eyebrows said. His face was as red as the tomatoes people were buying.

Maise wiped her brow again. *Turd brain.* Maybe if you weren't wearing long grey socks with those horrible green shorts, you might not be so red in the face. "I'm trying, sir. Please be patient."

He scoffed. "Patient? This is a goddamn lesson in patience. If you people tried any harder you couldn't go slower."

Stef had left. She couldn't handle the pressure; it had never been in her character. Some of the shelf stackers had walked out too. Now it was only she and Mr. Olsen at the checkout.

At Maise's insistence, they had been able to get the manual credit card machines working. That was something. Several patrons had paid in cash and Maise had done what she did for Keith and wrote out a receipt. She told the customers if they had any issues with a specific item to bring it back for a refund, although, given she didn't think they'd have much stock left soon, people wouldn't be bringing things back unless they were poisoned or given diarrhea. The queues were already near the entrance doors, which now stood permanently open, their electrical mechanism no longer functioning. If they'd been able to keep them closed it would have helped contain some of the cool air from the handful of refrigerators still running on old generators.

"That'll be twenty-four eighty-five," Maise said, adding a third carton of milk to the total for a young woman with a black ponytail.

"Shouldn't you be using a calculator for that?"

Maise turned and picked up a calculator from the shelf, handed it to the woman. "You can do that check separately if you like, but, I assure you it is one-hundred percent accurate." The woman stuffed a twenty and a five-dollar note into Maise's hand, took the milk and glared at her as she left.

It was now twenty-six minutes since her shift had ended. She didn't want to leave Mr. Olsen in the lurch, but she wanted to get out of the oven and go home, find out what Mark was doing, what else was affected and when the goddamn power might be back on. She left the checkout and went to Olsen. Several people called out asking what the hell she thought she was doing.

"Mr. Olsen?" He looked up at her, frantically trying to process goods for customers and bag them with some semblance of efficiency. His face was flushed, and sweat dripped from the end of his nose. Any semblance of the Lego hair from earlier had long vanished, greasy black strands hanging down over his forehead.

"Hey, Maise. I really appreciate you hanging around like this. I'll be sure to let the store owners know how committed you are."

"Thanks, Mr. Olsen. Uh, when do you think we'll be able to shut the store? I really need to get home."

Olsen looked around, glancing at the faces of the customers growing angrier by the moment. "Gee, Maise, I'm not sure. We still have plenty of people waiting to buy groceries. I know your shift ended almost half an hour ago, but…"

She was impressed by his ability to talk with her, take stock of the situation and keep calculating and bagging items at a rapid pace.

Someone called out from Maise's line. "Get back to the checkout!"

She turned but could not see who said it. A woman at the end of the queue—someone Maise had thought she'd seen in there before with her kids—walked out with her groceries. "Hey," Maise called out, "you can't do that."

A man at the front of her queue said, "come on, lady, write up my goods, will you."

She glanced at Olsen and he nodded. "Just a bit longer, Maise. If you disappear, I'm worried they'll riot." He smiled, something she had only seen him do once or twice. "I'll pay you double time, for sure."

Finding it difficult to refuse, Maise returned to her register and began pricing up goods again, trying to keep up with Mr. Olsen's frenetic pace. Her arms had begun to ache and her lower back felt like she had a hot poker stuck in it. Normally she'd have had a break or two by now—normally, she'd have finished her shift. She had to grit her teeth and do what her dad had always told her when something became difficult—suck it up. But it did nothing to allay the comments and ridicule from the people in line, some of which she'd known since she was a young girl, that she had served many times before and in other parts of Whittlesea over the course of her life. She wouldn't forget their acidic tongues and annoyed faces. The growing anger drove her to work faster.

A racket sounded outside the grocery store entrance. Glass shattered and she heard the screeching impact of metal on metal. People gawked.

"Fight between two men," another said, returning to his spot in line. But the person behind him had taken the spot and wouldn't let him back in.

"You snooze, you lose," a young man with his hair tied up in a man-bun said. Maise despised the look. "You left the queue."

"But I just wanted to take a look at what was happening. You can't steal my spot for that."

The kid, who Maise knew from her high school days, turned away, still refusing to shift. The older man looked around for support, but nobody spoke. Nobody was willing to give up their spot, since many of them had been there for too long already. The man puffed out his chest, then turned and walked from the store with his groceries under his arm.

"You can't do that, Arthur," Olsen said. "I'll be reporting you to the police when this is all over."

Arthur stopped at the door. "No problem, Jerry. I'll be happy to pay for my goods then *and* any fine they want to impose just so I don't have to spend another moment in this bloody store with that ponce in front of me." Man-bun said nothing. Olsen threw his hands up in the air.

Three more people stuck in the line did the same thing. Maise didn't know two of them and wondered if Olsen did. Otherwise, they'd likely get the goods for free.

"Oh, come on, people. Have some integrity!" They did not look back. "This is worse than when COVID first hit. At least then, people waited to pay."

"At least the registers worked then."

Nobody else left without paying. A pretty, middle-aged woman with blonde hair, too much makeup and sunglasses on her head, spoke from third place in Maise's line. "It's because of this thing on the news about America and Europe Everybody's freaked out."

"What are they saying?" Maise asked.

"It's a terror attack. And if it's a terror attack, the power might not be back on in a few hours or even a few days. No power means no more deliveries and who knows how long it will go on for. That's why we're here for as long as it takes."

Olsen's face seemed to go a shade paler. Maise kept working the bag and calculating the cost of each basket in her head. Some people attempted to purchase large amounts of single items—things like toilet paper, flour and water, but Olsen knocked the people back and limited them to one item per customer. Maise tried not to listen to the chatter in the line, questions about what would happen when the food ran out, or the water, or when so and so needed medicine and the pharmacy had no more stock. The one that concerned her though was what happened when the police presence just wasn't enough to make sure people were following the law. She'd have to go and see her uncle down at the police station later on. He might know if it was just the power or if something bigger was going on.

When a tall middle-aged man tried to buy two lots of salami, Maise told him it wasn't allowed, and he could only have one. He tossed the extra salami at her and it struck her right arm, sending pain through her elbow.

"Go easy, fella," another man said.

Maise bit back a response that included the words *biggest asshole in the world*. She pushed on, but the lines of people cradling bread and rice cakes, biscuits and soups, because they couldn't fit them in their baskets or trolleys, only grew bigger. After a time, a man wearing a blue singlet top displaying the BINTANG BEER logo entered the shop and started yelling.

"Listen, everybody, stock up while you can. They reckon this thing is gonna last for a while."

Just as Bintang finished, a swarm of people converged through the sliding doors, bumping the man as they created a bottleneck into the aisle ways. Many of those remaining in the queue were pushed sideways. They pushed back and an older man fell over onto one knee. Olsen stopped bagging. So did Maise. People filled the aisles with trolleys, smacking them into each other with metal clangs.

"You better hurry up," someone called out from the line.

"Maise!" Amongst more people entering the store, she watched Mark, bustling his way towards her. "You all right?" He asked, as he reached her. Maise nodded, but she didn't feel all right.

"I just want this to be over," she said, slouching, hands resting on top of her dark hair.

"Let's go then."

Maise looked perplexed. "What do you mean?"

"Leave."

"I can't leave."

People in the line began calling out for her to start processing goods again.

"Just wait a minute," Mark snapped at them, holding a fierce stare at the people in the line, daring any of them to counter him. He had a reputation in the town for tough words and even tougher actions. He frowned at Maise. "But you just said you want this to be over."

"I do, but I can't *leave*. I can't bail on Mr. Olsen, or my job." She waved a hand. "These people."

Mark considered this. He brushed his fingers across his forehead, then wiped them on his shorts. Absently, he said, "Bloody hot in here. What time's it close?"

"What time are we closing up, Mr. Olsen?"

"Eight," he said. "Not a minute later. It'll be too dark to work in here by then."

"Fine. I'll pick you up at eight." She gave him a thin smile. "If anybody gives you any trouble, let me know." Maise nodded. He turned and walked out of the store, snarling at the people in the line as he passed.

FIVE

Mark was back at the IGA supermarket just before eight. People continued filing into the store, but Olsen did a good job of ushering them out and providing encouragement to return tomorrow, reminding them that there was still enough food and supplies if they arrived early. Mark waited outside the entrance for Maise. She walked out through the doors with Olsen and they watched the older man as he secured the entrance with a padlock.

People were out; more than usual, even though it was still warm, probably twenty-eight on the Celsius scale. The streets had a low key party vibe—maybe New Year's Eve, or even Australia Day—which was later in the week—after a long afternoon of swimming in pools and eating sautéed lamb off the barbecue. Mark lost count of the number of wooden stakes holding cups of citronella burning thin wisps of black smoke along the streets. They were usually used to keep mosquitoes away, but now, without streetlights or porch lights, people were using them as lamps to light their front yards.

Maise had a bag full of supplies and they walked towards the service station. Mark wanted to check on his car again, maybe even push it out of sight and away from the bowsers if he could.

"You have any more trouble?" Mark asked, crossing Laurel Street, where the remnants of two car accidents sat within view of the intersection of Church Street. All four cars had been pushed to the side of the road.

"No," Maise said, adjusting the groceries. Mark held out his arms and took them from her. She smiled. "I didn't tell you that Keith came in earlier."

Mark's eyebrows went up. He wasn't surprised Keith was still lurking around. He'd heard through another mate that he talked about getting back with Maise all the time. Not if Mark had anything to do with it. "What'd he have to say?"

"Basically said he wished we were still together." Mark sighed. Jesus. That's all he needed.

"Don't be like that."

"Like what?"

"Annoyed."

"I'm not annoyed." He tucked the groceries under one arm, brushing flies away with the other.

"Would you prefer I got back with Parker?"

Mark rushed the next sentence out. "I'd prefer you didn't go out with either of them."

"Well I'm not. Right now, anyway."

"Maise? Parker's no good for you. He's unreliable. He's selfish. He always put himself first when he should have put you first." *And he did something I can never tell you about, either,* Mark thought.

"He can be. I know that; he knows that too. But so can you."

"Not like him, though." Maise made a face as if she partially agreed. "And Keith has his own faults. You know he has a massive temper."

"I never saw it."

"Lucky you." Mark had seen Keith lose control too many times. Sure, he'd been drunk most of them, but when things started going against Keith, he quickly got nasty and sometimes, there was no going back. He put a bloke in the hospital when they were still teenagers. The man was older. Nobody could stop Keith after he started throwing punches and he didn't stop until the bloke was almost dead. Mark actually looked at him differently after that. Started hanging out less. Mark could handle himself but he had always wondered who would win in a fight between them. "You're too smart for him, anyway."

"Huh. That's not nice."

"At least Keith offered to check on you. Where's Parker?"

"He's camping. With Sam."

"I know." He felt some level of comfort that Maise was no longer interested in Keith, but Parker was the real worry. "Up at Hell Ridge. Near the old Hazeldene General store."

"That's not illegal."

"We'll see if he comes back to check on you like Keith."

Maise said nothing for a long time, only the sound of her shoes crunching the gravel.

"You really were happy when I broke up with Parker, weren't you?" Now it was Mark's turn for silence. "How long are you gonna hold onto your dislike for him? It wasn't all his fault, you know."

"Mostly."

They reached Plenty Road. It was strange to see no traffic on such a major roadway. The United service station was another hundred yards further south. They began walking past darkened shops, places that might have still been trading under normal conditions: Whittlesea Tire and Battery, Just for Pets Plenty Valley Stock Feed. As darkness enveloped the town, it was a strange feeling; there were no streetlights; no shop fronts lit up. A few people had torches, most carried candles, and many houses had several out on their front steps or porches where lights would normally shine. The world was strangely unlit.

Ahead, people were milling about outside the service station. Mark noticed a policeman standing within the group. They approached as some of the people drifted away.

"It's Uncle Jim," Mark said.

Their Uncle—their mother's brother—was Senior Sargent at the Whittlesea Police Station. He'd worked there for thirty years and most people in town and the surrounding area knew him. James Findlay was a huge man, a slice over six foot three, just under two hundred and fifty pounds in the old scale. He had a huge stomach, slabs for biceps and a thick neck that as kids, Maise and Mark used to hang off. He was looking older now, with his neat, formerly dark hair turned mostly grey. He recognized Mark and Maise and turned their way. "Two of may favorite people in the world." Maise hugged her Uncle; Mark shook his hand. "You just finished up work?" he asked Maise.

"Yes, thank goodness. It was crazy."

"Don't you know that panic brings the crazies out?"

"What brings you out?" Mark asked. Maybe his uncle knew a bit about what was happening. "Haven't seen you walking the beat for a while."

"Tryin' to round up a few cars," Jim said. "Anything older than about mid-eighties or so." He leaned closer to them, turned his back on the other people standing nearby, and added, "keep it to yourself, but right now, the Government has no idea how to fix the power issue and if they can't resolve it, they will call a state of emergency and we'll have the power to seize any working vehicle for police and emergency services use."

"Really?" Mark asked. He glanced at Maise, who said nothing. He had recently paid a deposit on a 1982 Holden Commodore from Keith Whitehead—though he hadn't picked it up yet—with plans to restore it. He'd really wanted the car given General Motors weren't making any of the cars locally anymore. It had been similar to the first car his father had brought him and Mark felt nostalgic about that. The thing was beaten up, dirty, and the engine was in need of an overhaul, but if he could put some time and money into it, he was confident the car's value would appreciate. All of that might be for naught, now.

"We've got some idea about the cause, though we're waiting for confirmation from the Government. In the meantime, we're compiling a list of everyone that owns an older vehicle. We need more mobility right now. We just don't have enough eyes on this town."

Mark sighed. He wanted to help. "Well, you know I'm buying one off Keith Whitehead, though I haven't picked it up yet. As of last week when I paid half, the plan was to collect it tomorrow."

Jim chuckled. "We know. Don't worry about it yet but be prepared to cough it up if we need it. You know what people are like when they lose essentials," Jim said. "The moment they think they've lost their freedom to do whatever they want, they'll do whatever they think they can get away with."

"What's the story though? I mean, when will the power be back on?"

Jim shrugged. "We honestly don't know. So far, there are no power lines down, no power stations with issues—other than they aren't functioning. What we also know is that anything with an electrical circuit after the mid-1980's is out. Phones, stereos, TV's—the power, of course. The government is trying to work it out, that's all they've told me so far. I'm just with the local cops, after all." He smiled. "The grids are out in all of Whittlesea Shire, Nillumbik, Banyule and Mitchell. Apparently a plane went down north of Beveridge up near the Hume Highway."

"A plane?" Maise asked. Mark felt his stomach turn.

"Lots of electrical circuitry on a plane."

"We've got car crashes all over the place. Seems at the instant the power went out, every vehicle with a computer chip in it just died." His eyes widened. "In some cases right in the middle of driving down a busy street. Part of what I'm doing is checking for any accidents."

"Could you ride a bike?" Maise asked.

Pointing at her, Uncle Jim said, "Good question. But I prefer to stay on my own two legs. A couple of the other constables are rounding a few up. We just have to keep any eye on things, make sure people don't start panicking over this. You know what it was like when COVID hit. People went a little crazy buying everything they could lay their hands on."

"Don't I know it," Maise said.

A loud voice sounded from further along the road. A man on a bike rode down the center of the street shouting. As he got closer, his words became clearer.

"… Chinese," the man said. "The Chinese are coming. They did it! Bobby Cripps saw an army vehicle full of them out on Ridge Road when the power went out." He passed them in a second, shouting to the next group that would listen.

"The Chinese? Don't start saying stuff like that," Mark said, face twisted with annoyance. "People will believe it." His ex-girl-friend was half Chinese.

"Well," Jim began, waving flies away from his face, "We did get reports of a "modern looking" Army truck coming down from Flowerdale way with several Asian military personnel. Now, it could be they're from the Puckapunyal base, and we're assuming it's an older model vehicle. That's yet to be verified, though." Mark and Maise exchanged a glance. "Look, I gotta go. Get home and stay inside. Safest place for now. Hopefully the power will be back on tomorrow, but if it ain't, you might wanna buckle down, cause people will get more restless the longer this goes on."

Their Uncle said goodbye and hurried away in quick, stubby strides heading back up Plenty Road.

"Doesn't sound good," Maise said. "I mean, what's this about the Chinese?"

"I don't want to hear about the Chinese. Raven's part Chinese. Her dad's Chinese. He's always been very good to me and our family."

"I know. I wasn't suggesting anything bad. Just wondering what it all meant."

"Let's check on the Ute and then head home. Uncle Jim is right. People can get a bit crazy when things go down."

They crossed the pavement of the service station where Mark had left his Ute earlier that day. It was the first time he had ever seen the fuel station closed. The store was dark, no attendant, full of bottled drinks, candy and other valuable assortments, only the silent shells of vehicles stuck at the bowsers, including his own Toyota Hilux Ute. He didn't like leaving the Ute there, but he had no choice—he could push it home—but that was not manageable for him and Maise alone. The other customers who'd been refilling when the electrics died were in the same boat. He did have an idea to keep it out of harm's way, though.

A narrow driveway connected the service station with a small restaurant on the next property. He stood, considering what to do. Whittlesea had a reputation for vandalism and car theft. Mark locked his car in the garage each night. Leaving it exposed at the bowser all night was a whole other level. He asked Maise to help him push it the twenty or so yards to the other parking bay, where it was partly concealed by shrubs and would be less of a target. Thankfully, the ground was flat, and with Mark pushing at the rear and Maise guiding the wheel, they were able to negotiate their way into the space.

With that done, they started home. Mark quickly resurrected the discussion about Keith; he wanted to be sure Maise wasn't going to rush into anything with him lurking around.

"Just to be sure," he began, "you're not getting back with Keith, are you? Or Parker?"

Maise was silent for a time. Finally, she said in a soft, controlled voice, "please just leave it alone, Mark. It's really none of your business."

He pushed Maise hard, admittedly, looking out for what he thought were her best interests, but he knew when enough was enough. If you pushed her too far, she was prone to losing her temper in a big way. Slow to anger, but a big explosion, their father used to say.

Still, he wasn't giving up on it. She might not want to talk about it now, but there'd be another time. Mark wouldn't be satisfied until he was certain Keith and Parker were out of the picture for good.

Maise asked, "what about Raven?"

"What about her?"

"Is it over?"

"I haven't given up on her yet."

He just had to devise a plan that would give him the opportunity to see her again.

SIX

The moon peered out of the heavens, casting a silver glow onto the water and the vast sky was speckled with stars when Parker came awake sitting in his chair by the King Parrot Creek. A few beers and a world of exhaustion had done the trick. He reached into his pocket for his phone and realized he'd left it back at the tent. He hadn't planned on falling asleep or being stuck by the water without a torch. Besides, he had a massive headache, probably from falling asleep in the chair and twisting his neck a certain way, or drinking too many beers without eating.

Using the faint light of the moon and his natural instinct, Parker lifted his rod and reeled in the line, then laid the rod down on the fork stick and turned to face the darkness of the scrub. He had a good idea of the pathway back, but wasn't enough to avoid using his body to push his way through prickly bushes and sagging tree branches where he'd be scratched and scraped. And if he was lucky, he wouldn't trip over any logs or fall into any half-dug wombat holes. He couldn't remember seeing any on the way down to the creek, but they had a way of concealing themselves in the terrain.

He started off, wondering where Sam had gotten too. His old mate should have been there by now. He was normally reliable, generally showing up on time—quite the opposite of Parker. Maybe karma had caught up with him. If Parker thought about all the times he had been unreliable—turning up late or not even turning up at all, it was embarrassing. Maybe Sam had just gotten sick of all the times Parker had let him down and decided to make him wait. He hoped his mate was held up for a good reason and would arrive early the following morning.

The trek back to camp was smoother than expected, with only a scratch or two, and momentarily, the outline of the four-man dome tent came into view. He was thankful he'd blown up the thick air beds and laid out the sleeping bags earlier; now all he needed to do was slide into his own and go to sleep.

Parker unzipped the tent, crouched over and stepped inside. He'd left the fly screen and the rear window open in hope of getting a cross-breeze, but it was still uncomfortably warm. After zipping up the fly, he slid across the silky cover of his sleeping bag, not even bothering to open it—the night was still too damn hot. As Parker did so, he buried his worries—they'd still be there tomorrow, whatever they might bring.

SEVEN

Monday, January 23, 2023
Day 1

It wasn't the heat or hunger or even thirst that woke Parker in the end, it was the need to take a pee. The half a dozen beers he'd drunk the previous night had gone through him, and although he'd tossed and turned the last two hours trying to out sleep it, a full bladder had caught up with him in the end. One thing he loved about camping was that he could sleep in late—if he wanted. Six out of seven days in the normal world Parker was up at five o'clock and with his eyes half closed and a coffee in hand, was driving to the work site for a six o'clock start.

He dragged himself out of the sleeping bag—a place he must have inadvertently snuggled into while asleep—a little after nine, he guessed, based on the sun's position. He didn't even know what time he'd gotten to bed because his phone was dead. That was going to be the priority of the morning. Sam still hadn't arrived. Parker needed to find out why he was so bloody late.

He relieved himself in the scrub, well away from the camp, and then staggered back to where he had set up the small butane gas stove. Normally, he'd walk down to the creek and fill the tin kettle with fresh, cold spring water, but his head still ached and his back hurt from sleeping on the edge of the air mattress, so he cracked the plastic top off a bottle of water from one of two twenty-four packs he'd purchased at the IGA store. With the kettle half full, Parker turned on the gas and waited for it to boil. Coffee was the first order of the morning.

It was going to be another warm one. Already, the heat was pressing against his skin, mid-thirties, he thought for sure. Still, the birds chirped as they always chirped, sitting in the trees, swooping low between flowering bushes. The heat didn't seem to worry them, and he suspected the wombats, wallabies, and the echidnas were out as they normally were, foraging underneath the vegetation.

Waiting for the kettle to boil, he slipped on a fresh pair of khaki shorts and a Cobra-kai t-shirt, then slid into a pair of short socks and old runners and snatched his phone from Sam's bed where he had tossed it the previous night. He did have a charging block but he wanted to save that for when they were down the creek or away from his car.

Parker opened the Ute's door and plugged the phone in, then inserted the key and turned it to the Accessories Only notch. Nothing happened. He turned the key back and tried again. Still nothing.

"Strange."

The car was only twelve months old and Parker had it serviced at South Morang Toyota a week before.

He popped the hood and moved around to the front of the vehicle. He lifted the lid, expecting to see one of the connectors had come free, but the battery was as securely connected as the day it came off the production line. Parker scratched his head. How many beers had he drunk the night before?

He sat back in the drivers seat and thought about it. He pressed the alarm button on the small remote attached to the key ring. Silence. Something wasn't right. This time, Parker turned the key all the way and tried to start the engine. Again, nothing happened. It was as though the battery had completely died. Climbing out of the drivers seat, he decided to wait until later and try again.

The kettle began to whistle, so Parker shut off the gas burner, and filled a mug with instant coffee, two sugars and a splash of milk. He poured in the hot water, gave it a long stir, and then sipped at the fresh brew.

"Can't beat the taste of coffee first thing in the morning," he said to the birds.

Coffee in hand, he rummaged through one of his bags to find the charging block for his phone. He plugged it in and waited for the light to flash on the block, indicating that it was charging the connected device. Again, nothing happened.

"What the hell?"

He unplugged it, tried again. Nothing. He looked around the block, checking he hadn't missed turning the thing on, but he had used it before, and it was a simple plug and use device.

He sat at the small table where they would eat their meals and dropped the phone and charger down, his frustration growing.

The way Parker saw the situation; he had three issues on the go at once. Firstly, his car wouldn't start. No rhyme or reason why, only that when he'd gone to bed last night—as far as he knew—the Toyota could drive him all the way to Sydney. Now, it wouldn't even charge his phone, let alone drive. Or that was the assumption he had to make. That meant he couldn't easily get back into town —or anywhere, for that matter. Secondly, his phone had died, and he couldn't recharge it. That was probably more important than the car because if his phone worked, he could call Sam and he'd drive up there and collect him. Thirdly, Sam hadn't yet arrived. Plausibly, his friend could have been held up—he might have a logical reason for it and he might have tried to contact Parker to let him know, but...

Parker thought back to the last time he had used his phone before running out of charge. He'd been talking with Sam. A small knot of unease uncoiled inside him. What if it hadn't actually run out of charge? His mate had mentioned something about the US and Europe having gone dark, no electronics working, all communications down. What if the same thing had happened to Australia?

If that were true, that situation trumped all others and he might have a bigger problem on his hands. Hell, all of them would have a bigger problem on their hands.

Knocking down the last of his coffee, Parker rose from the table and put the kettle on again. He had to think his way out of this; what might have happened? There was Sam and... Maise. Sure, they might not be a couple anymore, but he still worried about her. If something had happened, Maise was potentially in danger.

The simple, yet difficult way to find out what had happened was to walk home. The thought did not provide any motivation at all. It was around forty kilometers or twenty-five miles of hills and bends down to Whittlesea. Thirty minutes by car, but probably six hours walking. Could he really walk that far? He had never walked that far in his life, not even close. He supposed he could walk to the nearest store—the one in Kinglake, which he new well—but even that might be three or four hours. What about a farmhouse? The houses were spread thin up this way, but someone might know something.

Parker slumped into one of the soft fabric camp chairs. He couldn't just traipse off yet. What if Sam arrived and somehow, Parker missed him in the crossover? That would be bad luck. For both of them. There was no clear solution, other than to wait it out and hope Sam arrived soon.

EIGHT

M aise and Parker were on holidays on the Gold Cost, in Queensland. It was sunny—not too hot—and waves full of white froth ran up the sand as the two of them walked along Surfers Paradise beach. They'd spent a couple of hours riding boogie boards and were heading back to a beachside restaurant near their hotel for lunch. Maise knew it was a dream. They had almost reached the hotel when shouts sounded. Maise looked around, realized it had occurred outside her dream, and then woke, leaving Parker behind and a pang of regret that surprised her. Why was she dreaming about him now?

It was coming from the back of the house. She leapt out of bed and raced through her bedroom door, hearing Mark shout again from the back patio. Mindy barked, that deep, guttural growl indicating danger.

She reached the entrance to the kitchen and living room and saw immediately that Mark was now standing outside the wide sliding glass doors shouting at someone. He had a golf club in his hand and Mindy stood by his side, poised to attack, her hackles up, tail stiff, teeth bared. She yelped repeatedly at a man standing frozen beside one of the big water tanks located at the rear of the house. He was dressed in a raggedy black tracksuit, had buzz cut blonde hair and a blotchy, pale face. A second man staggered across the backyard with a plastic container full of water. He was much taller; broad shouldered, with scruffy brown hair, shorts and a purple t-shirt, long white socks with sneakers.

Maise ran to the back doors.

"Stealing our water," Mark said. "From the tanks."

A third man stood on the other side of the fence in their neighbor's property, only his bald head poking over the top of the palings. He took the container of water from the second man and disappeared.

The man at the water tank had stopped filling another container and now stood, hands up as Mark threatened him with the club.

"Gimme back my water, asshole," Mark said, pointing the weapon at him.

The man turned and ran across the backyard towards his buddy. Mindy scampered after him. The dog was fast and before the man could reach the fence, she dug her fangs into his backside.

He screeched and fell forward onto the grass, curling himself into a ball for protection. Mindy stood over him growling, glancing back towards Mark. Maise couldn't help but smile.

The second man ran back from the fence and kicked Mindy in the chest. The dog cried out and leapt away.

"HEY!" Mark lifted the golf club and ran at the man, swinging the stick the way Happy Gilmore might take a tee shot. It struck the man in the leg, but he caught it and pulled Mark towards him. He was taller and wider than Mark, though shaped round and heavy at the waist. They wrestled for control of the club, and in seconds, tumbled to the grass.

The first man had crawled to his feet, and spotting Maise, started towards her. She thought about stepping inside and closing the doors but didn't want to leave Mark alone. She spotted several lengths of wood stacked near the barbecue. Maise snatched the longest one up; realizing it probably wouldn't do much, and turned to face the man.

His emaciated face, peppered with red sores and reeking of ill intentions, leered at her. She tightened the wood in her hand; anger mixed with terror, and waited, her heart racing.

Before he could reach her though, Mindy—barking ferociously

—leapt up and crashed into the man's side. He stumbled, swung at the dog and missed, tried to retreat, but Mindy attacked again, and he had no choice but to flee for the fence, Mindy barking and nipping at his heels.

The golf club thrown aside, Mark and the other man had abandoned their ground wrestling and now stood toe to toe, the difference in size more obvious now. That had never bothered Mark in the past, Maise knew. There was a pause as they each sized the other up, then, teeth gritted, Mark leapt forward and pushed the man fiercely, throwing him off balance.

"Come into my house and steal, you ass." The man grunted as he battled to regain his footing. "I'll give you three seconds to get the hell out before I whack you one."

Leave while you can, Maise thought. She had seen this before and it never ended well for Mark's opponent.

The man stepped forward and struck a great looping fist at Mark's head. Her brother avoided it with grace, and before the man could retract his hand, Mark had twisted at the hips and swung a hard left, his tightened knuckle connecting with the man's right cheek, making a thick, fleshy noise. The big man swayed on his feet, eyes wide with surprise. Then, like a striking viper, Mark shot another left jab—no hip twist this time—and hit the man flush on the tip of the nose. He went down on one knee and collapsed on the grass.

"Lucky I only hit you with a left," Mark said.

The man's hands covered his face, rolling from his back to his side in painful silence.

Mark leapt away and picked up the golf club, then stood over the man, club held high.

"Get out of here now, otherwise, I *will* put you in the hospital.

The other two men had disappeared. The man climbed onto his knees. Blood dripped from the tip of his pointy nose.

"I've got kids," the man mumbled, wiping blood on the back of his arm. "We've run out of water already."

Mark shook his head. "Don't give a crap, mate. This is not the way to get it." The man grunted, made it onto his feet, then staggered towards the fence. "Besides, there's not much left in the tank.

You gonna take our last bit of water?" The man turned and shrugged. "And don't hang around in the Buckley's backyard, either. I'm gonna come over there in a moment and check you've left."

With the golf club raised, Mark stood behind the man as he tried to climb the palings. On the first two attempts, his foot slipped off the middle ledge and then finally, he pushed himself up, arms and fence shaking, and slid over the other side. He must have landed badly as a thud sounded from the Buckley's backyard.

Mark turned to Maise and shook his head. He wasn't even breathing heavily. "Idiot. Let's go out the front and check they're leaving."

Maise followed Mark through the sliding doors and each of the rooms to the front door, where he opened it, and they went out and stood at the end of the driveway. Mindy sat beside them, appraising the state of the situation.

The street was quiet, a few people out of their homes poking about their front gardens. It was hot already, the deep blue sky promising another scorcher.

They watched the street towards the Buckley's house expecting at any moment to see the men emerge. Mark was about to start walking when the three men appeared—but not from the Buckley's house—much further along, maybe three or four houses. They were each carrying a container of water.

"How long since the blackout?" Mark asked, watching the men. The man that had been bitten by Mindy looked back over his shoulder and stuck his middle finger up at them. "Fourteen, maybe fifteen hours since the power went out and we've got people stealing water already."

"You think they've really run out of water?" Maise asked.

"Probably. Those guys looked dumb enough not to realize there's only so much in the pipes. Probably took a thirty-minute shower last night. Woke up this morning with no running water. God knows what else is going on in this town."

"This town? Not to mention all the others," Maise said.

"I suppose."

"It's human nature. You remember what happened in the early

stages of COVID? People have an instinct for self-preservation. At least twenty-percent of the population is selfish. They'll take what they need and not worry about the next person. It's going to get worse, Mark. You can only protect the house so much. If this thing goes on, more people will come. And they'll be looking for something other than water next time."

"I'll be waiting. I'll have the place ready." He gave her a stern look. "I promise, sis. You've got nothing to worry about."

But Maise wasn't sure she wanted to be there when more people came. She'd watched a lot of international news over the last few years, and she knew when people had fundamental things taken from them, they went into survival mode. It was a basic human reaction. If the government couldn't get the power back on, it meant no water, no food, and merged with summer heat, inevitably a lot of lives lost. People would be angry.

The door of the house next door opened and an elderly man shuffled out. It was Mr. Buckley. He waved to them. "Mornin', Turner kids."

"Morning, Mr. Buckley," Maise said, chuckling at the fact he still called them kids, even though they were in their early and mid-twenties. "How's Mrs. Buckley?" She'd been unwell for the last couple of days.

"Not too good, I'm afraid. She's runnin' a fever."

Maise felt a pang of concern. She was one of the nicest people Maise knew. "Sorry to hear. I'll come over later and see how she is."

Mindy trotted up the path and climbed the steps, pressing herself against Mr. Buckley's leg. He reached down and gave her a scratch behind the ears. Mindy's tail wagged.

"Say, did you see those men in your backyard? I saw them coming over the fence from your place."

"We were just seeing them off," Mark said, holding up the golf club. "They won't be back."

"Do you have enough water and food?" Maise asked.

Mr. Buckley nodded. "We just did a big shop. Had it delivered yesterday. Bottled water, lots of tinned stuff, June loves keeping the pantry stocked."

"Hey," Mark said, stepping forward. "Don't lose the old Ford you've got hidden away in your garage, Mr. Buckley. At the moment, none of the newer cars are working. Yours is probably one of the few that will still run."

"Is that so?" He said, stopping in the doorway. "Funny that. They say the new stuff is better. Huh. Seems I was right. Pity I don't drive the thing anymore." He shuffled back inside and gave them a wave as he disappeared through the doorway.

Maise followed Mark back up the driveway with Mindy in tow. "I'm gonna put some boards up on the fence to stop people climbing over. Secure the side gate that leads around to the yard so nobody can get back there."

"Really? Isn't that a little extreme?" It was just like Mark. She was sure by the end of the day the house would look like a fortress.

"I don't think so. People are already climbing into our backyard looking for water." He stopped and faced her. "You haven't thought anymore about what we talked about yesterday?"

Maise frowned. "What did we talk about yesterday?"

Mark shrugged. "You know? Parker? Keith?"

"What? Why would I think about that?"

"Good," Mark said, leading them up the front pathway. "If I know Parker, he's sitting by the creek at Hell Ridge totally oblivious to this thing, or even if he was aware, he's probably thinking 'stuff it, I'll stay up here'."

"That's a bit unfair."

"You'll see."

Maise didn't want to get into an argument right now. "I'm going inside. I'll go and check on Mrs. Buckley later after I do my shift at the IGA."

But the scowl on Mark's face told her they were going to have another discussion at some point.

NINE

Phillip Lee sat on a faded wooden bench beneath the shade of a large oak tree in a quiet park on the outskirts of Whittlesea. He'd walked the mile and a half to the remote park, passing people walking on the street or hanging in their front yards with a smile and a nod. He was pleased to see the park was empty. It would make the rendezvous smoother. That was something. It was ten o'clock, the air was already hot, and Phillip took no joy at being outside at this time of day. But this wasn't just any meeting. He'd been waiting three years for this one. Three years of meetings in China, phone calls and e-mails, and now he was sitting alone in the heat, feeling more nervous than he'd ever felt before. The time had come. The button had literally been pushed.

Normally, he'd be sitting in an air-conditioned office some-where in Melbourne's north, working on another real estate deal, convincing a potential buyer to handover an ever-increasing pile of money for a property. He always loved the real estate game, but over the last few years, his love had grown even more as he found ingenious ways to sell more properties to his Chinese associates. Ever since his acquaintances had approached him about the their plan

It had come down to this, Phillip thought. Three years of planning. Three years since that fateful day in Beijing, when a government offi-cial had approached him after he passed through immigration with dual Chinese and Australian citizenship. He'd almost cut and run in that first meeting. Chinese government officials were not to be taken lightly. He'd sat in a room, wondering why they had pulled him aside. But the official had been pleasant, flattering, and the deal with which they had presented him—fragments only at first— to be the eyes and ears of the Chinese government in the region in which he resided, had proven to be immensely valuable so far. Since that meeting and his subsequent agreement to join their cause, Phillip had built his understanding of the Chinese plans and a network of Chinese connections in Australia that would now carry out their purpose.

A teenage girl walked across the opposite side of the park. In a moment, she had disappeared, but it got him thinking about his daughter, Raven. That morning was the first time Phillip had been home in two days. Raven had left already. He'd barely seen her over the last few weeks as they ramped up things for the go-live. He'd tried to persuade her to go with her mother on vacation, but she insisted that working long hours at the veterinary clinic was more important. Phillip hoped she'd be safe with the current challenges the town and broader state faced. His wife, Mary-Anne, and son were taking separate short vacations; at least they were in less populated areas. It was unfortunate they were so separated.

Phillip didn't want to think about his family now. He had to concentrate on the task. The nuclear weapon had been detonated and now his job, a very important role the Chinese government had seen fit to bestow upon him, was imminent. Phillip was honored by the trust they had shown him and would not let them down.

Soon after, Phillip spotted a man walking towards him from a laneway between two rows of bushes. He stood, watching the man approach. Until now, the only local contact had been via phone or e-mail. Phillip didn't know what his contact looked like, other than that he had to be Chinese.

As the man approached, Phillip recognized the camouflaged colors of a soldier's uniform. A pistol sat in a holster on his hip and he wore a peaked cap. It struck him then that this was really happening; after years of planning, the Chinese Army was invading Australia. Though, not many people would know about it just yet.

On approach, in Mandarin, the man said, "Mr. Lee?"

Phillip walked forward and greeted the man, who, with a soft handshake, identified himself as Lieutenant Wang. They walked back to the shade.

They exchanged pleasantries about the heat, and then the man said, "the nuclear detonation at three-hundred and fifteen kilometers above the earth has been a success." Phillip gave a thin smile. He knew this. "All electronic equipment and systems in the three largest capital cities have been terminated."

"Good to have clarity that it all went well. Nothing works at my home, nor does my car."

"We'll have replacement vehicles and communications devices available soon. Our ships have landed at major ports along the east and south-east coast. Planes are landing at more than forty airports on the east coast, many are remote and vacant so local scrutiny will be minimal. Still, even if we are noticed, its difficult for anybody to alert the authorities right now."

"Where did you arrive?" Phillip asked.

"To the north. We landed at a vacant country airport last night. I have a small squad in a single vehicle parked nearby. More will follow, but we are not allowed to begin the true invasion until D+3 —three days after the nuclear detonation. We are trying to maintain an element of stealth for the next day or two. Allow the locals to create their own challenges."

Phillip could see the sense in this. During the early COVID-19 outbreaks, many people were selfish and he suspected the Chinese government was hoping for more of the same, which would reduce their ability to resist the planned invasion.

"What's the next step?"

"All our local contacts—like yourself—will be activated. We won't meet them all, but training and process has been very clear. We're confident everybody knows their role. Are you clear about your first tasks?"

Phillip nodded. "Capture the local authorities that can help organize the people. Prevent the first stages of emergency response."

"Yes. Anyone or anything that will help them resist our plan must be sabotaged."

"And the military will support us?"

"Of course. We will have a substantial presence in the town by Wednesday afternoon. They will start to arrive tomorrow morning. It will be a gradual buildup as they set up their different positions at strategic locations. The water facility is one of the first."

They discussed more of the mission targets that Phillip had read in his instruction booklet. He knew them well and didn't need much clarity.

They shook hands again, before Lieutenant Wang twisted away, then turned back, eyeing Phillip, as if considering his next words carefully. "You know there might be some collateral damage in all of this."

Phillip thought about his wife, son and daughter. His handler had told him of the potential for collateral damage early on. Phillip's wife and son were relatively safe, but Raven was still local. She'd been home more than usual in the last few weeks, aside from working, and he hoped it stayed that way. He needed keep an eye on her. He didn't want her to come between him and his mission.

"Mr. Lee?"

Phillip shook his head as if to clear it. "Yes, sorry. I understand."

Lieutenant Wang watched him. Phillip smiled. Eventually, Wang said, "There won't be an issue carrying out your tasks, will there?"

"No." He stuck out his hand. "No issue at all."

Lieutenant Wang reached out slowly and shook it. "Power and riches, Mr. Wang. And fulfilling a great duty to our motherland."

TEN

Parker decided the best thing for him to do while waiting for Sam was to grab some more bait, head back down to the creek and hopefully stock up on fish. What else was there to do? He could wait at the campsite where it was only going to get hotter, or he could sit by the stream and enjoy the occasional breeze that floated off the water. Sam would know where to find him when he arrived. Besides, he felt a little peckish and a nice pan-fried trout with salt and lemon juice would go down well.

It was a little too early for a beer—even for Parker—so he took a tub of bardi grubs and a small cooler of soft drink with him. He even set up a second fishing rod, which he placed roughly fifteen yards away from his position. A bell on the end of the tip would alert him to any bites.

Parker sat in the same spot as the previous day, confident there were a couple more trout hiding in the deeper holes beneath half-submerged trees or the faster water at the head of the pool; that was why it was still his favorite piece of water between Kinglake and Flowerdale. It was a bit of an effort to get the car and trailer— if you brought one— down the ragged dirt road to the campsite, but once you reached the flat, grassy section, it was difficult to find a more fruitful spot.

After threading on a grub as bait, Parker cast the light rig—with two tiny sinkers—upstream and across the width of the creek toward a mossy chunk of timber stretching diagonally into the eddying water. He released a little slack from the reel, then turned the bail arm over, and placed the rod on a forked stick dug into the grassy bank.

This was the life, he thought as he sunk into the chair. The birds sung in the trees, the grasshoppers chirped in the long yellow grass on the other side of the river bank, and insects hovered over the grass and water, seeking to satisfy their thirst. Parker watched the clear water ripple and bubble over the shallow rocks in the pool ahead, which gave way to a slower, green-black body of water directly out from his chair. If only Sammy were here with him.

Parker soon fell into thought about what might have happened. If some sort of terrorist attack had hit the US and Europe how likely was it that Australia had been hit, too? Australia was generally too far away from anyone or anything for people to care. It had born several minor terror attacks over the years, but nothing major. But who would want to hit Australia? Al-Qaida? ISIS? Maybe it was the Chinese. In recent times, the relationship with China had soured. China had stopped importing Australia's iron ore, and that had hurt both countries. China was paying more for lower quality coal and their factories just weren't running as efficiently. Many of the factories were on restrictions because they couldn't obtain enough electricity. The Chinese had applied tariffs on Australian beef and barley too, and other less essential items. But coal was the big one. China needed good quality coal and lots of it. What if China had decided to take over Australia so they could access the coal? It sounded extreme, even for Parker's sometimes vivid imagination.

Parker reminded himself that Sam might arrive at any moment. He was a resourceful guy and might find an old motorbike or even a push bike, at least to make it up to Hell Ridge, to let Parker know what was happening. Best thing for Parker to do was just wait. He thought about Maise again. *Not your problem, mate.* But Parker couldn't help feeling a little uneasy when he thought of her.

There was movement in the scrub on the other side of the bank.

Parker watched, waiting for a cow or a kangaroo to appear. Instead, it was a man, dressed in a shirt that had once been white, green pants and a pair of black gumboots. He was a head taller than Parker; his hair was snow white; messy, long tendrils floating in the breeze. His had a short white beard and wore black sunglasses. A long, solid stick protruded from his right hand.

"Howdy, young fella," the man said.

"How goes it?" Parker asked.

"Couldn't be better. You?" Parker made the hand sign for fifty-fifty. "Up for a spot of fishing?"

"Yeah."

"Catch any?"

"A small one last night."

"Been here before?"

Parker sat forward in his chair. "Since I was about five years old. My dad and I used to come up here in the spring and camp in his station wagon." The man tilted his head slightly. "You from around here?"

The man waved backwards. "I live up on Hell Ridge, a little way beyond."

A thought struck Parker. "You're not Normy King are you?"

The man smiled. "I am indeed."

Parker stood, laughing. "Wow. My dad and I used to come up and visit you when I was a kid."

"John Richardson. I'm Parker, his son."

"Lovely fella, John. How is he?"

"Travelling right now. Up north."

"Half his luck."

"You had the coolest place."

Normy stood straight. "I still do."

"You had no electricity or sewage or anything. The best garden I can ever remember."

"You wanna come up for a look? I don't get many visitors these days."

Parker considered this. He might kill a few hours, but what if Sam arrived while Parker was away? He'd just have to wait.

"Sure," he said finally.

"Cross the river a little further downstream. It's about knee deep."

"On my way."

ELEVEN

M ark decided he would beef security up a little bit as a deterrent for anyone thinking about stealing from their property again. He started with a couple of laps of the back and front yards, working out the weak links and where he could add some boards or reinforce a fence paling. The side gate between the edge of the house and his neighbor's fence was only five feet tall. Mark took a hammer, several old timber fence planks and a box of one-inch galvanized nails and went to work on making the gate taller. He added another foot and a half to the height, making it about six and a half feet—too tall for most people to bother climbing over. He hoped they'd decide it just wasn't worth it. He also added a padlock on the bolt for double protection.

By his measure, society had already begun the slow descent towards to chaos. In less than twenty-four hours, people were already stealing tank water from backyards. The pipes would be empty in most houses by the end of the day. Not everybody had water tanks. Bottled water would be stripped from the grocery store and it was a good thirty-minute bike ride or two hours walk to Yan Yean Reservoir, the town's water supply. Water tanks would be a more sought after target. And the food? What happened when that started running low? He'd ride his bike over to the service station later and check on his Ute, but the more he thought about it, the more worried he became. Cars were mostly useless right now. He supposed people with older model riding mowers or motorbikes could still get around.

This was all based on the assumption that the government and emergency services couldn't get the power back on. It was probably a fair assumption, given some of the power outages the state had seen over the last few years. Mark recalled a few years back when a windstorm swept through the eastern ranges of Melbourne. Some residents waited more than a month for the power company to restore electricity. He had a feeling that this time, things might be worse. It wasn't just the power that was down—cars weren't working either. And a storm explained the power loss back then. Imagine a month without power?

One of his neighbors, a middle-aged man with a couple of kids that lived two houses along the street, stopped out front. He wore a hat, a moustache and glasses. He reminded Mark of Ned Flanders from *The Simpsons.*

"Hey." Mark gave them a wave. "What're you doing?"

"Just having a look at the place," Mark said. "Had a break in earlier." He didn't want to say anything about having water tanks.

"Is that right? Rodney asked, his eyes wide under his red and blue baseball cap. "So did Gino. He lives on Cassidy Street, one over."

Mark nodded. "Sounds like it's happening all over."

"You hear about the Woolworths' truck on Plenty Road?" Mark shook his head. "It stopped running when everything shut down. Slammed into a tree and tipped over. People have been raiding it, stealing all the food and supplies. A bloke got stabbed fighting with another over a case of water."

"How'd you hear about this?"

"Dave Tiffen, one of the Whittlesea cops who does these big bike rides all the time was out riding his bike this morning and saw some people where the truck had crashed."

"Geez. People panic when stuff like this happens."

"What about the plane crash at Beveridge?"

"I heard about that."

"Dave was up there on his bike. Said everyone died. It's like a battlefield. Bodies everywhere; grass is scorched black, pieces of plane all over the place. First commercial airliner crash ever in Australia."

"That's really bad." Mark imagined one of those scenes he'd watched on the news every few years in a far away country. It always made him imagine what it would be like being on a plane that was heading for crash, the fear in the final few seconds before impact. Very little scared him, but that idea gave him a cold shiver. "You should start your own newspaper, Rod."

"Nah. I just want this thing to be over." The conversation fizzled out. "I better keep moving," Rodney said. "Catch you later." He wandered on from Mark's property.

Mark kept thinking about the stories Rodney had told him and he decided to leave fixing up the house for now and head down to the service station and check on his Ute. He had a bad feeling it would be a target for the bored and scared people who had nothing better to do than wander the town at night.

Bicycle seemed to be the best way to get around. At least he had a decent mountain bike. He took the bike from the garage—he hadn't ridden it in more than twelve months, since last summer, when he and Raven had followed the track around Yan Yean Reservoir—and wheeled it out onto the driveway.

The reminder of Raven was depressing. It had only been two weeks since she'd said they needed a break, but Mark still had that sickly feeling in his gut when he thought about it. The first few days had been difficult, plaguing his thoughts from the moment he woke until the time he fell asleep. He'd always handled break ups without much afterthought, but this time was different. He discovered he genuinely cared about Raven—not that he didn't know that when they spent time together, but not being with her meant there was something missing in his life. He'd never told her—that was part of the issue. Mark wasn't a great communicator. He knew that. *Raven* knew that. But knowing something and being able to fix it were sometimes a world apart, especially for Mark. In the end, it had all gotten too much for Raven.

With Mindy trotting alongside the bike, Mark rolled down the driveway and out onto the street, where he joined others—kids and adults that had determined the same thing. He spotted two cars—a Ford Cortina—it might even have been a show car from the late 70's or early 80's, and an old Holden Kingswood. It reminded him to go around to Keith Whitehead's house and speak with him about taking possession of the Commodore for which he'd already paid half the money.

There was an unusual amount of activity around the service station. Two more vintage cars were parked at the bowsers, the owners filling their tanks with a manual siphon apparatus. A big brown and white Ford truck that looked like a Matchbox car Mark had when he was a kid, and a little white Holden Torana with rust holes across the trunk. Others were filling up their red and yellow plastic containers—the kind you used to hold your lawn mower fuel. One of the Singh brothers who owned the service station patrolled the pumps to make sure people did the right thing, taking cash in hand for the fuel. At the far side of the big awning, two more brothers had a long pole in one of the big underground fuel tanks, measuring the amount of fuel that remained. Mark ignored them and rolled across the concrete through the connecting driveway towards his Ute.

There were two men hanging around his Hilux. Both had on hi-visibility polo shirts, black shorts and heavy work boots. They might have been tradesman. The first, who looked like he worked in the sun all day, had short dark hair and a grubby five o'clock shadow. Thick tattoos covered both arms and legs from hands and feet to the clothing line. He peered through the driver's window. The other, whose dense mousey hair spilled from the back of his peaked cap, poked around the rear of the Ute, looking for a way into the big tool chest.

Appearances didn't concern Mark. "Hey!"

Both men snapped their heads around. The man at the window said something to the other. They stepped quickly away from the car and slipped through a row of bushes at the rear.

Mark cycled up to the Ute, eyeing the spot where the men had disappeared. The car looked to be in the same condition. Mindy leapt up into the tray and sat on her haunches, tongue rolling from her mouth. Mark scratched her head, suppressing the need to chase after the men. He wasn't surprised, just glad he came along when he did. But what was he going to do about it? There was every chance the moment he left the men would return. Although, there wasn't much to steal—most of his tools were either on site or at home in the garage—the men might have something with which they could tow the Ute away. It might not work right now but it was still his car. If he could pick up the Commodore from Keith Whitehead, Mark might be able to use it to tow the Ute home.

"Mark," someone called out from the other side of the road beyond the restaurant. Mark turned. It was Brian Fitzgerald, a local mechanic, who ran a shop near the fuel station. He worked on both Mark and Maise's cars when they needed a service or had any mechanical issues. Brian jogged across the road. Mindy approached, wagging her tail, and Brian stopped to pat the dog as he reached them. "How goes it? I see ya car's been there all night."

"Yeah. I pushed it out of the way, but I just saw a couple of blokes poking around."

"I saw them too. Dodgy looking characters. We can push it over the road to my shop, if you like," Brian said. "You can keep it there for now."

"Seriously? That would be bloody awesome, mate."

"Not a problem. I've a got a bit of space left."

Together, the two men rolled the Hilux down the fuel station's gentle slope and across the road to the parking area outside Brian's shop. With a little finessing, they negotiated it into place beside several other vehicles.

"Mate, I can't thank you enough," Mark said, shaking hands with Brian. He felt immense relief that the car would be safe now.

"Your family have always been good customers. I remember your old man giving me a chance when I first started my business back in the 90's. Just collect it when this thing is over."

They bid each other farewell, Brian returned to his shop, and Mark pushed off his bike and moved back towards the service station and underneath the awning to get out of the hot sun. The shade felt good and he wondered if it would crack forty degrees Celsius today.

Several people were talking near one of the pumps. Mark tried to ignore them and veered left towards the IGA where Maise was working.

One of the men talking in the group stepped away from the others and called out to him. "Hey, Mark." He looked around and spotted Keith Whitehead. "Got a minute?"

Keith and Mark chatted whenever the saw each other, but the relationship hadn't been the same since Maise and Keith had broken up. Before going out with Maise, Keith was one of Mark—and Parker's for that matter—oldest rivals. They had grown up playing football and cricket against each other; taking turns each year to win grand finals. Keith wasn't a great loser—neither was Mark—and most of the time Keith wasn't a bad guy—on the surface, anyway—but he could be wild and unpredictable. Maise might not have seen it, but Mark had witnessed Keith have some serious meltdowns and Maise was lucky enough to have avoid it so far. Mark wanted to keep it that way.

Mindy began to growl. "It's all right, Min," he said in a low voice.

Now was Mark's chance to discuss the car and avoid having to track Keith down to finalize the timing of the handover. He wondered if Keith knew how much the car's value had increased since the blackout. He wasn't dumb, which only put Mark a little more on edge.

"How goes it?" He asked Keith as they shook hands.

"Yeah, all right. This blackout thing has got a few people spooked. Be interesting to see what happens over the next few days."

"You guys got plenty of food and water?

Keith shrugged. "Enough for now. You?"

"Some ass tried to steal water from one of my tanks this morning."

"For real?"

"Three of them."

"I bet they copped a whack."

"The two in my backyard did."

Keith laughed. "Suckers. Hey, I heard about you and Raven. Sorry to hear, man."

"Yeah, well, I don't need her," he lied. "Hey, what's the go with the car. When can I pick it up?"

"You got the rest of the cash?"

"Safely secured with your name on it."

"Tomorrow then. Around midday."

"Cool. See you then," Mark said as he started to push off on his bike.

Keith turned after him. "What about your sister?"

Mark rolled to a stop again. "What about her?"

Keith walked to him. "I need a little inside info, man." Mark cocked an eyebrow. "Well, I was thinking of asking her out again. Just wanted to know if she's gonna get back with Richardson or not."

Discussion about Parker and Maise usually sent Mark's blood pressure up. " I dunno, man."

"Are they cozying up with all this drama happening? Wouldn't surprise me." Keith looked genuinely unhappy about the prospect. It was a rare expression on his otherwise cocky face.

He could ease Keith's fears in a second by telling him Parker was in fact far away from Maise and there was little chance of them cozying up right now. It might help put Keith in a better frame of mind to hand over the car. Keith might even do Mark a favor and head on up the mountain and camp right near Parker; annoy the hell out of him.

"I may know something," Mark said with a sly smile.

"Yeah, what's that?"

"Parker's not around at the moment. He's out of town for the next two weeks."

"Is that right?" Keith smiled.

"Camping."

"Camping? Nice. Good time to get out of here. Where? Eildon?"

Mark hesitated now. Did he really want to divulge where Parker was set up? Part of the reason they went to Hell Ridge was because not many people new about it. Although, he wasn't exactly giving away the location. Hell Ridge was a decent sized area. It could be anywhere along the creek near the bluff.

"Come on, man. Where? It's not like I'm gonna drive on up there and annoy him. I got better things to do."

"He's up at Hell Ridge."

Keith's smile ripened into one Mark had never seen before. It was almost gleeful. "Good spot." He thought on it a moment longer. "You believe the stories about the treasure up there?"

Mark shrugged. "I dunno. I don't pay much attention to that sort of stuff."

"Yeah, me neither. Anyway," Keith continued, turning to leave, "If you could put in a good word for me to Maise, I'd appreciate that, mate." He called back over his shoulder. "See you tomorrow at midday."

Mark watched Keith disappear with a look of incredulity. There was no way he'd let Maise get back with Keith Whitehead. Never in a million years. He just hoped Maise wouldn't do it, either.

With Mindy following, Mark rode back up Plenty Road towards Laurel Street and the main set of shops where the IGA Supermarket sat. Maise was working another shift and Mark wanted to make sure she wasn't getting harassed by greedy customers who expected her to have stock of something they had cleaned out. He also wanted to check how much food and supplies were left. He suspected people would have overloaded their homes and cleaned out the shelves by now.

As he rode along with Mindy, Mark thought about Raven again. They hadn't spoken for more than two weeks. She had suggested they spend some time apart, and he wondered now, why he had agreed. They had been arguing more than usual and it had seemed like a break was sensible, but Mark wished he could go back and not agree so quickly. He wondered how she was coping wit the blackout. If only there was a way he could contact her besides visiting her house. She lived with her parents on the other side of Whittlesea, on the outskirts, where land sizes—and houses—were considerably bigger than in the central town area where it was more like the suburbs. Maybe he should just ride on over there? The idea that she might not want to see him, that when he arrived at her door she told him he had wasted his time, was too much to test. He had to sit on it a bit longer.

The IGA Supermarket was functioning. A large sign had been stuck to the open entrance doors stating: CASH ONLY PURCHASES. *Cash was king*, Mark thought, wondering how all the people that only used plastic would be faring right now.

People were lined up through the entrance. Mark stuck his head through the opening. Maise's hands were moving and darting about as she scanned items through the register, serving a long queue of people. Two other girls, much younger than Maise, worked the extra registers. The only time Mark could remember ever seeing so many people in the store was Christmas Eve, and even then, he didn't think the queues were this big.

The town was holding up—for now. Two of the main services were functioning. He wondered what would happen when the food and fuel ran out, and as he rode with Mindy running along beside his wheel, Mark lapsed into deeper thought about the situation. Negativity had enveloped him since the blackout began. As much as he hated being so pessimistic, he couldn't see a short-term solution, and it was only a matter of time before things started going downhill if the power wasn't operating soon. The heat was the major issue. It seemed to have climbed even more since he left the house. He was sweating in more locations than he could count, and the sun—even this early—felt like it had scorched the tips of his ears and back of his neck. And what about all the elderly people? It happened every summer when the power *was* working —the elderly suffered through the heat, a small portion of whom died from heatstroke or heat exhaustion. With the power out, the temperatures well above thirty degrees—probably touching thirty-five on a day like this—the fatalities would be even higher in the town. Added to that, if cars and trucks weren't operating, food and medicine wouldn't be replenished to stores and pharmacies. What about all those folks on life support in the hospitals, or at home on medication that had expired, or was about to run out? Mark and Maise had a cousin closer to the city that was a diabetic—what happened when she used up all her insulin? The elderly and comprised were at serious risk. Then there were pets... Mark's head hurt. His other big worry was the car of which Mark was now part owner. Keith had seemed reasonable when Mark had discussed pick up, but he suspected that had only been because Maise had been a topic of conversation. Mark still had his doubts as to whether Keith would hand it over. Old cars suddenly became more valuable. Somehow, he had to get ahold of that vehicle.

TWELVE

Parker reeled in his fishing rod, rested it in the forked stick and then hurried along the shoreline, weaving his way in and out of thick gums and ground cover until he reached a section of the creek he could easily cross. Here, several big rocks formed a pseudo bridge across the water and he was able to jump from one to the other without getting wet. Had Sam been with him, they probably would have just swum across the creek.

Old Normy met him at the base of a slender, bumpy trail, where they shook hands. Normy was taller than Parker remembered, maybe six-three or four, and his long legs forced Parker to work hard to keep up as they climbed the lower slope of the hill. Parker spotted a crack in the hillside—perhaps a cave—with grey, weathered boards nailed across the opening in a rough attempt to keep people out. He wondered if it was natural or man-made.

"I don't remember seeing caves around here," Parker said between breaths. Normy stopped with his boot leaning on the cracked trunk of a small tree that appeared to have come down in fierce wind. "Are they natural or man-made?"

"Bit of both," Normy said, turning to start again. "I've got a few of them about. Come on."

The scrub grew thicker and the terrain steeper as they worked their way between twisted trunks and fallen, crumbling logs—some the size of a telephone pole—and Parker began to notice mounds of dirt piled at intervals throughout the undergrowth, as though somebody had been digging into the side of the hill.

"What are they, Normy?"

Normy hesitated, and then said, puffing, "Ask me another time."

The hillside grew steeper. Parker climbed from one big rock to another, stretching the large muscle of his thighs, knowing that tomorrow, his legs would ache from the unusual effort. He tripped on the rough edge of one boulder, catching his foot before smashing his knee. He felt lucky, knowing it might have been worse and he would have retained little hope of getting back to Whittlesea. Before long though, the vegetation threw a final, desperate hurdle at them; blackberries, growing in wide, awkward sections that Parker wouldn't have bothered trying to get through without Normy's help. They took small, cautious steps, but Parker still caught a few scratches on his lower legs, despite Normy's warning. Finally, the undergrowth began to thin, and soon they reached a set of stairs that had been scratched into the hill, fortified with vertical cuts of wood the thickness of old phone books. The bush threw long and heavy shadows over the climb, but the air was thick and oppressive, and by the time Parker reached the last step, he was puffing, sweat running down the middle of his back.

"Give ya a good workout," Normy said, breathing normally.

Parker clapped him on the back. "You got a glass of water?"

Normy chuckled. "I do indeed."

Parker followed with the wide-eyed wonder of a kid in a toy store. Parker loved camping; hadn't missed a caravan and camping show at the exhibition buildings in Melbourne for years. The inventive ways people made their camping lives easier fascinated him. He knew Normy lived alone and had little contact with the outside world, and he thought that if the older man had worked in business—design or something like that—he would have made a lot of money. He had a mind like an engineer.

There were cables and PVC tubes, springs and clips, barrels and buckets. The house was a flat structure with a fine slope on the roof. There were no downpipes because all the gutters ran into multiple water tanks. One side of the house had four large solar panels that produced electricity when the sun was out.

"I'm not on the grid," Normy said, "and I haven't' gotten around to getting myself one of those big batteries, so I only get electricity when the sun shines. Suits me fine."

He filled en empty glass from a barrel sitting on a wooden bench outside the kitchen. A thin PVC pipe ran up to one of the larger water tanks, filled via a gravity feed system.

Parker drank it quickly. "Tastes fine."

"'Course it does. I have to treat it though; birds crap on the roof and it can wash into the water. Not good for you."

It was still hot, but the combined house and the placement of numerous medium sized trees around the building threw pleasant shade. They weaved between trees and shrubs, Parker wondrous at the number of contraptions Normy had either working or under construction. Parker had no idea what purpose half of them served.

They circled the building and ran into Normy's most prized possession—his vegetable garden. Parker remembered it being a large rectangle of craziness when he was a kid, but now it looked enormous. He guessed eighty square feet, and it was chocked with luscious summer vegetables. All the produce was big and bright: yellow, red and green capsicums, cucumbers, tomatoes the color of ketchup, zucchinis, and corn. Though, just as many vegetables that could be harvested were in other stages of growth.

"How much time do you spend on this?" Parker asked, his mouth agape with wonder.

"A lot."

"What do you do with it all?"

"I eat most of it. There are a million things to make out of it and it's my primary source of food. I have eggs from the chickens, too —and the occasional chook, but I pretty much eat veggies for lunch and dinner. Helps me stay lean."

"How often do you go into town?"

"Once a month. I buy flour, any seeds I might need in the next six months, meat, sugar, small batteries."

"Sugar?"

"For certain specialties I enjoy."

"Well, the place is better than I remember," Parker said.

"It's changed a lot since then." Normy led Parker back towards the house. "Stay for a bite to eat?" He asked, turning back as he walked. "As you can see, I've got plenty."

"Sure," Parker said. "I've got nowhere to be." He thought about Sam again, and wondered if he should return to the camp in case he arrived, but he dismissed it; the chances of Sam being there were low.

Old Normy served up leftover vegetable frittata like nothing Parker had ever tasted. They ate outside under a lemon tree. While Parker was eating, Normy hurried away and returned with a cold bottle of beer. "Home brew," he said, pouring Parker a glass. "This is why I need the sugar."

They sat out in the heat, which was bearable, and drank the rest of the bottle after finishing off the frittata in record time.

"You hear anything about the blackout?" Parker asked.

"Blackout?" Parker explained what he knew. "Didn't even know about it," Normy said. "My closest neighbor is more than two clicks away. I've got nothing tied to the electrical power grid. Everything I use is solar running independent. I don't have a phone. My refrigerator and freezer are leftovers from the nineteen-eighties. I've been fixing them myself for years. Helps being a mechanic by trade." He took a swig of beer. "My motorbike is thirty-five years old. My car is forty, although I don't know if they're still working. And you say your car won't start?" Parker shook his head. "I guess I'll find out when I head back into town next week."

They traded stories about the area for another hour and a half, Parker reminiscing about the fishing he and his father did, Normy about living at Hell Ridge on his own. Parker found it fascinating and could have listened all day, except he knew Sam might have arrived and would be waiting for him.

The sun was edging towards the western horizon when Parker

finally stood to leave. Normy could talk. Parker realized he probably never saw anyone.

They shook hands and Parker started for the steps leading
down to the creek. "You need anything over the next two weeks
while you're camping, just walk up and let me know," Normy said.

"Thank you, sir. And thanks for the hospitality. I love hearing
all your stories. You've got an incredible property up here. A
perfect haven away from the rest of the world."

"Just the way I like it."

Parker started to walk off. Then he turned, remembering what
he had seen and what Normy had said climbing up to Hell's
Ridge.

"Hey, Normy, one more thing."

Normy raised his brow. "You're gonna ask me about the mines
and the piles of dirt, aren't you?"

"Mines?" Parker said, feeling a tinge of excitement. "I didn't
know it was a mine."

"Yeah," Normy said, nodding. "Few of them about. Were dug
out back in the forties, after the second big war."

"What for?"

Normy smiled now. "You come back and visit me before you
leave and I'll tell you. Deal."

Parker chuckled. He wanted to know now, but he would wait.
"Sure. I'll see you then."

He picked his way back down the rough stairs, took a few
minutes to find the almost invisible path through the blackberry
bushes, and then slid down the boulders to avoid tripping as he
had done on the way up. He stopped for a few minutes where the
dirt was piled, inspecting the holes from which it was dug, at a
distance, concluding a person had tilled them, after spotting an
old, rusted short handled shovel leaning against a wiry trunk.
Soon, he moved on, using the slender trees to brace himself as he
again slid his way down the steepest section of the mountain,
ducking and weaving the scraggy, dangling scrub, brushing things
out of his hair he didn't want to know about. At the mine, he
crossed the ground and stood about ten yards away, trying to get a
glimpse of the dark, murky air beyond the stained wooden fence

planks. Part of him wanted to pull the barrier away and poke his head inside. The other part of him though wanted to keep on moving. He did that, eventually finding the narrow, windy trail leading to the rapids of the creek. The path from Normy's was easy to remember now he had done it twice.

Parked stepped across the wet, slimy rocks, worked his way back along the bank to where he'd left his fishing rod, then walked the path back to his camp, feeling a slight anticipation that Sam might have arrived and be waiting.

But the campsite was empty and unchanged from when he'd left it that morning. He tried to charge his phone again, but the screen remained dark and he threw it into the tent in anger. The car was just as unresponsive. Worry crept into Parker's gut. He had expected Sam to have arrived by now. It made him almost twenty-four hours late. And thoughts of Maise, who he probably had no business thinking about anymore, grew stronger. Was she okay? She worked at the IGA and if the power was out there, people would be demanding and Maise would wear the brunt of it. Parker wondered if he had buried his feelings for her deep enough following their break up. He pushed the thought away.

At what point did he walk back to Whittlesea? Maybe he could leave now. Six hours would see him home well after dark. It probably wasn't the safest option. If he ran into trouble and needed help, he wouldn't find his way without a torch.

No, he would give Sam until tomorrow morning and if he hadn't arrived by then, Parker would start the long walk back to town.

THIRTEEN

I t was late Monday afternoon, 24 hours since the power had gone out and it had been the craziest period of shopping for the Whittlesea IGA in its history. Maise had worked the last three hours and if she thought it had been busy the day before, it had nothing on this. People were buying whatever they could get their hands on, sometimes basketfuls of products Maise doubted they would ever use. The limits Mr. Olsen had placed the pervious day ensured most people got something, but the stock had almost run out.

Maise's head pulsed as she fought to keep up. Part of it was the heat, no doubt, but also the constant thinking and adding up in her brain. By not using the calculator, she was much faster than the others girls, but that meant she served more customers. She gave thanks that everything in the IGA had a price sticker. Several people challenged her adding abilities, so again, Maise provided them the calculator and after that, they said no more.

They'd run out of paper on which to process manual credit card transactions and had reverted to cash. Numerous people reached the checkout only to ask Maise if they could use card, despite Mr. Olsen taping a big sign at the entrance stating cash only purchases. The lines had been out the door, reaching the Lime Street corner a little past the Commonwealth Bank. She'd glanced up and spotted

Mark at one point, but other than confirming she was managing, didn't have time to speak with him.

A younger woman with a kid clinging to her leg started yelling at Maise, accusing her of trying to keep food from the mouths of her children. While Maise didn't know every person in Whittlesea, she knew many, as most shopped at the IGA. This woman though, she had never seen before.

"What are my kids gonna eat? We've only got rice bubbles and Tim Tam biscuits left at home." Maise tried to look apologetic. The standard operating procedure when customers argued in such a way was to apologize. "They're waiting for me to bring food home." The woman continued. She fished a plastic card from her purse and flicked it at Maise. "Why can't you just let me use credit? Surely you've got one of those old clunky machines that take a copy of the card details?"

"I'm sorry," Maise said. "It's store policy. Cash only now."

"This is rubbish. Absolute rubbish. I know Bert Fraser very well, he's on the council and I'll be having a strong word with him about this store."

Mr. Olsen arrived. "Please, ma'am, if you don't have cash I'll have to ask you to leave the store. We have other customers waiting patiently."

With that, the woman dropped her basket where she stood and walked out. Others waiting in the queue rummaged though her goods and it was empty in moments. Maise bit her tongue, wanting to scream at the lady that she was a whiny baby.

Maise made herself a promise, then. She was sick of taking people's crap; sick of keeping her mouth shut and disagreeing in silence. She would never be Jas and she'd pick her battles, but Maise pledged that from now on, she'd stand up for herself, wouldn't sit back and keep quiet, waiting for the world to come to her. She would voice her opinion, fight for what she wanted and not let anyone else suppress her voice. She knew she was often right. She felt somewhat better after that.

To his credit, Mr. Olsen had not stopped moving or talking, working tremendously hard to keep the place functioning. One of the older generators was still operating and once the frozen food had sold out, he used it to power a couple of industrial fans with their faded paint and ancient logos to blow hot air at the registers. It made a difference for Maise and the others. Just having a breeze, even if warm, was refreshing. The sweat on her skin began to cool her body. Anything was better than standing there in the still heat. Mr. Olsen had given them bottles of water from a stash out back and even set up another lady to serve—since the registers weren't working and it was cash only, it didn't matter where stock was counted. Still, the lines took forever to reduce.

Working the register, Maise usually heard bits and pieces of small town talk—what trouble kids were into, who was sick, which married couple were breaking up this week. Now, it was about what was going to happen in the coming days. She heard that the government was stumped reconnecting the power, but that the power would be reconnected at five o'clock that night. She also heard the State Premier had died of a heart attack and that the police couldn't cope with the amount of crime occurring. Maise didn't know what to believe.

The most concerning piece of information she heard came from a woman who lived on the other side of the Plenty River, beyond the Little River Street reserve. The conversation between her and a man in line was supposed to be private but the woman's voice carried.

"Chinese are invadin'," the woman said in a slow, annunciated Australian accent. "They've taken over the Yan Yean Reservoir."

The Yan Yean Reservoir was built a hundred and sixty-five years earlier, at the height of the gold rush days and was the oldest water supply for the city of Melbourne. It was nine hundred and sixty-three meters long and had a capacity of thirty thousand megaliters. It supplied many of the city's north-eastern suburbs and towns. On completion in 1857, it was known as the largest artificial reservoir in the world.

The lady was talking to the man directly behind her in line. "What's going on there?" The man asked.

"Army trucks with more wire fences and big gates. Tents. Lots of vehicles—army jeeps full of soldiers dressed in uniforms carrying machine guns."

"So? It's the Australian Defence Force (ADF). Set up to protect our water supply and help the town get through this."

"Bit early to being the military in, isn't it?"

This piqued Maise's interest. She tried to listen while adding up her customer's grocery charges. Other people had pushed in closer to hear the conversation.

"And you saw this yourself?"

The women hesitated. "Well, no, not me personally, but—"

The man laughed, turned to the others around them and shook his head. "So you haven't actually seen it. Who has seen it?"

"My neighbor." The man's eyebrows were raised, waiting to know who had witnessed the potential incursion. "Betty Hart."

The man clutched his belly. "Betty Hart? She's the biggest gossip in all of Whittlesea. I wouldn't believe anything *she* said. And how did she get over to Yan Yean?"

Others were nodding and murmuring their agreement and that seemed to put an end to the discussion. Maise wasn't sure either way.

Eventually, supply began to run out, and when the queue reduced to the point where Maise was able to take several swallows of her warm water, Mr. Olsen suggested she leave the register and do a clean up in the store. Maise happily obliged, preferring to move about than stand there a moment longer. The other two girls watched her leave with faces full of envy.

Several people still wandered the aisles, looking for product that wasn't a favorite among shoppers or that might have been missed behind vacant cardboard boxes or dead stock. Maise slipped on a pair of disposable latex gloves and carried an empty rubbish bin with her, picking up broken packaging or discarded shelf-ready cartons and broken product that had been trampled or dropped in people's haste to get stock into their baskets or trolleys. She took a roll of black garbage bags from the supply room— noting that Mr. Olsen had covered a stash of soft drinks, bottled water, and about six cases of canned goods behind a wire screen— and filled three of them, then took the big orange scissor dust mop and began walking the aisles collecting dust and smaller pieces of rubbish.

The shop was almost empty now, both of customers, and stock. Mr. Olsen called them together at the front of the store.

"I'm closing up," he said. "We've got nothing more to sell, really." None of the girls argued. From one of the cash boxes, Olsen took a wad of notes and handed them out to the girls, much more than they had earned, by Maise's count.

"Are you sure, Mr. Olsen?" Maise asked. "This is more than double what I would normally earn for three hours." The other two girls frowned.

Olsen smiled. "The way I see it, Maise, you three worked under incredible duress today—and yesterday, for that matter. It's damn hot. There's no air-conditioning. People have been very demanding. You all toughed it out, did what I asked." He gave a slight nod. "You're earned it, believe me."

Maise left the store and went back up Church Street towards home. She passed a number of other shops, dark and empty: the Whittlesea Pharmasave, a tobacco shop, and a thrift store. The pharmacy had its front window broken and someone had covered it with some temporary wire fencing, the kind used for building sites to prevent accidents. The Commonwealth Bank was of course shut. If all the stores remained closed, where would they spend their money? The automatic teller machine was dark too, but she wondered how long before someone tried to break it open and take all the cash. She passed Lime Street; the real estate company, the bakery, the fish and chip shop. People were out riding bikes, walking. It had cooled a little, but not enough to be comfortable. A group of pre-teens had congregated on Walnut Street, just around the corner from the Amcal Pharmacy, talking in small gangs. Most wore long board shorts, singlet tops, and hats, and they had the sun-kissed look of kids at the end of six weeks' summer holidays.

On Beech Street, Maise spotted a large number of people lined up at a stall outside the Royal Mail Hotel where they served cups of water from one of the hotel's large water tanks.

When she reached home, Mark was sitting under the pergola out the back, sipping on another warm beer.

"You're home early? I was gonna come down and grab you at eight again."

"No more food," Maise said with her palms up.

"Nothing?" Mark asked, sitting forward with surprise. Maise shook her head. "Well, we've still got a bit left. Should keep us going a few more days yet."

"What about after that, Mark? What are people—not just us—going to do when the food and water runs out?"

Mark shook his head. "I don't know." He considered this for a moment. "Hey. Any word from your ex-boyfriend?"

Maise had thought about Parker several times today. He probably had the best spot in town up there by the creek. He would have stocked up for the two-week trip beforehand, and he had an endless supply of fish and water.

"No. And I don't expect to. Why would he?"

"'Cos he's worried."

"We're not going out anymore, remember?" She made a hand motion. "Besides, if I was him, I'd be staying put. He's stuck up there for now, anyway. I doubt his Hilux will work and I don't expect he'll walk all the way back."

"Keith would have," Mark said with a smile.

Maise's face pinched into disbelief. "What? Bull crap."

"He asked about you today." Maise's brow lifted. "He still likes you."

"You shut it down, though, right?"

Mark shook his head. "I'm going to get the Commodore off him tomorrow afternoon so I need him on my side."

Maise eyed Mark. "You still think he'll actually give it to you?"

"I've got the rest of the cash. Why wouldn't he?"

She shrugged. "Great. After that you can tell him I'm not interested."

"I think you can tell him." Mark winked.

Maise stood up to leave. She needed to wash before the sweat became ingrained into her skin. "There was a lady in the store, lives on the other side of the Plenty River that said she knew somebody who had seen the army at the Yan Yean Reservoir. But get this—she reckons they're Chinese."

"Chinese?" Mark chuckled. "The Army is Chinese?"

Maise shrugged. "That's what she said they said."

"What's that—" Mark leapt forward and stood. "Maybe it's an invasion," he said with a smile. "Maybe they caused the blackout and now they're moving in on our turf. Although, why would they bother setting up in Whittlesea?"

"Our water supply, of course."

"True. Well spotted."

"Technically we're on the outskirts of Melbourne."

"Perimeter, you reckon?"

Maise turned to leave. "Shoosh. There's no invasion." I'm going to have a shower with my bucket of cold water. I've sweated more today than ever before."

"Three buckets, max," Mark said. "That's about all you'll get out of the tank water."

Maise waved him off and left him alone with his warm beer.

FOURTEEN

Tuesday, January 24, 2023
Day 2

T he tent door flapping in the breeze finally woke Parker. He rolled off his air mattress, having not bothered to use the sleeping bag for the second straight night, and staggered out of the tent with bed hair and sleep in his eyes.

Stretching, he peered about, and guessed from the height of the sun in the sky, it was about eight o'clock. *Still no Sam.*

He had made the decision the previous night after returning from Normy King's place to walk back to Whittlesea if Sam hadn't shown up by morning. Parker might sit around waiting for Sam only to have him never show. That wasn't the holiday he'd planned. Worst case scenario, they rode their mountain bikes back up to Hell Ridge. But it was more than just Sam. Maise was down there too, and although he'd tried to ignore thoughts of her, he found himself lying awake wondering how she was managing. Even if they weren't together anymore, he still cared deeply for Maise and he wanted to check in on her.

After returning from old Normy King's magnificent property, he'd nestled into his canvas chair beside the bubbling creek and fished the afternoon away. At one point, after his third or fourth beer, the heat had worked him into a state of rest and he fell asleep for an hour or so, then woke with a headache, for which the only cure was another beer. But the joy of drinking alone quietly dissolved. He cooked a couple of sausages on the butane stove before it got dark and then laid down on the air bed thinking about what was going on in the world before quickly drifting off.

As he gathered supplies to carry in a pack, Maise's image kept infiltrating his thoughts. She worked at the IGA, taking shifts to supplement her mature age student study allowance. Sam had mentioned the US had gone dark. Potentially *all* the power was out. Houses, grocery stores, hospitals, hotels… and if cars weren't working, did that mean trucks were out too? Surely. So, what happened after the stores ran out of food? Would people be stealing from each other? If one person had a stock of non-perishables and another didn't, would it become a fight to the death? It sounded extreme, but Parker thought that might happen eventually if food became so scarce. Because at their core, people would do what it took to survive, with consideration only for those part of their immediate circle. He remembered the news footage of people fighting over supplies in early 2020 after COVID first hit. Supermarkets ran out of toilet paper first, then staples like flour, sugar, and rice. Nobody gave a shit that Bob Smith's family down the street had nothing with which to wipe themselves. If things had gone the way Parker suspected, these people would be cramming the stores now, shoving as much product as they could into their shopping trolleys. And Maise was right in the front line. Sam could look after himself. Maise was no longer his girl, but he didn't want her to face it alone.

"Stop it," Parker said as he zipped up his backpack. "Just stop talking rubbish. You don't know anything, yet. The power might *not* be out. Maise will be fine."

Parker wasn't convinced though. The small knot in his gut continued to grow. His instinct for this sort of stuff—his father called it his survival instinct—was generally on the mark. Late in his teens, he'd been partying with a group of kids, when the only one with their license offered to drive them back to the caravan park. The driver had been drinking, and everyone climbed in except Parker. He couldn't explain why he turned it down, but some deep inner voice begged him not to do it. He'd pleaded with his girlfriend to stay, but she'd laughed him off—as had the others —and they'd left him standing beside Lake Eildon to walk back to the caravan park alone. The car had crashed soon after, the driver hitting a fox crossing the road, and two of the passengers had died.

Now, Parker felt a similar pull of trepidation, and he worried about what might await him when he reached Whittlesea. He pushed it away and focused on getting himself ready, working through his mind how he would deal with the long journey in the heat.

Parker considered being away from the site. He expected to be gone at least a night, since it would take him six hours to walk there and probably two hours to ride back. He would need to secure the campsite. Possums and even water birds weren't afraid of getting into food stores. And there was always the possibility that if people ventured down the track they could steal supplies or trash the campsite. In all his time camping at Hell Ridge, nothing like that had ever happened. Parker hoped now wouldn't be the first time.

In the end, he decided to leave the generator out, lock the fridges in the tent and run the cable through a small hole in the rear. He zipped up both tents and locked them with small padlocks he kept in his supply case. He secured the non-perishable food, the gas cooker equipment and anything else lying around inside the secure boot of the Hilux and took his charger and phone.

He did a final sweep of the campsite to ensure he hadn't forgotten anything, and as he did, he considered his set up and how he would fare if the rest of Whittlesea had no power either. He had the old generators that ran on diesel, of which he had two forty liter, or ten-gallon tanks, and it didn't seem to be affected by whatever had happened to his car and phone. The car fridge was the same; it ran off the generator and was still pumping out cold air. He had butane gas, and plenty of it, to cook food, boil water or even start a fire. He had a gas light, an extensive first aid kit tucked away under the front seat of his Ute, bedding, spare clothes, even the ability to wash the clothes if needed. And he had a heap of food, mostly non-perishables, and an infinite supply of the freshest water and trout you could find. He was set, and even if a few of them ended up back at the camp, they could survive for several weeks

Parker slipped on his pack and started up the dirt track towards the main road, wiping a lick of sweat off his brow. If something had in fact gone wrong in the world, as he suspected, there probably wasn't a better place to stay than Hell Ridge. He just had to make it to Whittlesea, check on the people for whom he cared, and convince them to come back up to the camp with him. And who knew? Maybe he could show Maise their time apart had changed him.

FIFTEEN

Maise woke with a start, and leapt out of bed under a cloud of confusion about whether she had heard someone shouting. She waited, hearing nothing, and realized that incident had been the day before. The tension across her shoulders eased. She noticed just how silent the world was right then. There were no cars, no electrical appliance noises, not even kids shouting out in the street. The world had not been fixed overnight. The room was baking hot and her digital clock was still dark. If the power had been on, the numbers would be flashing. She slumped back down on the bed and lay there staring at the ceiling. It was going to be the third day without power. The heat would drive people—

Mr. and Mrs. Buckley. "Bugger."

She had told Mr. Buckley yesterday morning that she'd come over and check on how Mrs. Buckley was feeling. Her work at the IGA had exhausted her and Maise had forgotten about it. She scolded herself for not being more thoughtful. It was one of the things she had criticized Parker about and she didn't want to be a hypocrite.

With renewed purpose, Maise dressed, cleaned herself up and rushed together a breakfast comprising fruit, yoghurt and juice. Mark had put the yoghurt in the freezer, and it had remained at a low enough temperature so far as not to spoil. After today though, most of the stuff that needed refrigeration would be lost.

Mark was out in the shed pottering around, so Maise left him and headed out the front door a little after nine according to the analog wall clock.

The youthful, stinging heat of the day kept the sidewalk and front yards empty. People's houses were already too hot without electric cooling, and she suspected they'd seek refuge in their back-yards under the shade of trees or pergolas, hopeful of a breeze. Those with pools would be popular. How many elderly people would suffer through the grueling heat? That was Maise's fear for her neighbors.

She climbed the front steps and tapped lightly on the glass panel beside the door. She waited, then repeated the action when she didn't hear footsteps from inside. Nobody answered. A thin worry crept over her. She reached out and rotated the door handle. The mechanism clicked open and the door swung away from her. Hot air rushed out, momentarily overpowering her. It was far hotter inside than out, much hotter even than Maise's house, where she and Mark had opened all the windows and doors to affect some kind of breeze. It was clear the Buckley's had done nothing of the kind.

She stepped inside, leaving the front door open behind her. "Mr. Buckley? Mrs. Buckley?" A faint voice called out to her. "Where are you?" Maise asked.

She moved quickly from the entry foyer into the passageway and saw right through the house and beyond into the backyard, where a small set of table and chairs sat under the cover of a pergola. She passed a neat dining room with an ancient wooden legged table on her left; the master bedroom with a frilly bed spread on her right, and finally reached the family room, where Mr. Buckley's voice greeted her.

"She's dead." Maise followed the sound and found him lying propped against a wall on the other side of the kitchen bench. Sweat covered his pale face; red, droopy eyes swum in tears that made lines down his wrinkled cheeks. He looked defeated, like a man who has lost the world.

"Mrs. Buckley?" He nodded. Maise felt her stomach drop and

her legs grow weak. *No, please.* "Where?" She managed, her mouth full of invisible cotton wool.

Mr. Buckley waved a weak hand towards a doorway off the living room. "Moved her to the back room away from the front of the house, but it made no difference."

Maise edged her way around a coffee table and between a set of recliners, where Mr. and Mrs. Buckley devoted their evenings to Eddie McGuire and *Millionaire Hot Seat,* then the nightly news. She passed through the door, her heart rate elevating; found a carpeted hallway with a series of dark rooms and picked the closest one.

The room was hot enough to cause Maise to grab hold of the wall. On the bed lay Mrs. Buckley. Her eyes were closed. Maise stared at her. Maybe she wasn't dead. Maybe Mr. Buckley had made a mistake and…

She approached the body, her pulse thumping, and stopped by the bedside. The older woman looked peaceful. She *might* have been sleeping. Maise watched for the rise and fall of her chest, holding her gaze for a long moment, willing the old woman's torso to move. But her chest remained flat and unmoving. Maise reached out and touched her hand, then retracted it. It was cold, disparity in such a hot world. After a few moments, Maise forced herself to reach again with shaky fingers and feel for a pulse that never came.

A swell of sadness overcame Maise as she watched the old woman who had been her neighbor—*their* neighbor—for all of Maise's life. She thought about the gifts Mrs. Buckley had wrapped for her and Mark when they were kids; the Easter eggs they had hidden in their yard, telling a pig-tailed Maise that the Easter Bunny had made a mistake and left some behind. There had been countless times where Mrs. Buckley had looked after them—when their parents had gone out for dinner on a special occasion, or even after school, before Mark and Maise had been entrusted with their own sets of keys. Mrs. Buckley was always up for a chat; happy to lend an ear, or provide that cup of sugar or egg when someone ran short while cooking. She was the kind if woman Maise hoped to be when she reached that age. She felt a stab of guilt that she hadn't checked on them yesterday like she had promised. What if—

"Maise?"

The call came from the living room, and she remembered Mr. Buckley was still sitting against the wall. She left the bedroom and found him in the same position.

"Are you okay?" Maise asked. He gave the barest nod; but his bottom lip trembled. "What can I do?"

"Help me up?" He groaned, starting the process himself.

Using both hands, Maise took Mr. Buckley under his left arm and lifted, shocked at the weight of his thin frame. They lurched onto the couch and Mr. Buckley fell into it.

"Can you open the back door for me?"

Maise hurried around the sofa and slid open one side, keeping the wire security door closed. There wasn't much of a breeze, but the air outside was definitely cooler than inside this furnace. She went directly to the bathroom beside the room where Mrs. Buckley lay, took a dry face washer off the sink and twisted the tap. A faint stream of water ran, under which Maise wet the cloth. It was the best she could think to do right now.

Back in the living room, Mr. Buckley laid back on the couch and Maise placed the wet towel onto his forehead.

"Cold water in the fridge," he said. "Don't know how cold it will be now, though."

She took the jug and filled a glass from the cupboard, then brought it to him. He thanked her, taking large gulps with a shaky hand. When he had emptied the glass, he handed it back to her and she placed it on the coffee table.

"What do we do now?" Maise asked.

In a gravely voice, he said, "The police will need to be notified. They'll probably organize for the hospital to collect her body. Although, I'm not sure how they'll get out to collect the body if none of the vehicles are working."

She felt a deep sense of loss for Mr. Buckley and for his sake, tried not to let the emotion of the moment overcome her. Tears touched the corners of her eyes, and her throat choked up. She wondered what could she do for him immediately and concluded there was only one thing he needed right now. She couldn't let Mrs. Buckley's body swelter in the heat for any longer than necessary.

"I'll go," Maise said "To the police station. Let my Uncle know what has happened. I'm sure they'll be able to tell me what to do from there."

Mr. Buckley put a hand over hers. "You're a darn good girl. She loved you, you know. Like one of her own."

Maise pressed her lips together, fighting back the tears. "Thank you. That means a lot."

She filled another glass of water for Mr. Buckley, then promised she'd be back soon with some answers. "Sure you'll be all right?"

He nodded. "Much better now I'm not stuck on the floor against the wall."

"Can you move around?"

"Yeah, I think so. Just hand me the walking stick in the cupboard over there, will you?"

She did, then bid him farewell until she returned. Her sadness at Mrs. Buckley's death and for Mr. Buckley's loss covered her in an invisible cloak. She had Mark to deal with; to tell him she was going down to the police station was bound to cause a discussion.

"Are you sure?" Mark said, standing at the kitchen bench with another warm beer in hand. "It's going to get crazier and crazier until this power is back on. I'm just not sure we should be out wandering around right now."

"I'm not wandering, Mark. Just riding my bike down to the police station to let Uncle Jim know Mrs. Buckley has passed and to ask how we should deal with it. They can steal my bike if they want. I'll walk home. Besides, you have to ride over to Keith's house, don't you?"

"Why do you have to tell anyone? Why can't you just leave her there for now? If this thing get's fixed tonight or tomorrow, I'm sure you'll be able to call and let them know."

Maise's face twisted with disgust, but her voice was low and calm. "I'm not going to wait until then, Mark. Mr. Buckley asked me to go," she lied. "What was I supposed to say?"

Mark made a grim expression and shook his head. "I don't like it." She had him, now; he'd gone from arguing she shouldn't go, to saying 'I don't like it'. She remembered the promise she'd made to herself while working the previous day. "I'll come with you then."

"*Seriously?* I'm not bloody twelve years old. I'll go, you stay. Anyway, I thought you had to go and get the car from Keith?"

Mark checked the old clock on the wall. "Yeah, I do. Very soon, actually." He took a swallow of his beer. "Just be quick about it, will you?"

"Of course. Besides, its hot, I don't want to be out there any longer than I need to."

Maise took her mountain bike from the garage and instead of a helmet took a grass-weaved Billabong hat from her room, which, with its wide brim, would keep the deadly sun off her face. She wheeled the bike out to the letterbox and glanced back to see if Mark was watching her leave. He wasn't there; at least that was something.

Before she took off, she saw several neighbors standing at their letterboxes holding a flyer. She checked theirs and found the same piece of paper. It was a message from the government, and it read:

Dear Citizens,

We bring you news of this unfortunate incident that has left us without power to any contemporary equipment with electrical circuitry, including the limited use of motor vehicles. At this stage, we believe some manifestation of energy – most likely a solar flare – has created a large-scale electro magnetic pulse that has damaged anything with electrical circuitry boards in the region. The State Government has convened an emergency meeting on Spring Street and we will continue to work on a solution. For now, we recommend you stay indoors with blinds drawn to reduce the effect of the heat. Remain hydrated through either your local water source or bottled water if it is available. We implore each person to avoid over-stocking from stores. We will keep you updated and intend to have more solutions in the coming hours.

Your premier,

Rex Matheson

·   ·   ·

Maise stuffed the flyer into her back pocket. She leant her bike against the letterbox, then jogged to the Buckley's house, took the flyer inside and handed it to Mr. Buckley, telling him she would return from the police station soon.

With that, and a sense of renewed hope that the government was working on a plan, Maise set off.

SIXTEEN

I t was a steep, rocky five-minute walk back to the main road from Parker's campsite. He climbed the furrowed track thinking about the chances of someone finding the place. It had several things going for it, including its difficulty to access. Making it down the path to the bottom was an achievement in itself, and should only be attempted with a sizeable 4x4 or a skillful driver. The track had deep, jagged ruts caused by heavy rains washing down from the top of the hill, and gnarled tree roots crossed the road at various places, undulating its surface. It could be done, but many people avoided it.

The heat crawled quickly under his skin. He had on shorts, a t-shirt and sneakers, along with a peaked cap to keep the sun off his face, but by the time he reached Whittlesea, he'd probably have a sunburn on his arms and neck. Sunscreen was the one thing he'd forgotten. He carried four six hundred milliliter bottles of water, knowing he would expend a huge amount of sweat on the trek. There was a general store along the way at which he'd probably have to refill.

He reached the blacktop and started along the left edge, walking with the flow of traffic—not that he expected much traffic. Gum trees nestled in against the road, leading away to a tangle of scrub on either side, the shadow of their towering bodies providing some respite. It really was a beautiful country, the scents of gums and grass, even the water, distant now, although it would wind its way back to the road soon enough, carried its own peculiar scent. The sunlight, hot and burning when directly under its wrath, painted dappled light on the bitumen through the trees. It might have been the first time in a long time that Parker had gone anywhere without listening to music, the radio, or talking on the phone. It gave him a chance to hear the surroundings, and he was pleasantly surprised at nature's songs. Birds chirped in the trees, a synthesis of fast and slow whistles, loud and soft calls, chattering only a couple of yards from where Parker walked, making audacious attempts to coerce each other. When he tuned into the moment, it was a magical place.

After a time, he unscrewed the lid from his first bottle of water and took a long gulp. He considered the impact of an EMP event. He didn't know much about them, if he was honest. Based on what Sam had said and what Parker knew, EMP affected electrical circuitry and modern vehicles were full of them. He supposed the computer chip in his car had been damaged and he imagined others were damaged in the same way, too. But what did that mean for older models that had no computer chip and a carburetor? Maybe they were still working. He knew a couple of people that had vehicles like that.

Leaves rustled in the shaggy, yellowish grass beyond the shoulder of the road. Parker halted, then stepped sideways into the center of the blacktop, watching the space from where he'd heard the sound. Snakes were common in the area, particularly around summer, and Parker had seen his fair share over the years while out in the bush. The last thing he wanted was to be bitten by a tiger snake or an eastern brown and have no way of getting to the hospital. He would die a slow, painful death.

A thin black sash glided through the gravel shoulder and onto the road. Parker watched, frozen. It slithered directly across the highway and stopped in the center, as if daring him to pass. Still, Parker held his nerve. Snakes could be lightening fast. He cocked the bottle of water in his hand, ready to throw it at the reptile if it felt threatened and attacked. Eventually, the snake glided the rest of the way and disappeared into the grass. Parker let out a sigh, unaware he'd been holding the tension in. He moved quickly past the spot, keeping a wary eye on the place where the snake had disappeared.

Eventually, the King Parrot Creek returned to the edge of the road, or at least to a viewing distance for Parker. The mostly dark-green body wound its way through the trees, curling and twisting, shallow in places where the sun poked through the umbrella of leaves and lit the rocky bottom. There were dozens of places to camp and fish along this section. He hoped that if somebody *was* out looking for a spot, these places would be appealing enough for them to try.

The highway dipped and climbed, and Parker couldn't escape either, avoiding the temptation to jog down the sloped sections, bending his back and feeling the strain in his calves and hamstrings on the hills. The isolation gave him more time to think and Maise was at the forefront of his mind. Aside from his father, who was travelling around the northern part of Australia—and Sam—Maise had been Parker's family. His mother had died the previous year and Parker knew he had struggled. His father had withdrawn into himself, dealing with the pain and loss; he had no time for Parker's grief when he couldn't deal with his own. Aunties, Uncles and cousins had hung around for the funeral and had stayed in contact for the first month or so, but then everyone's lives had continued, leaving Parker and his father without their mother and wife. It had been Maise, by his side day and night, who had gotten him through the time.

He still missed her. Badly, at times, as much as he tried to ignore it, even deny that she had left a huge gap in his life. That rock he'd been able to lean against was gone. Their relationship had become difficult near the end, he knew that, and accepted it was mostly his fault, but now, it seemed worse not to have her at all. He was selfish at times, choosing to attend social events without Maise so he wouldn't have to justify staying longer or getting smashed. Since his mother's fairly sudden death, he had decided to live as much as he could, do the things that he wanted before he got married and had kids. It wasn't that he didn't want to spend time with Maise. He had just needed his own space. His independence. Maise never quite understood that. She wanted them to spend all their time together. Parker wasn't ready for that. It didn't mean Parker loved her any less. She wanted to talk about settling down and having a family. Parker imagined those things in his future, but for now, the timing wasn't right. He still wanted the flexibility to do things as he pleased.

Although he'd been able to do the things he wanted since they split up, he wasn't any happier. In fact, he was more miserable. Single life happiness was a fallacy. It occurred to him in the isolation of walking back home, and with the potential issue happening in Whittlesea, that he was better off with Maise. *Much* better off. He enjoyed her companionship. She was reliable, supportive. She made him laugh. She was smarter than he'd ever be, and he loved learning things from her. There was always a discussion to have with Maise, and regardless of the content, Parker enjoyed it. He had avoided the thought since the break up, but now, he admitted to himself that he still loved her, no question, and up until their break up, despite any challenges, he had always seen himself spending his life with her. Having kids. Growing old. Regret shrouded him.

He made the decision then that he would check on Maise, even if it risked her slamming the door in his face. He would tell her how he felt and see where it led from there. He would have to be careful around her brother, though. They had once been best mates, but that had ended like a catastrophic plane crash. Parker felt his mood shift. He hated thinking about Mark because it filled him with negativity. The situation was unresolved, even after six months. It had adversely affected both their lives, and although Parker knew he should accept part of the responsibility, he believed Mark should too, and he didn't think that was ever going to happen.

A sound drifted to his ears and Parker thought for a second he was imagining it. He stopped and listened, waiting for the hot northerly wind to cease and silence the whispering trees. When it did, he guessed it was the sound of an engine, coming towards him from the Whittlesea direction.

Anticipation growing, Parker walked quickly along the edge of the highway towards the noise. Suddenly, from around the corner, a large orange tractor appeared, bobbing along the road, an elderly man with a flannel shirt and a brown-rimmed hat in the driver's seat. When he spotted Parker, the engine whirred down as the man dropped a gear. Parker felt hopeful. Maybe whatever had happened had been fixed.

The tractor slowed until it halted beside him. The old man put the thing into neutral and the engine quieted to a low whine.

"Hey, fella," the man said. "How goes it?"

"All right," Parker said. "You live around here?"

"'Bout three mile that way," he pointed in the direction from which he'd come. "Off to my neighbors to do some grass slashin' for her. Where you off to?"

"Whittlesea."

The man whistled. "Long walk. No car?"

"Not working. Is yours?"

"Last time I checked."

"When was that?"

The man looked along the highway into the distance, considering the question. "Yesterday afternoon."

"You haven't checked it since then?" He shook his head. "Bugger. So, you don't know what's happened?"

"Power's out. Know that much."

"Your mobile phone work?"

He chuckled. "Don't have one, son. Got a landline, but to be honest, haven't used it today."

Geez, Parker thought, of all the people he could meet who might be able to give him more answers, this guy was last on the list. "Okay. Fair enough. Well my car's not working and my phone's not working and I'm walking back to Whittlesea to find out what's going on."

"You check your battery?"

"Of the phone?"

"Or the car."

"Yeah. I checked both. The car is fine, the phone won't charge."

The man shrugged. "Oh well. Sorry I can't help. And sorry I can't give you lift into Whittlesea. Going the wrong way."

Parker raised the palm of his hand to indicate it was fine. He glanced over the tractor again, noting the faded orange paint, the rust and the chipped and faded logo. It looked nearly as aged as the man himself. "How old is this tractor?"

He thought for a moment. "Built around eighty-eight. Still going strong. They built these things to last back then. No computers or fancy stuff that can go wrong." Parker nodded as expected. "Well, I have to get movin'. Neighbor's expecting me. Stay safe, young man. I hope your trek back to Whittlesea is an easy one."

"Thanks," Parker said. "Safe travels."

The man put the tractor back into gear and it jerked away with a rumble.

Parker's pace quickened. Suddenly, he wanted to get to Whittlesea—or at least the Kinglake West general store—as quickly as possible, and find out more about the state of things. He had his answer to the question about older vehicles at the least.

He knocked off his first bottle of water, took a pee in the bushes on the side of the road, his modesty sailing away on the hot breeze. But as he rounded a bend and started up a long hill, another sound softened the call of the birds and the whispering trees, this time from the north. He momentarily wondered if it was the farmer and his tractor, deciding to offer Parker a ride to Whittlesea. But the sound was not the deep rumble he'd heard earlier.

He turned to face the oncoming noise, waiting for its arrival from around the bend. He felt a mix of nervous excitement. Maybe this was his ride into town. He'd appreciate not having to walk the remaining five or so hours.

A small jeep appeared—an *Army* jeep—complete with three soldiers. It wasn't an older vehicle, either. The sun twinkled of the fresh green paintwork.

Relief washed over Parker. There *were* modern vehicles that still worked. He waved as he took two steps out onto the road. To his absolute amazement though, the Jeep did not stop. It swerved around him, maintaining its steady fifty miles or eight kilometers per hour. Parker dropped his hand as it passed. The front passenger glanced at him. But that wasn't the strangest part of it. What Parker noted as most disturbing was their appearance—they were Chinese, and the vehicle had the Chinese flag painted on the door.

SEVENTEEN

Mick Hickey sunk into the plastic fold out chair with a can of beer and a packet of cigarettes. He slid one from the pack and stuck the tip into his mouth, then withdrew a metal zippo lighter from the pocket of his jeans and lit the end, drawing the smoke in deeply. Around him, in a circle of similar plastic chairs, sat Billy Burgemeyer, Aaron Fillipone, Heath Chin and Les Finlayson. Les signaled for the lighter and Mick tossed it to him. It continued around the group until everybody had smoke drifting from their cigarettes.

They were in the murky building at the back of Les Finlayson's house, probably the coolest place to be with no power. It was a four-car garage, and Les had one side taken up with a 1972 Holden Kingswood and a four-month old Harley Davidson Fat Boy 114. Although Les didn't actually have a permanent job, he was able to pay cash for the bike; that both annoyed and inspired Mick.

"Beer won't be cold for much longer," Mick said. "No more ice."

"Don't friggin' remind me," Les said. "Nothin' worse."

A medium sized blue cooler sat in the center of the circle, a half-dozen green beer cans floating in the last remnants of melting ice. They often used Les' garage as a meeting place, outside of official club business, when they would drive across Whittlesea to the larger clubhouse where dozens of bikers could assemble. But Mick preferred the smaller group. He wasn't yet convinced a motorcycle club was for him. He'd joined for the bikes and the camaraderie, and while there was plenty of that, often, there was more that he didn't enjoy so much. He tried to stay out of the peripheral activities, but sometimes it was unavoidable.

Aaron asked, "Have we heard from the others? Potsy and Rick?" Full of tattoos, Aaron had a round pale face with a poor excuse for a beard, and his red hair was already starting to recede, exposing a shiny forehead. He was the second oldest of the group behind Les.

Les took a drag. "Nuh. Nobody yet. Prob'ly stuck without a car. Too far for those lazy bastards to walk."

Today, with power and electrical equipment down, they had all made their way to the hangout looking for answers. Les was the man they usually looked toward for such. He was a senior member of the club, tough, street smart and feared. Although he wasn't the highest ranked member, he was considered the toughest and nastiest. Mick was always wary of Les, especially when he had too much to drink. What Les said, Mick and the others usually did. No questions asked. Stories floated around about Les' past deeds, several involving the disappearance of men that hadn't paid their debts or had wronged the club. Pocked skin on his cheeks and an ancient, faded scar down the left side of his face added weight to his demeanor. Most of the crew hung on his every word. But even he fell short of answers today.

"Government is taking us for a ride again," Les began, leaning forward from his chair, smoke and beer in hand. He had a scruffy beard, dark, grey-streaked long hair tied back in a ponytail, and his ubiquitous black sunglasses rested on the top of his head whenever he wasn't outside. "Dropped the ball somewhere. Now we'll have to pay for it."

"Whadda you think happened, Les?" Heath said, pushing strands of long glossy black hair back onto his head. Heath had a thick torso, forearms like small legs of lamb. He was a few years older than Mick and Billy, but not as old as Les, and loved a fight as much as anyone.

Les shrugged. "Dunno, mate. Electricity's out. Phone's not working. Your guess is as good as mine."

Mick had some ideas. He'd watched his share of science fiction shows in the last few years. "What about an EMP?" Les' expression told Mick he had no idea to what he was referring. "An electromagnetic pulse. Comes from a bomb in the sky. Knocks out anything with an electrical chip, basically."

"I don't know about that," Les said. "Sounds like something out of a movie." Mick opened his mouth to say something, but Les continued. "Who'd drop a bomb in the sky?"

"Chinese," Aaron said.

First smart thing Mick had heard from Aaron's mouth in a long time. "That would be my guess. If it had in fact happened."

"Well, might be so," Les said. "But the most important thing right now is that we get up to Hell Ridge to check on the crop. We should have made it there last weekend, 'cept for Digger's bash." He chuckled. "Glad we didn't miss that." The others agreed. Les lit another cigarette, but he recognized from Mick's furrowed brow that he had more to say. "What is it?" Mick considered his words. Les looked at Mick. "You reckon this EMP thing might go on for a while?"

"Nobody can know. Everything I know about 'em though, it ain't an easy thing to fix."

"What do you know?"

"Maybe we got to prepare that this thing might go on longer than we think."

"How long?" Aaron asked.

"I'd be guessing. Might be a day, might be a week."

"That's no bloody help," Aaron said.

Les switched his gaze from Aaron to Mick, took another swig of beer.

Mick figured he had nothing to lose; nobody else had any ideas. "Well, try this," Mick began, looking at Aaron. "Imagine for a minute we don't have any electricity for another week."

"As if that's gonna happen," Heath said.

"Why isn't it back on yet, hotshot?" Mick snapped. "There were no storms. No high winds. The whole goddamn state is out. Don't take a genius to figure out something bigger is going on."

"I don't buy it," Heath said. "Come on, man, surely the government will fix this soon."

Les was surprisingly silent. Mick half expected Les to challenge his thinking. Usually, Les was more skeptical, although, he was the kind of guy that had a contingency for everything. He grew dope plants in an isolated part of the scrub up near Hell Ridge and sold it to local kids. Les had a plan in case the dope was discovered, a plan if somebody squealed on them, and a plan for the possibility that they couldn't supply to their regular customers.

Les looked around at the others. "I think Mick is right." Aaron and Heath's eyes widened, showing surprise. "It's not like a we had a big bloody storm and all the power lines got knocked down."

"Yeah. Good point," Aaron said. "Didn't think of that."

Mick didn't bother to tell Aaron he'd made that point.

Les took another drag and continued. "Wouldn't hurt to take a few precautions. Which means making sure we have enough food, smokes and grog." He raised his eyebrows. "Yeah?" The others nodded. "Anyone know how the supermarket's lookin'?"

"I went past on the way here," Heath said. "Still a few things about."

"Won't last long."

"Bloody foreigners probably took most of it," Aaron added. "Greedy bastards have no shame."

Mick didn't know who qualified as a foreigner, and he had seen plenty of locals taking more than they needed, too.

"We can't wait on this," Les added, letting smoke drift from the corner of his mouth. "Bloody toilet paper ran out first when COVID hit. Had to steal it from the footy club. We gotta act straight away, right?"

"For sure," Aaron said.

"What're you thinking, Les?" Billy asked, bouncing in his seat with enthusiasm. His arms and legs were also covered in tattoos, and even though he wasn't working, he still wore an orange high-visibility shirt synonymous with tradesmen, storemen and truck drivers. He vied for the title of Les' number one supporter.

"We need to get our hands on some grub, smokes and beer, like I said. IGA should still have some supplies. That's the first step. We can take the Kingswood." He waved his beer towards the vehicle in the garage. "But we'll need to steal another one to move stuff around."

"Yeah," Billy said. "I like that. Make things a bit more exciting."

"I need to get up to Hell Ridge and check on the crop. Make sure it's getting water from the creek in this heat and that nobody's getting nosy."

"You worried about that old guy up at Hell Ridge who was snoopin' around the plants?" Aaron asked.

Les' mouth twisted with anger. "That old bastard's gonna get what he deserves if he's messed with my stuff."

"Lot a bush up there to bury him in," Billy joked.

"Wouldn't be the first," Les added, taking another swig of beer.

"What about the dope Keith Whitehead has?" Billy added.

Nodding, Les said, "Good point, Billy. That little bastard hasn't paid me for it yet. We'll have to visit him, won't we?"

"I bet he's sold it already."

"Then he's gonna have a problem, Les said, tossing his empty beer can aside. He leaned forward and took another from the cooler, cracked the ring and took a swig. Then he leant back in his chair. "Right. This is what we're gonna do." He held out one hand to count with his fingers. "One, we need to find another car—one that actually still works."

Billy said, "Saw a couple near Church Street on the way over."

Still with his thumb sticking up, Les said, "Who do we know that has an older model?"

"Old couple not far from here have one of those 70's VW combi vans," Aaron said, crushing his empty beer can in one fist."

"Good. Go get it. Fast."

"What about after that?"

"We head over to the camping store and see what we can muster."

"What if it's shut?" Aaron asked.

Les stared for a long moment. "Half our luck," Les said. "We'll make ourselves welcome."

Heath chuckled. "And no cops drivin' around, either."

Aaron said, "What's at the camping store?"

"Gas bottles. Tents. Anything we can use for camping."

"We camping?"

"I got a bad feeling about my plants so I wanna hang up there for a few days."

"All of us?"

Les shrugged. "Suit yourself. We get the drugs or the cash from Whitehead. Last I heard he hadn't sold the dope so he's probably still got it."

"A belting might do him some good if he won't cough it up," Billy smacked a fist into the palm of his hand.

"We'll see. Lastly, we get on up to Hell Ridge and check on the crop. Maybe hang there for a few days, make a go of it like we do up at the King River."

"A camping trip?"

"Don't get too excited, Billy. Priority is making sure the crop is in good shape."

They all sat waiting for Les to go on. After a moment, he stood out of his heat and went to a corner of the room where a pile of guns lay—shotguns, rifles, several handguns. He picked up one of the shotguns and turned to them. "Well? What are you lazy bastards waiting for? Get out there and find me a vehicle that still runs."

EIGHTEEN

M aise directed her mountain bike up a driveway and off Church Street, then followed the cracked footpath the last twenty yards to the Whittlesea Police station. It was a wide, single-story structure built in the 1980's, with a tiled roof and a low wire fence running slightly longer than its width. An uneven concrete pathway led from a gate in the fence to the front door where a single officer stood, protecting the entrance from a group of people gathered on the lawn. The people lingered with umbrellas and brimmed hats to keep the sun off their faces. Some had bottles of water; several had clear plastic or reusable containers. Those without looked at the others with envy. Half the folk had given up standing and were sitting cross-legged on the grass. They also had signs too; painted mostly, proclaiming TURN OUR POWER BACK ON and NO MORE LOCKDOWNS. Maise wasn't aware they were in a lockdown.

Several folks looked at Maise as she pushed the squeaky gate open. She guided her bicycle through and across the lawn where she leant it against the station's brick wall. The gaze of the crowd never left her. She moved through them—they didn't appear to be trying to get inside—it was as though they were waiting for information or just assuming their right to protest. The officer standing beside the door smiled at her.

"Hey, Maise."

"Hello, Officer Wales." She knew Nathan Wales from previous visits to see her uncle. There were ten full time officers working at the station and Maise knew most of them by face.

"Here to see your uncle?" Maise nodded. "He's a busy man, today."

"I won't be long." Mark and Maise had unconditional access to their uncle since losing their father—even in a crisis.

Officer Wales opened the door and Maise went in, hearing an echo of commentary questioning why she was allowed to enter the station.

Ahead of a brief entrance, a small reception room with a white counter, behind which, a policewoman with red hair tied up in a bun scribbled on a pad. Since their father had died, Maise had been coming to the police station on a weekly basis. Constable Janine Westall looked up from her writing as Maise approached and smiled.

"Hello, Maise. Here to see your uncle?"

"Yes and no. I also wanted to report a death." The policewoman's face stiffened. "My next door neighbor, Mrs. Buckley. She passed away overnight. She's elderly and her house is terribly hot."

"Okay, hold it there," Officer Westall reached for another notebook. "Can you give me all the details?"

Maise recounted what had occurred and provided the address.

"Still have several ambulances working the area. They're doing this sort of thing to retrieve others who have passed," Officer Westall said. "As soon as it's available, we'll send someone out along with an officer to take Mr. Buckley's statement. If you can let Mr. Buckley know to stay there until we arrive."

"I will, thank you. How long do you think it will be?"

"Sometime later today, I expect. You want to stop in for a quick chat with your uncle?"

Maise nodded. "Please."

"Go right through."

Beside the reception area, a doorway led to a corridor and a number of enclosed offices. The door was electronically locked and the only way to get through normally was via a security pass.

Maise didn't have one of these, but now, it was redundant as the place had no power. Someone had stuck a small wooden box between the door and the frame. Maise pulled on the handle and it swung open. She slipped into the hallway.

A burly policeman almost knocked her over.

"Sorry," he said, slipping past.

Officers moved along the corridor in both directions. It was like a busy freeway. Maise leapt across the width and pressed herself against the far wall, and then, keeping her head down, walked quickly along the hallway towards her uncle's office.

She poked her head around the doorway. He was sitting at his desk using what looked like a CB radio. The mouthpiece had a cord that was connected to a large black box on the desk return. A power cable snaked over the floor and out of the room. Maise assumed it was connected to a generator somewhere out back.

"I want that road cleared, Ron. Get another dozer from Freddy Albress. He's got a heap of old ones on his property. Surely more than one of them works. Over."

Uncle Jim looked up and spotted Maise. He gave her a smile, then waved her into his office towards a blue fabric armchair as Ron continued in a drawl that Maise couldn't quite understand.

Jim waited for him to finish, then responded. "Two things: the ambulance needs to be able to get through. There's already a backlog of dead we need collected and brought back to Hall's Funeral Services. Second, if the power comes back on and we have to rush around with medicines and food, we need the roads cleared. Make it happen, Ronny. Over and out." He switched off the CB and tossed the mouthpiece onto the desk, then picked it up and hung it on a small hook attached to the main box. "Better look after it, hey? We've only got a couple of them working right now."

"I didn't think anything electrical worked anymore?"

"This is a really old one we had in the basement. Izzy Gallagher did a clean up when she first joined the force two years back and remembered stuffing it onto a shelf. Dug it out along with another one and they both worked. A couple of people around the town have older models too. Gives us some form of communication. Without that, we'd be in even deeper poop than we are." He sat up straight, smiled again. "Anyway, how are you, darlin'? And your brother?"

"We're okay."

"You got water? Enough food? You know if you run short, you just head on down to the high school. They've got water and a little food. They're distributing to those that have run out. We tryin' to get an ancient water carting truck working so it can ship from Yan Yean Reservoir up to the tanks at the school."

"We have our two tanks. They're full, although someone tried to take some yesterday morning." Jim pressed his lips together and shook his head. "Mark gave them a send off."

"I bet he did."

Another policeman stuck his head through the door. "Jim, we've got three more burglaries on Jeffrey Street. It's getting' worse. Homeowners are away. I'll ask Detectives Kelly and Phelan to head out there."

"Maise said people were already taking water from their tanks yesterday mornin'. Might be worth getting a communication out about that, too. We had any more vehicles come in yet?"

"Still only the three. I've got Mitchell, Danley and Andy Newell on foot looking for more."

"Keogh come in today?"

"No, sir. Either did Tiffen."

"Maybe check on them, too. We need all the people we can get right now, even the part-timers and trainees. Get Westhall off the reception desk and out on the beat."

The Officer disappeared out of the doorway. Maise smiled at her uncle. She was about to open her mouth and tell him the reason she was there when the CB radio crackled again with an incoming request.

"Sargent Findlay."

"Yeah, Sarge, we've got a problem down here at the Broadview Residential Aged Care."

Jim took a deep breath, glanced up at Maise. "What is it, Larry?"

"We got people dropping like flies down here. Three more dead this morning. The generator we got from the football club has conked out. Half the medicine is dependent on refrigeration. Over."

"What about the generator at Gilly's Meats? Neil must have almost sold out by now and he won't be getting any more stock. Go and see if we can borrow that for the residential home. Tell Neil if he won't cough it up, he'll have me to deal with."

"Okay, Sarge, over and out."

Jim didn't even bother hanging the mouthpiece back on the receiver. "Now, you didn't just come down here to see me, did you?" He said, smiling again.

"No, I didn't," Maise said. "I—"

A woman appeared at the door. She was a little older than Maise, with blonde hair tied back in a ponytail, sharp blue eyes and finely proportionate features. "Sorry, Sarge," she said, looking sheepish.

"What is it, Izzy?"

Izzy glanced at Maise, then back at Jim. "You might want to step outside for this one."

"All right," Jim said, pushing his burly body out of the seat. "Bare with me, hon."

Maise waited as her uncle stepped out into the hallway with the female officer. Maise didn't deliberately listen, but she heard the gist of the conversation. The Premier of Victoria had died of a heart attack while trying to help distribute water and food. The Deputy premier had taken over. The latest message from the Government in Canberra was that right now there was no clear understanding of how to restore power. People had started looting stores in the city and the metropolitan police force was completely inundated.

Her uncle returned to the rolling chair and slumped down. It creaked and whined as he swiveled to her. "Sorry about that."

"It's okay," Maise said, sitting forward. "I came down to tell someone that our elderly neighbor, Mrs. Buckley, passed away. I already spoke with Officer Westall. She took all the details."

"The couple on the left of your place?" Maise nodded solemnly. "I am sorry to hear that. Unfortunately, she isn't alone. We've had almost ten die this morning. Seven last night and they won't be the last. The heat is a problem. People are running out of medicine. We had four die from car crashes when the blackout hit."

"I'll get out of your hair. I just wanted to let you know what had happened and on behalf of Mr. Buckley, find out what we have to do."

"I'm sure Janine will let the ambulance crew know. They'll come out, collect her, and take her back to the funeral parlor. She may not get a normal funeral, but they've got an old generator there and they will keep her body for a little while anyway. Hopefully we get the power back on before then.

Maise stood. "Thanks, Uncle Jim."

"Sorry I haven't been able to get out and see how you and your brother are going. It's been—" He shrugged. "Busy."

Izzy Gallagher was back again. "We need you in the conference room, Sarge."

"I was just leaving," Maise said. "Tell me though, why do people go so crazy when something like this happens?"

"Even though they won't admit it, people like order. It allows them to function. They mostly like rules; that things work and just happen. When it stops, or doesn't work anymore, they panic. It's normal."

"Makes sense."

Jim stepped around the other side of the desk and opened his arms for Maise. She slipped in and wrapped hers around his ribcage. He hugged her like a little bear. "Take care," he said in his gravely voice. "Stay at home for now, only leave for what's necessary, you hear?"

"Yeah." He trailed her out the door and headed the opposite way, following the other officer.

Maise waved, then turned and headed for the exit, thankful she had alerted someone to Mrs. Buckley's death and that Mr. Buckley wouldn't have to sit with his wife's body for too much longer. She also learned that she wouldn't want the responsibility her uncle had for any amount of money.

NINETEEN

The sun towered in the sky, bright and scorching and not quite at its summit as Parker guessed it was just short of midday, which meant he had less than an hour before he reached the Kinglake West general store. It felt like a great ball of heat had cooked him from the inside out and the hottest part of the day was still several hours away. His feet ached, both the heels and the balls, and his calves were tight with stabbing pain shooting up his shins with every step. Still, he reasoned, he was far closer to Whittlesea than when he had started.

He thought about the army vehicle that had driven past him earlier. It meant the military had working vehicles, but they sure didn't look old. If modern technology was affected, why were they not? Maybe they were old, and he simply couldn't tell. Or perhaps some cars and trucks weren't affected. The other point—probably the one that concerned him most—was the sight of the Chinese soldiers and the Chinese flag on the doors.

He reached the Kinglake West general store after almost four hours of marching along the lingering, windy blacktop, up and down slopes, along the gravely edges, and even the white lines for a time. The ache in his heels and the balls of his feet had deepened. He'd knocked off three bottles of water and had sweated them out just as quickly, his t-shirt soaked through at the chest and upper back. If his hat and the shade of the towering gums hadn't protected him, he would have been in much worse condition.

Although still hot and stuffy, the inside of the low, wooden-roof store was a welcome relief, taking away the blaring sun and perpetual brightness Parker had battled all morning. Rows of shelving, stacked with the basic items one might find at a grocery store covered dark tiled floors. The population out here was far less and save the twenty or thirty-minute drive into Whittlesea, locals could stock up on most items. There was a small fresh food section with local grown vegetables and fruit, two giant glass refrigerators, snack food trays, three bays of canned goods, shelving for personal items and a final bay for cooking and cleaning utensils. Parker was surprised the store still had so much stock and an idea popped into his head.

The store owner was a man named Ron Johnson that Parker had known since he was a kid, and with whom his father had traded fishing and war stories over many years. Ron had a mop of white hair, a reddish complexion and a wide smile. He was well known in Whittlesea and Parker had never heard a bad word said about him.

"Hey, young fella. You look like you just did a marathon."

"I feel like it," Parker said. "Walked from Hell Ridge. Near the old Hazeldene store."

Ron whistled, wore a genuinely surprised look on his face. "That's a long way. What'd it take ya, four hours?"

"Just under," Parker said.

"Good time indeed."

"If you had told me I could walk that far yesterday, I would have laughed."

"It's amazing what a bit of purpose does for you. Where you headed?"

"Into Whittlesea. Check on my friends."

"Ah, say no more."

"Any idea what exactly is going on?" Parker filled Ron in on what he knew.

"Well," Ron said, sipping at a coffee he had in a cardboard cup sitting on the counter. "Electricity is still out. Phones are dead, landlines and mobiles. I ain't seen one car since yesterday afternoon. Saw a bike rider come through this mornin'—one of those cyclists with the tight clothes. Normally get a lot more of them."

"Where was he coming from?"

"Further south, maybe Greensborough or Eltham. Said the power is out everywhere, no phones or anything. Police are on foot or seconding old vehicles where they can. Thought he'd take a ride and see what else is affected since the radio and Internet are dead too."

"Doesn't sound good."

"No way to get hold of the energy company, so I guess we just wait for them to get about and restore the power. Haven't had many customers, either. The few that have been in are buying up a bit though."

"What about the army?" Parker asked. Ron raised an eyebrow. "You didn't see a military vehicle roll past here earlier?"

"No, nothing. Mind you, I've been in and out all day. No point standing around when nobody comes in. Military truck, you say?"

"Strangest thing. An army jeep—new one, too—drove right by without even noticing me." Ron shook his head. "But the thing was, the soldiers were all Chinese. Even the vehicle had a Chinese flag on it."

"Chinese?" Ron thought about this. "That makes no sense." Parker agreed. "Either they're doing some sort of joint military operation or..."

"Or what?"

Ron waved it off. "Or nothing. That must be right. Some sort of joint thing. Maybe the Chinese are helping fix this problem."

"I hope you're right."

Parker was keen to keep moving, but an idea had developed once he saw how much stock Ron still had on the shelves. If the power was out and vehicles weren't working, there might end up being a food shortage at some point, especially if the government couldn't get the power back on quickly enough. Two years of battling COVID made a person think differently now. Although he had plenty of food back at camp, if this thing dragged on and a few more people joined him, they'd eventually run out. It would be sensible to buy a few more things now, while Ron still had them. Problem was, he couldn't take the supplies with him.

"Look, Ron, Can you do me a favor?"

"Ya know I like to help."

"If I buy some things now, can you store them here for me until I get back?"

Ron tipped his head sideways. "Sure I can." He narrowed his eyes and added, "I got a cellar out back. I normally leave people's stuff there for pick up. I can leave your items down there and you can collect it when you return."

"That works for me."

Parker selected several bags of flour, half a dozen tins of baked beans, a two kilogram bag of rice, three cartons of long life milk, headache tablets, salt, sugar, and a big bag of greenish potatoes. He paid in cash and Ron fitted it all into two boxes, stacking them behind the counter.

As Parker handed over the cash, Ron asked, "Where are your two mates, the guys I normally see with you in here?"

"One of them was supposed to drive up last night but he never showed. That's one of the reasons I'm heading back to Whittlesea. Find out what happened to him."

"Sure he'll be okay." Parker nodded. "And the other one?"

"Nah, he's not around anymore. We sort of had a falling out."

Ron raised one eyebrow. "Charlie Turner's kid? That the one?" Parker nodded. "Funny that, he was in here not long ago and mentioned you. Couldn't stop talking about the good times you guys had up there on the King Parrot."

"Mark Turner? Sure you've got the right person?"

"Big guy, tough looking? He's got a sister. May or something."

Parker said nothing. He couldn't imagine Mark saying that. It made no sense. He hated Parker now. Ron must be confused.

Ron continued. "Must have been start of December. We were talkin' about how he missed the beginning of the September fishing season. He was disappointed. Said those times were the best with you."

"Me?"

"Parker Richardson. Heard it from his lips myself."

Parker shrugged. "Guess I'll have to take your word for it. I'm surprised though. He hasn't had much good to say about me of late."

"Well, these things go in circles, my man. Friends come in and out of your life. They say there's a seven-year cycle. Good friends though, the ones that have been with you a long time... even if you don't see 'em for a time, when you finally catch up, it's like you were never apart. And when you need 'em, they're there for you, as though the were waiting in the shadows for their chance."

"Yeah, not this one. Not Mark. He had his chance. When I needed him, he wasn't there." Ron only nodded.

Parker said goodbye and started away from the general store in Kinglake West. He still had another two hours, but he was closer than when he had begun and he held onto that amidst the growing pain in his feet and legs. He didn't think much about Ron's comments. If Mark said those things, Parker could only imagine it had been for theatrics rather than genuine feeling. It reminded Parker that if he had any chance of winning Maise back, he would have to go through Mark first, and that wasn't something he was looking forward to.

TWENTY

M aise decided to head back down Church Street, then take
Whittlesea-Yea Road and go home via Wallan Road. It was
a little further, but she wanted to survey the town center to understand how people were coping. She imagined Mark scolding her
for not going straight home. She understood why he did it; since
their father had died, he'd been super-protective. But he seemed to
forget she was still working in the IGA almost every day. She could
handle herself.

The streets were busier. People were out in small groups; kids
on bikes riding in twos and threes, several women pushing
strollers under the shade of the shop front awnings. A small
number of shops were still operating, including the butcher, the
medical clinic and the pharmacy, though, Maise heard people
complaining about the availability of medicine as they walked out
thought the blue doors. A small group of people walked down
Church Street holding signs similar to what she'd seen at the police
station.

Just before turning west into Walnut Street, she saw an old lady
coming from the south end of Church Street, her gait and cane
unsteady as she moved slowly in the heat. She was dressed in her
Sunday best—as many elderly people seemed to do whenever they
left the house—a long, flowery dress and a thin blouse. It reminded
her of Mrs. Buckley and Maise was stung with guilt. She must be

cooking, Maise thought. It would take her all day to get wherever she was going at that rate.

Maise passed her, then circled back and pulled up alongside the curb.

"Hello, ma'am."

The woman stopped and craned her neck around. "Hello, love," she croaked. Her wrinkled cheeks glowed red and her thin grey hair was dark with sweat.

"Where are you headed?"

The old woman raised an unsteady hand and pointed ahead. "Medical Clinic."

Maise had passed it on the opposite side of the street. "Can I walk with you?"

"If you like," she said, smiling.

Maise climbed off her bike and walked along the curb beside the elderly lady. She learned the woman, whose name was Nancy Wood, had come to live in Whittlesea with her husband in the 1950's, when it had been little more than a country town. She'd raised three children and sent them all off to various parts of Australia with university educations and imminent professional careers. Her husband, Frank, had lived until he was ninety-three— they were married for seventy years. She was ninety, and had only lost him ten months before. She was a fascinating lady who had a quiet, soothing charm about her.

They reached the Medical Clinic. Maise rested her bicycle against the bricks surrounding a wide glass window.

"I'll be okay from here," Nancy said.

"Nonsense." Maise smiled. "Let me come in with you."

Nancy returned the smile. "You're a dear. Remind me of my daughter, Pamela. She was always helping strangers."

Maise had never seen the clinic so packed. Each of the dozen or so seats was taken. In some cases, kids were sitting on their parent's laps, while a handful sat cross-legged on the floor. Everybody looked at Maise and Nancy.

"Three hour wait if you don't have an appointment," the lady behind the counter said.

Nancy shuffled forward. "I have an appointment."

The woman smiled. "Hand me your appointment card, Mrs. Wood."

Maise sighed with relief. She couldn't imagine having to wait three hours. The heat inside the room was gagging. A middle-aged man sitting at the end of the row of seats gave his up for Nancy and Maise was able to squat down beside her.

"You don't have to wait for me," Nancy said. "I'll be fine."

"Do you have some water?" Nancy reached into her bag and produced a 600ml plastic bottle sold at the IGA. Maise had scanned a million of them. "I'll wait a bit longer."

They sat in silence for a while. It became apparent that just one doctor was on duty as only two people went into the consulting room in the twenty minutes Maise sat with Nancy. Her appointment was well past, but she seemed content to sit there and rustle through old copies of TV Week.

Maise was preparing to leave when Nancy said in a lower voice than her usual discreet tone, "You know they say there's treasure buried around here." Maise raised her eyebrows. Nancy looked around, as if to make sure nobody was listening. She gave a soft nod, as if to reinforce everything she was about to divulge. "I like you, dear. My kids are all grown up and have left and my grand-kids rarely come and visit."

"I'm so sorry to hear that."

"Besides, my kids heard the stories when they were younger and it didn't seem to inspire them to go exploring."

"Exploring?"

"I don't know if it's true or not, but apparently a wealthy man left the city and came to live in the area after the end of World War Two. He brought along with him his expensive collection of jewels and artifacts. Nobody saw him for a long time and he died some-where up the mountain. Police never found anything with the body, and plenty have gone searching for it without any luck. The story goes that he had buried it in and around the mountain."

"Hmm," Maise said. I've never heard of that."

"My husband believed it. He and his friends did a few trips up there over the years. They never found anything, but he swore they were close."

"Where exactly?"

She whispered, "Somewhere around that Hell Ridge."

"Thanks for telling me," Maise whispered with a smile.

"Well, don't tell anyone just in case. But you've been so kind to me and it's all I've got to offer you." She took Maise's hand and gave a gentle squeeze.

"Will you be okay getting home?"

"It's not far. Normally I'd get a taxi. I've got a concession card so I only pay for half the fare." She brushed a slick of grey hair from her forehead. "Besides, my friend Beryl is over there. She lives near me. We'll walk home together."

It wasn't long after that Nancy was called in. They bid each other farewell and Maise was glad she'd stopped to help the older woman. It was just what she needed to help redeem herself for neglecting to check on Mrs. Buckley before she died.

As she opened the front door of the Medical Clinic, a young woman, named Arlette Davis burst in, whom Maise had served a few times at the IGA. Arlette was tall, with streaky blonde hair, a friendly, narrow face and an extensive summer tan. Maise stepped back into the waiting room as Arlette rushed to the middle of the space.

"They're here!" She shouted. Some asked who "they" were. Arlette caught her breath and bent over, hands on her knees. "The army. I saw one of their jeep-thingys driving around near the Showgrounds. They're gonna set up tents and everything and start serving food when we run out."

Finally, Maise thought. Things were starting to look up.

TWENTY-ONE

As Parker's feet grew blisters, he couldn't stop thinking about the idea of confronting Mark. Maise's older brother hated him and he suspected Mark had been a contributor to Maise's decision to end things. Any hope he had of getting back with Maise rested on reconciling with Mark. That was going to be one massive challenge on top of another. The whole thing left him feeling uncomfortable.

Soon, his momentum and motivation began to wane. The highway and surroundings had been almost the same for the last four hours, with the occasional opening between the trees revealing a dirt driveway leading to a property hidden behind thick scrub. He'd done several quick scouts of properties with buildings close to the road but found nothing he could use to hasten his journey. He was sick of walking, sick of drinking water and sick of the flies that chased him. He needed a circuit breaker, something to speed up his passage before he lost his mind completely.

As Parker reached the next driveway—no more than a two-lane dirt track—with a posted white letterbox and the dark trunks of ironbark trees lining the route inwards, he stopped, wondering whether there might be an old motorbike or at worst, a push bike, that he could borrow.

He entered the property, minus any kind of gate, walking

beneath the overhanging trees and their friendly shadows. Tangled scrub invited him on either side, beyond the well-beaten, flat packed mud track.

There was a gate, after all, but it wasn't padlocked, and Parker unhitched the hook and slipped through. He closed it, re-latched the metal clip, and continued on, watching cautiously for signs of the owners. He would ask their help, to borrow a bike if they had one, and hope they would allow it.

But the house was empty. Dark, silent, doors locked, no sign of any people or even pets. That might make it easier, Parker thought. There was nobody to deny his request. He didn't usually take things without asking, but he thought the circumstances warranted it.

He left the wide timber verandah and spotted a large shed close to the main house with its maroon roof and dirty cream weatherboard panels. The door was jammed, tilting off the upper hinges, and when Parker finally shoved it open, the hinges creaked as though it might not have seen a drop of oil in years.

Inside, gloomy shadows promised cobwebs, spiders, and other critters desperate for new flesh. Junk filled all corners, old beds, a mattress, even the shell of a piano. Parker picked his way through the items, watching his step, cautious not to end up with a bigger problem than having to walk another two hours to Whittlesea. But there was no motorbike, or even a bicycle. There was only a child's trike that reminded him of the scene in Goonies where the older brother must ride a little girl's bike to catch the younger brother and his friends. *No thanks*, Parker thought.

He left the large shed and wandered around behind it, peering about the property. Although the house had been empty, Parker half expected somebody to jump out from hiding and scald him. It felt weird being on the property, going through the shed. He was ready to give up, accepting he was destined to walk the remaining distance and develop a further appreciation for once having an automobile.

Then his luck finally turned. At the end of the shed stood an overhang, no walls or floor, just a roof for cover, and underneath it, were a series of rusted push bikes, a half decent mountain bike, and the million dollar prize, a discolored motorbike with faded yellow paint and cracked mud guards. It was a Yamaha 125 and from the style of the logo and design, Parker was hopeful it might work, given what the farmer had told him. It even had a key in it. He rolled it out, checked the fuel lines were open, and set the choke to halfway. He screwed the lid off the tank to make sure it had fuel, but it looked dry and he felt a pang of disappointment. He hoped there was something in the bottom, or that the reserve tank was still wet. After putting the bike in neutral, he pulled the kick starter out, then straddled the seat and dug his heel into the lever. It sounded old and sick. He tried again, with a little more promise, until the third go, when the bike turned over and chugged into life. It quickly died though, so he set the choke to fully open and made another attempt. Nothing. He had two more failed attempts and then turned the fuel lever from ON to RES. He repeated the procedure and this time it barked to life, before coughing momentarily and then flattening out. Parker waited a few moments before twisting the throttle, then set the stand down and let it idle, waiting for the 4-stroke engine to warm up. There was nothing in the main tank but some fuel in reserve. He only hoped it would get him into Whittlesea.

In a few minutes, the idle speed began to rise so he closed the choke. The bike dropped its idle to a nice, steady level. He was ready to go.

Parker made one more check for fuel, but he couldn't spot a drum. Did he keep looking, or chance he'd make it home? In the end, he decided to waste no more time, and leave. As he drove down the driveway, Parker sent a silent apology to the owners for taking their bike; he was sure they'd understand, given the circumstances.

Without a helmet, he was more cautious, taking it slower than he might have normally done, staying in the middle of the highway as he descended the windy slope leading out of Kinglake West towards Whittlesea. It was normally about a fifteen minute drive—compared with two hours, on foot—but at a reduced speed, it took him slightly longer to breach the town's outskirt, just past Humevale and the Toorourrong Reservoir, a place he had frequented a number of times for a barbecue or picnic with his parents when his mother was still alive.

Once he hit the flatter stretch outside the town, he opened the throttle, feeling the hot wind in his face. *No flies out here*, he thought with some joy. About three miles short, he felt the bike slow as the power disappeared. He even took his hand off the throttle, trying to use the momentum of the bike, but it soon sputtered and then rolled to a stop, giving a final, helpless shudder as it went silent.

"Stuff it," Parker said to nobody in particular.

He stood in the middle of the road for a time, the sun pasting his shoulders. Wide paddocks greeted him on both sides, wire fences set with thick, rotted posts that had watched cars drive along the highway for decades. A cow or two eyed him, chewing grass as though they had nothing else to do in the world. Did he hide the bike and pick it up on the way back, or walk it into town? He didn't want to leave it, but pushing it all the way would slow him down.

Still torn, he decided leaving it was safest. He'd pick it up on the way back. Parker looked back along the highway about a hundred yards to where the scrub had finished, gums and iron barks creating thick coverage on the other side of the guardrail. That was the best place to conceal the bike. He pushed the Yamaha along the blacktop and reached a spot where the paddock fence line was invisible to the road through the brush. He found a small gap in the guardrail and wheeled the bike through and down the slope, feathering the brakes to stop it gaining too much momentum. Using loose branches lying at the base of the gum trees, Parker covered it and returned to the highway to assess whether it was visible. He walked both ways to ensure a person coming from either direction could not spot it. He was satisfied that for now, it was safe. He would return with fuel and collect the bike for an easier trek up the hill.

Although only a couple of miles, the remaining section of the walk was the most difficult for Parker. The back of his legs and his forearms continued to burn. Forgetting sunscreen had been a mistake. His energy began to fade, as though the sun had liquefied it. He had a chocolate bar and a fourth bottle of water, but he'd simply walked too far for his body to cope.

On the outskirts of Whittlesea, Parker witnessed the first incident that told him there might be a bigger issue at hand. Someone had driven a car into a power pole. The wooden post had split the hood; the windscreen had ended up spread over the road like confetti at a wedding. There was no sign of the driver, but somebody had wrenched open the left side of the hood and removed the battery.

Further along the highway, several people stood on the far side of the road in the vast front yard of a property full of trees and the rusted relics of several old vehicles. They eyed him warily, but did not invite him over or engage in any discussion. Parker stayed on the far right side of the highway.

Soon after, the pain in his feet forced him to stop. He did so on the rocky shoulder under the meager shadow of a sign that indicated Kinglake was twenty-eight kilometers away. Exhaustion closed in. Every movement was an ache. He removed his sneakers and massaged the balls of his feet, wincing at the pain. He wondered how much longer before cramp took him down.

Eventually, the thought of Sam and Maise drove him to slip his runners back on, stand up, and start walking again. The more he thought about Maise, the more it strengthened his resolve to make it back to town and check on her. He couldn't shake the thought that something had happened to her and if it had, he'd never forgive himself for letting her go so easily.

At a small family-run camping store on the outskirts of town, a cream-colored Holden Kingswood and an ancient mustard colored kombi van sat parked at the entrance doors, which had been pried open, the chains used to lock them tossed aside on the concrete pathway. Two men sat behind the wheel of each vehicle. A third and fourth with tattoos covering both arms, wearing high-visibility shirts, shorts and sneakers, walked in and out the entrance with arm loads of gear, loading it into the back of both vehicles. A fifth man, dressed the same, but with a ponytail and dark glasses, smoked a cigarette and held a shotgun downwards at his side. *Bikers*. There was a motorcycle club in Whittlesea, several more in surrounding towns. They generally didn't bother anyone, but Parker knew they pedaled drugs and undertook other illegal activities.

Watching the store as he passed, Parker resisted the urge to ask the bikers how they were paying for the goods. Two of the men carried a long cardboard box from the store. The man with the gun blew smoke in a cloud above his head. Parker had stopped to watch. As if sensing this, the man looked his way. "Keep walking. Don't want you to get accidentally shot."

Parker glanced back once and the shotgun man waved him on. *Didn't take long*, he thought. He hoped it wasn't the theme in town. Some people were opportunistic and with the Police presence limited, it was open season.

Parker didn't look back again, focusing instead on the long highway ahead, but soon after, he heard tires screeching as both vehicles skidded away from the store. The old Kingswood raced past him with the engine roaring, sounding like it might blow up at any moment, shotgun man's leering face large and satisfied in the driver's window. The Kombi followed moments later.

Parker walked on, wondering if he had seen the worst of it.

TWENTY-TWO

The big clock read just before midday when Mark set off for Keith Whitehead's house. He hated leaving their place, but getting his hands on the car was important if this thing went on any longer than a few days. He remained hopeful of heading up to Lake Eildon to camp if he could secure the car from Keith.

He decided to leave Mindy at home for protection; the heat would be too much for her. Maise was out and he would have preferred to wait until she had returned, but if he didn't show up at Keith's on time for the transaction, he worried that Keith would use any excuse to change his mind.

It was about three klicks, or just under two miles, to Keith's house, and on any other day when the heat and humidity weren't suffocating, he'd have run over there for fitness. Thankfully, he had his mountain bike, which would cover the distance in about a third of the time. He took three thousand in cash from a shoebox behind a hole at the back of his wardrobe cupboard, split it in half and tied it up in two rubber bands. From the garage, he wheeled the bike out, wondering whether he should have taken something for protection while carrying so much cash.

The midday heat bashed his skin and even with a hat and sunglasses, he felt it's sting. There weren't many adults out, but he saw plenty of kids, some sitting in those little plastic clam shell pools full of water in their front yards trying to keep cool.

Anybody with a pool, he thought, was in luck, at least while it was still clean. After a few days without any filtration, the water would start to turn.

On the silent roads, alongside lines of parked cars it didn't take long for Mark to reach Keith Whitehead's place. Even from a distance, Mark could see the paved driveway was empty, and he knew the Commodore he came to claim was missing. As he reached the crossover, he saw the detached double garage at the end was open and unoccupied.

Mark rolled the bike up over the footpath and down the driveway, stopping outside the garage. There was a workbench running along one side cluttered with tools and boxes, a hand lawn mower tucked away near the back, tables stacked against the other wall, and bicycle parts strewn across the floor on one side. Mark kicked at a deflated football lying in the corner and it went skidding across the floor. They had agreed midday for the collection time. Keith had been very clear about that. The slight suspicion Mark had about Keith not intending to give up the car grew. Something had changed his mind. Perhaps he had doubts, and had come to realize how valuable a vehicle was when most others were not running. Or perhaps the police had possessed it. Though he couldn't imagine Keith letting that happen.

Mark decided to wait, just in case Keith was running late. He left his bike against the garage and poked around the outside of the house, climbing through the garden and over a five-foot wooden fence to get access to the backyard.

He did two laps, looking through the kitchen window, the study, two of the bedrooms and the family room. The place had been trashed. Beds were overturned, the mattresses slashed, clothes, dressers, bedside tables, lamps, had all been tossed onto the floor. In the kitchen, chairs had been knocked over, the flat screen television lay face down on the rug, and myriad of other items had been strewn across the family and dining area, including now empty plastic containers and discarded packets of food that had probably been in the pantry. Mark began to worry about his own house again. What if the same thing happened?

There was no sign of Keith, or any of his family. He had two brothers and both his parents were still together—but none of them were at the house. Mark tried to recall if they all went away on the Australia Day long weekend. But if they'd gone away, why had Keith agreed to the midday meeting?

After almost twenty minutes, the sun began to annoy him, burning his forearms and the back of his neck where his hat didn't cover his skin. What were his options? He couldn't wait around all afternoon.

Snatching his bike from against the garage, Mark climbed onto the seat with his pockets still full of cash and pedaled back down the driveway and out onto the road. He suddenly felt deflated. His chance of making the exchange today had evaporated in the heat. Mark suspected that Keith had wizened up to the fact that an old motor vehicle that still worked was worth far more than what Mark had offered to pay for it.

He pedaled hard along the streets, guiding the bike via Church Street, paying little attention to anything that didn't resemble a white Commodore. He only spotted one car—a Datsun sedan with patchy paintwork and a squeaky drive belt. He circled back towards home, and as he hugged a bend at high speed near the Whittlesea Community house, he spotted a car idling on the side of the road ahead and jammed on the brakes. The tires chirped and the bike slid as he hit some loose gravel, but he managed to keep it upright and bring it to a stop. Mark hung in the gutter, trying to look inconspicuous as he took in the scene.

It wasn't a car after all—it was one of those small SUV's—like a Jeep—army green, and it appeared to be military, with two passengers and a driver.

The back of Mark's neck prickled. A man in a suit stood at the side of the road talking to the people in the vehicle. It looked like a guy whose face he had seen in the local newspaper—Bert something. Mark thought he was a councilor, one of the local members for the Whittlesea Shire. Mark couldn't hear what they were saying, but the conversation continued between the suited man and the driver, who was dressed as a soldier, and appeared to be Chinese, or at least Asian. The driver made a hand motion, as if the councilor should get into the vehicle. The man stepped back from the curb and put up both hands up as though indicating he wanted no part of whatever the driver was suggesting. The man in the front passenger seat said something. Suddenly the back door opened and the third man climbed out of the vehicle. He *was* a soldier, dressed in a khaki uniform and had an automatic rifle in his hands.

"Jesus," Mark whispered. He thought about moving back out of sight, but it was too late, he might draw attention.

Mark glanced around to see if anybody else was watching, but the street was vacant, full of lifeless vehicles and parched front lawns, not even any bored kids idling outside their houses. Prodded by the machine gun, the suited man climbed awkwardly into the back seat and the soldier followed. Mark had a thought; he climbed off his bike and squatted down beside it, pretending to fix the pedal. The car took off from the curb with a screech of the tires and Mark ducked his head, but he couldn't resist a quick glance up as the car passed. He saw two things in the moment; the councilor in the backseat's stiff, fearful expression had gone pale and man in the front seat looked familiar. Recognition settled over Mark and his skin crawled as the man's face came into view, a man roughly his own father's age, that he'd had dinner with and drunk beers, watched football and cricket. The man turned his head slightly and looked at Mark. This time, fear struck him motionless. The man looking back at him was Raven's father.

TWENTY-THREE

P arker walked the remaining distance into Whittlesea looking out for any sign of the bikers. He passed two more small sets of shops but both were shadowy and soundless. As he reached the Whittlesea Football ground, he noticed that somebody had placed steel barriers around the pavilion as if to cordon off an area. Further back, he spotted two large trucks with camouflage paint parked on the edge of the Showgrounds. They had two giant, serrated wheels at the back and one at the front beneath each cab. A tray—ten meters long, had a green canopy stretched over it. Parker stopped to watch for a minute, waiting to locate any military personnel. The place was quiet, so he pushed on.

He had emptied the last drops of water from his bottle, and because Sam's house was near the IGA, he swung past; figuring by now the shelves would be empty. He also hoped that Maise was working, and he'd meet her there without having to visit their house, to avoid a potential confrontation with Mark.

Maise wasn't working though, and the inside of the IGA was thick with stinking heat. The shelves *were* almost empty. He wandered the store looking for a single bottle of water, imagining people arriving like a plague of locusts, stripping the shelves of supplies. Anything that might constitute survival goods were gone. And there were no replacements coming anytime soon. The people restocking the shelves were out of work because the trucks bringing the products weren't operational. Most likely, the warehouses that picked the goods and loaded the trucks weren't operating, either. The forklifts picking the pallets of stock from the shelves were dead, and the plants where the goods were made might even be shut down. *For how long?* Parker wondered. It was the billion-dollar question. Lives depended on it. If people were at the end of their shopping cycle, they'd be running out of food and what would they do then? The timing of their camping trip was fortuitous. He and Sam were stocked up. He could afford to add a few people, but the higher the number, the quicker supplies would run out.

In the end, Parker had to settle for an energy drink with enough caffeine to kill a horse, which he normally wouldn't touch. It was probably a good thing though because his energy was depleted.

Olsen, the IGA Manager, was the only one working. Parker paid for his drink in cash. Olsen looked like he might fall over from exhaustion at any moment. He had large black circles under his eyes. His face was flushed and sweat trickled down his forehead. He looked as though he'd lost weight since Parker had been in the store buying up supplies three days ago.

"Has Maise been in?"

Olsen wiped his brow with the back of his arm. "Not since..." he had to think about it. "Yesterday? Wow. It feels like longer than that."

"Take a break, mate, you look exhausted."

Olsen grimaced. Another customer lined up behind Parker, who took his drink, and left.

Small groups of people congregated along the street outside the IGA. Parker spotted Sam and Jas heading towards the main road. He called out and hobbled towards them.

They found the obliging shade of an elm tree, one of several growing along the street. He shook hands with Sam and hugged Jas. She had cut her long hair to shoulder length, and it had naturally gone wavy. "Glad to see you guys. Love the hair too, Jas." She nudged his arm and gave him a bright smile.

"How did you get back?" Sam asked, his blue eyes wide. He was taller than Parker—taller than any of them by three inches—

and heavy, without being too overweight. They'd started a local basketball team a few years back and until Sam had started playing, they barely won a game. With him in the center position, they hadn't lost. Sandy hair topped a wide, friendly face. It took a lot to annoy Sam—he was usually agreeable—but stay out of his way when he lost his temper. Unlike Parker after his mother died, Sam was always reliable. Parker knew the big man had his back. Loyalty and dependability were high of Sam's list of values.

"Walked."

"Geez, that's a long way, mate."

"Couldn't wait around for you forever."

Sam dug his hands into his shorts pockets. "Yeah, sorry about that. I got caught up with work until late and then the whole blackout thing happened and I spent a while trying to get my car working, and then Jas—"

Parker put up both hands. "It's all right. I get it. You get a free kick on this one." He smiled. "As long as you're okay. That's one of the reasons I left Hell Ridge. Could have stayed up there forever."

Parker explained that his phone wouldn't charge, the vehicle wouldn't start, and the different points of understanding he had found along the way.

"I can't believe you walked all that way," Jas said. "Was checking on Sam the only reason you came back?" You never wondered what Jas was thinking. Parker loved that about her.

Parker nodded. "Maybe not."

"Oh, how romantic."

"She might tell me to bugger off. Have you seen her?"

"Not since yesterday. She was fine then."

"What the hell's happening down here?"

"It's getting worse," Sam said. "People have been going crazy buying everything again. Just like when COVID hit. The IGA imposed buying limits but most of the stuff still went. I'd hate to see what it's going to be like in a few days if they can't get the power back on and the vehicles running."

"I hope people have got enough to last."

"We got a few more things earlier."

Parker commenced his plan. "I've got heaps back at camp."

"All the ferals are coming out," Jas said. "Last night there were groups of people roaming the streets. Vacant houses are getting broken into. It'll be worse tonight."

"What are the police doing?"

"Cops are walking around. They have a couple of older cars they're using for real emergencies, but they can't keep up."

Sam said, "the government sent out a flyer. It basically says they're working on the problem and to just sit tight."

"Not much else to do, is there? No timeframe on when they might have it fixed?" Sam and Jas shook their heads. "You guys see any army vehicles driving around? There's two big trucks parked at the Showgrounds and I saw one drive right by up on the mountain. They didn't even notice me. And the strangest thing was the soldiers were all Chinese."

"Nothing mate. No army trucks," Sam said. "But I was talking to old Dave Harding and he reckons the Chinese are gonna invade." Sam laughed. "Reckons it's a ploy by them to take over since we won't send them any coal or wine anymore after they imposed all those tariffs."

Parker smiled, but he wondered whether old Dave Harding might not be too far from the truth. "So what's the plan for you guys now?"

"We were thinking about riding our bikes up to see you—if you were still there. We just want to get out of Whittlesea for while."

"That's what I was hoping you'd say. We're well stocked, but bring as much food from home as you can."

"What are you going to say to Maise?"

Parker shrugged. "Just that if she wants to come with us, she can. No strings attached."

"What do you think she'll say?" Jas asked.

"You'd know better than me," Parker laughed. "I mean, normally she'd probably tell me to bugger off, but with this thing going on… maybe."

"I can tell you now she still has feelings for you."

Parker felt a jolt of excitement. "How do you know? Did she say something?"

"Not exactly. But girls just know these things."

This gave Parker fresh hope. He tried to sound calm. "Okay. That's good."

"Just be cool, okay? Don't go in there guns blazing and expect to get back together straight away. Let things happen and if it does, great."

"Yeah. Thanks, Jas. Good advice."

"So, you're going to Maise's?" Sam asked.

"I could go home, but there's nothing there. I might as well go and see her and Mindy."

"Just wait here a sec," Jas said. "I just want to check the store for something." She hurried away, leaving Sam and Parker alone.

The moment Jas had left, Sam's face split into a wide smile.

"What is it? Parker asked.

Sam stuck his hand into his pocket. He had to dig deeper, but finally, he snatched his hand out and held a small box. With his other hand, he snapped it open, revealing a thin, sparkling ring.

"What's that?" Parker asked. Then it dawned on him. "Oh, shit, man! You're gonna pop the question?"

Sam nodded. "Too right. Been wanting to do it for ages."

"So you're sure?"

"Never been surer. What do you think she'll say?"

Parker clapped a hand on his shoulder. There was no doubt in Parker's mind. Nothing was more of a certainty than Jas and Sam lasting. "I think she'll say yes, mate. For sure."

Sam beamed. He snapped the box shut and stuffed it back into his pocket. "And mate, I want you to be my best man, when we finally get married, all right?"

Now it was Parker's turn. His face cracked into a smile. He stuck out his hand and they shook vigorously. "It'd be my honor, mate."

Jas appeared from the IGA and walked towards them. Sam and Parker stepped apart as though they'd done something wrong.

"What are you two looking so dodgy for?" Jas laughed.

"That's our normal look," Parker said.

"True. Right, we'll grab our things" Jas said, "and meet you at Maise's in an hour or two?"

"Unless of course she tells me to nick off."

They shook hands and embraced again, Parker flashing a knowing smile at Sam, and then he left the shade of the elm tree and headed towards Maise's house. He thought about checking on his own home again, but nobody was there, and he had all he needed with him or back at camp.

He was on a mini high after Sam revealed his plans to ask Jas to marry him, but his edginess soon crept back in having to confront Maise after what Jas had said about her still liking him, as though he had more to lose now. Would she even listen to what Parker had to say? His plan was simple: ask Maise to come with them back up to Hell Ridge. He'd show her he had changed since they were last together and hope it worked. Jas coming along would help cement the plan. Mark might be the problem though. He didn't have Raven anymore. Would Maise trudge off with the rest of them and leave Mark alone? Maybe Parker would have to offer an olive branch and ask Mark to go with them.

He drank another swallow of energy drink; his head throbbed; pain stabbed his legs and ankles, heels and toes as he took each step. He just wanted to get off his feet and rest. *Just a little further,* he told himself. He would soon find out if Maise would turn him away.

TWENTY-FOUR

M ark made a detour via the police station before he pedaled home, providing his uncle with a detailed account of what he witnessed with the councilor and the army vehicle. He did not mention Raven's father.

By the time he arrived home, he was relieved to find there was no damage or break in attempts at the house. Mindy was overjoyed to see him, wagging her tail and barking excitedly. Mark knew that no matter what he did, Mindy would always receive him with unconditional love. Was there any better companion than a dog?

He was surprised Maise hadn't returned though. Worry surfaced, but he pushed it aside when he considered that she was visiting the police station and in all likelihood, having to wait to see their Uncle Jim had caused her delay. Mark knew he was overprotective and it bothered her, but he felt an obligation to look after his sister. It had been one of his father's last requests and he wasn't going to let the old man down.

In the garage, Mark stood over his pile of camping gear and supplies and felt dejected. Even with things that were happening, if he'd been able to secure Keith's Commodore, he still could have gone camping up to Lake Eildon, as he had planned. Now, the pile of gear was useless. It was just taking up valuable space in the garage, space that he would now need to store things laying around the outside of house. Mark's plan was to remove any incentives for potential burglars and secure them inside.

He started with the Weber barbecue, and as he rolled it across the patio, he fell into thought about seeing Raven's father and the two soldiers taking the Politician away in the military jeep. What did it mean? Mark wasn't sure but he couldn't reconcile how it was anything good. They didn't just have to survive with limited food, water and medicine until the power was back on and cars worked, they now had a potential further threat. Mark had to find out more about what it meant. That initial instinct developed. Whittlesea grew more dangerous and would continue to do so the longer the situation continued.

He took the coiled garden hose and a motorized blower he normally left under the pergola and placed them into the garage beside the barbecue. Stacked underneath the workbench was a store of old wooden planks, remnants from construction of the side boundary fence that was replaced some years ago. His father had kept them, and Mark hadn't the heart to throw them out. Now, he was glad. Using the planks, his DeWalt drill, and a packet of ¾" inch screws, he used the boards to patch holes and replace broken sections around each of the three boundaries of the property. One the right side, he peered over the fence into his neighbor's backyard. They were a young family travelling in Queensland for the last two weeks. Mark wasn't quite sure when they were supposed to return, but he expected they might have an extended holiday now. Their backyard looked neat, but he immediately saw their barbecue and gas bottle had disappeared. Mark had spent plenty of evenings standing around it with a cold beer as Henry grilled sausages and burgers while Leesa fixed cold potato salad and coleslaw. They were great people, and Mark hoped they were all safe. It was a reminder though that anything left outside was at risk of being stolen. Motivated by his neighbor's loss and with ten or so boards remaining, Mark doubled the protection on the gate he'd earlier worked on, so the thing could no longer be opened.

When he'd finished, he did another sweep for anything that might appeal to burglars. Mindy sat before him, waiting for a pat, eyes wide and eager. He bent, scratched behind her ears. She laid down and rolled over, exposing her belly. Mark chuckled. "You're a player, you know." Her tail wagged.

The idea of getting out of the township and heading for the hills began to grow. He just needed that vehicle. Parker, as much as Mark despised the guy, had the right idea—stay up the mountain by the King Parrot Creek. Plenty of fresh water, shade from the gum trees, enough fish to keep their bellies full. His mind drifted to Parker, and for the first time in many months, he considered their broken relationship. What if Parker was to show up now? Mark had lost respect for the guy, and would probably never trust him again. They had barely said two words, having only crossed-paths at the house once or twice in the last six months, Mark going out of his way to avoid a confrontation. They'd almost come to blows, when the whole episode first took place. And he didn't want to give Parker the chance to apologize.

He turned back for the house, satisfied he had removed all opportunities for someone to steal something besides the water in the tanks. As he approached the back door, Mindy gave a low growl. Her normally floppy ears went pointy and she darted off towards the sideway. Mark snatched the golf club from against the brick wall and raced after her, moving it into a strike position.

His first thought was that somebody was climbing the fence again. He was sick of people right now; sick of their lack of values, stealing from the McKenzie's next door; trying to steal his water earlier in the day.

Mark turned the corner just behind Mindy; her teeth bared, the growl now coming from the back of her throat. If somebody were trying to enter the property, they would have teeth marks or worse on them in seconds.

At the end of the narrow sideway, a man had climbed over the gate and was lowering himself down into the backyard. All Mark spotted was a floppy hat, a t-shirt and shorts. His legs looked burnt, and when he dropped over the gate—a much greater drop than usual since Mark had added wooden planks to the height—he cried out in pain as his ankle twisted. He collapsed onto the concrete path and grabbed his lower leg.

This guy's gonna get hurt, Mark thought. He'd seen Mindy kill big, angry possums and even Mark hadn't been able to call her off when she was protecting him or Maise from what she perceived as a threat.

But Mindy went from attack to joy in a split second. Her tail started wagging and her ears went back as she approached. The guy turned, crawling onto his knees and Mark's stomach dropped.

"Parker?" Groaning, Parker climbed to his feet. He looked like he'd just walked through Hell. Mark felt a flash of the old stuff, recalling the way they'd always greeted each other prior to the rift, with a strong handshake and a slap on the back. It would have been easier having the old Parker on his side now, taking on this situation as a team, the way they had always done before their dispute. The good old days, and damn they had been good. Mark had to suppress the urge like a bad memory. "What are you doing?"

Mindy smothered him, pressing her flank against his legs. He scratched her in a spot on the top of her tale near the base of her torso. She grinned; nobody else seemed to be able to replicate it.

Parker took off is hat and wiped his brow. He looked as though he'd been swimming, his hair was saturated, his red face and sweaty. "Looking for Maise." He noticed the golf club. "What were you going to do with that?"

"She's not here." Mark lowered the weapon. The bitter sting of betrayal resurfaced. "Why do you want to see her, anyway? You're not together anymore."

Parker placed the hat back on his head. "I know that. I just wanted to make sure she was all right."

Mark squinted, anger building in his expression. Parker and Maise weren't together *anymore*. Parker had ruined that the same way he ruined their friendship. "She's fine. And she doesn't need you to make sure she's all right."

Parker put up his hands. "I know that. I just wanted to—"

"Save the sob story, man. This thing's been going on for nearly forty-eight hours now. You only just arrived. Run out of beer, did you?"

Parker shook his head. "Oh yeah. I forgot. I was enjoying myself."

"I know. I told Maise that. Told her that's how you roll, looking after yourself first before anyone else."

"Gimme a break, man. I came as soon as I could. It took me six hours to walk back here."

Mark hesitated. Then the words came out before he could stop them. "You walked all the way from Hell Ridge?"

Parker nodded. "Yeah."

"Jesus. That's further than…" He let the thought drift. This was one of the many reasons he didn't like talking to Parker anymore. A thought crossed his mind briefly and he shut it out, focusing on his anger. This guy had done the wrong thing by his sister—even if *she* didn't know it—and the wrong thing by him.

"Further than the time we walked back from Mick Axton's party up on Silvan Rd." Mark gave a reluctant nod. Parker waited for him to say more. "What? You can't say too much in case you remember the old times and how good they were and start to get over your anger?"

Mark pressed his lips together. "That'll never happen."

Parker scoffed. "Of course. How stupid of me."

"What do you want, man?"

The dog sat at his feet. "I told you, I came to check on Maise."

"Well, you can't wait here."

"Fine. I'll wait on the street."

"Great. That's settled." Mark started for the back door.

Parker shifted forward. "Hang on. It's half Maise's house anyway. Surely she gets a say in who stays and who goes?"

"She doesn't want you here. Don't you get that? You did the wrong thing by her, man. Remember?"

Parker's face twisted in a grimace. "That wasn't my fault, you know that."

"We'll see if she sees it the same way."

"Don't you dare," Parker said, raising a finger. "You promised."

Mark waved him off. "Relax. As if I'd say anything. It would hurt her too much." He started for the door again. "Leave now, would you?

Parker took two steps forward. "It wasn't my bloody fault, you know that. Besides, what about your old man?"

Mark whirled. "Don't you talk about him."

"Bullshit. I know he was your dad, but he was *my mate*, too. What would he say about you kicking me out now?"

"What would he say about you ruining my life?" Mindy started barking at Parker. "There. Now you've done it. Even she's turned against you." Mindy turned and barked at Mark.

Parker scoffed. "You sure about that?"

"Settle down, Mindy," Mark growled. Her tail stopped wagging. To Parker, he said, "And then what, after Maise gets back?"

Parker shrugged and started walking up the sideway towards the back of the house. "I want her to come back to Hell Ridge."

"*Like hell*," Mark said, as Parker passed him. "As if I'm gonna let my sister disappear into the hills with *you*." He laughed, a high, crazy cackle, the anger letting loose. "And as if she's gonna wanna go with you."

They had reached the lawn at back of the house. "Nick off, mate. Just let me wait in peace. But if it makes you feel any better, Sam and Jas are coming too."

"Man, you're stupider than I thought if you think I'm gonna let her walk out of here with you, or Sam, or Jas or anyone for that matter."

"Afraid you'll be alone, Mark? Life tough without Raven?"

Mark pointed the golf club at Parker. "You're gonna cop a whack for that." He started forward with the club cocked, the fury taking over, Mindy running in circles as she barked at them.

TWENTY-FIVE

Maise pedaled the last thirty yards along her street beneath the burning sun, using the last of her energy to reach the Buckley's house. The air was breathtaking—literally—she had underestimated just how much the heat would affect her having to ride all the way down to the town center and back. She would never take a car for granted again.

It had been such an eventful morning, she was glad to make it home. No doubt, Mark would remind her of the risk, but she had also found out some important information. Although not without its challenges, her Uncle and the police department were working hard to secure the town. Though, they were no closer to knowing how quickly things would be back to normal. And finally, after helping Mrs. Wood to the Whittlesea Medical Clinic and redeeming herself partly for not checking on Mrs. Buckley yesterday, she'd discovered the military had finally arrived to help.

Maise laid her bicycle on Mr. Buckley's scruffy lawn beside the pathway and walked to the front door, where she tapped on the frosted glass three times. She was about to try the knob to see if it was locked when it turned and the door swung open. Mr. Buckley stood leaning against it, his thin frame covered in brown pants and a striped polo shirt.

"Hello, Maise," he croaked. The misery in his voice broke her heart.

"Hi, Mr. Buckley. How are you feeling? I'm glad to see you're up and about again."

"Yes. I'm all right. Hanging in there," he said.

Maise gave a pained smile. "I wanted to let you know I'd been down to the police station."

"*Thank you.* Thank you very much."

"The police and the ambulance will be here as soon as they can. Probably later today."

"That will be a relief. I hate leaving her there in the heat. Her body is starting to feel the effects."

Maise wished she could do more. There was nowhere to keep the body cold. "I'm sorry I can't help."

"You've done enough, dear girl."

With a thin smile, Maise said, "You're not too hot in here?"

"I've got all the windows open and I'm keeping a wet towel on my forehead. That seems to be helping. And you know you feel the cold more as you get older so the warmth is not so bad. For me, anyway."

"You've got enough water?"

"For now, yes."

"If you need anything, let me know," Maise said. "Even just call out over the back fence."

Mr. Buckley thanked her and Maise left. She was keen to find out what Mark had been doing and update him on what she'd discovered. She was surprised, having taken so long, that he hadn't come looking for her.

She heard Mindy barking and raised voices as she walked up the driveway of their property. The garage door was locked, so she entered through the front and not willing to leave her bike outside, leaned it against the wall in the foyer, then walked through the house towards the rear. It sounded as though people were having an argument in the backyard.

Mark was the first person she spotted; he had a golf club raised and was moving quickly towards another person. *Parker.* Her stomach dropped. He looked sweaty, dirty and disheveled, as though he'd been out working for days on end. Mark was about to whack Parker with the club. Mindy was frantic, barking as she ran from one to the other, begging them to stop.

"Mark?" Maise yelled, opening the sliding door. Mark turned at the final moment and the golf club froze mid-air. Maise turned her gaze directly on Mark. "What are you doing?" Teeth bared, lips pulled back, Mark looked ready to kill.

"Maise," Parker said, and turned towards her.

Mindy stopped barking and ran to Maise. She reached down and let the dog lick her hand. It had been weeks since she last saw Parker at a New Year's Eve party held by a mutual friend. They had exchanged brief greetings but not spoken again since. "What are you doing here?"

"Its good to see you. I'm glad you're okay." Maise said nothing. When Parker realized she wasn't going to respond, he added, "I just came by to make sure you were all right."

"Why?" She immediately regretted asking that. She understood it was because he still cared, at least in some little way. Parker's silence made her turn to Mark and ask, "What's going on here?"

Parker said, "Just a little disagreement. Doesn't matter now."

"Too right it matters," Mark added. "I want this asshole out of here."

Maise put up a hand. "Hang on, Mark."

"You're not with him anymore. Why is he here?"

"I want to know why you were ready to hit him with a golf club first?"

"We just had an argument," Parker said.

"He wants you to leave. Go back up to Hell Ridge with him." Maise stared at Parker. Was that true? "He wants to divide us, sis."

Parker held up both hands. "Hold on, Mark. I don't want to divide anyone." He gave an uneasy laugh and turned to Maise. "I just think staying down here is a bad idea. This place is going to get crazier if they can't get the power and water back on soon." He turned back to Mark. "You're welcome to come. Jas and Sam are coming, too."

About that, Parker was right. Getting out of Whittlesea for now might be a good idea.

"It's not that bad, yet. You were just at the cop shop," Mark said to Maise. He tossed the golf club aside on the grass. "What are they saying?"

Maise felt the tension relax in her shoulders. Nobody was hitting anyone with a golf club. "I spoke with Uncle Jim. Things *are* getting worse. People are committing more crimes. And older people are dying."

"Caused by what?" Mark asked.

"The heat. The stress of it? Older people are more susceptible to heat. And others are dying, too. There are another four dead at the aged care place on Laurel Street. At least three people died when the blackout happened. Their cars just stopped running in the middle of the road. They ended up having accidents. And Uncle Jim said the ambulance has to pick up a dozen dead people around the town. That's in two days, Mark."

"That's a hell of a lot," Parker said.

"Do they know when the power will be back on?" Mark asked.

Maise shook her head. "No, not yet. They're waiting for advice from the government. Honestly, they seem flat out trying to cope with people stealing stuff and vandalizing property in Whittlesea. There's a lot of people doing the wrong thing right now. You saw what happened here yesterday morning. There are more and more burglaries going on every day. People will get more desperate."

"See," Parker said. 'I'm telling you, we don't want to be down the mountain in the next few days if things don't get back to normal."

"And what happens if you spend all that time going back up to Hell Ridge and then everything is fixed?"

"We get to camp for a few days. Read a few books. Catch some fish. Cool off in the creek."

Maise watched them both, conscious of the competitiveness between them about being right as much as the search for a safe outcome. She did not want to look like choosing against Mark, but Parker had a point. Could she be around him for a few days, or even a week, if it came to that? Sam and Jas were going too. That was something. Maybe she could convince Mark. Once, she might have stayed silent.

"I tend to agree with Parker, Mark. I don't think we can rely on the government. That's the other thing I heard—the premier died last night. Despite all their efforts so far, it seems like getting the power back on is harder than they thought. That's the impression I got from Uncle Jim. I think we're stronger sticking together in a group."

"Of course you pick his side. Jesus Christ, Maise, you're not even together anymore."

"That's got nothing to do with this," she shot back. "Use your brain, for Pete's sake."

"It's got everything to do with it. He's back for two minutes and you're happy to run up the mountain with him."

Maise stepped towards him. "Not true. This is not about choosing Parker or you, Mark. It's about the what's best right now. It's not an emotional decision, it's a logical one."

"Like I said, Mark, you can come along with us."

Maise raised her eyebrows. "Mark? What do you think? If Parker can comprise, can you?"

Mark laughed. "I'm not going anywhere with the guy that tried to steal my money and almost ruined my business. I don't trust him. And you'd be smart not to, either."

He stormed past them, calling for Mindy to follow, snatched open the sliding glass, and went inside with his dog, slamming the door behind him.

"Sorry about that," Parker said. "I'm trying to put our crap aside, but …"

Maise shook her head. "I know. It's tough on everyone right now."

They stood looking at each other. "It's good to see you," Parker said.

"I'm glad you're okay." Maise managed a slight smile. A part of her was glad to see Parker, but she had begun to adapt to life without him, push aside the strong feelings of their relationship. It had been a conflicted decision to break up with Parker; logic over heart had won in the end. She thought he would never change and breaking up had been a way of dealing with the inevitable. The memories and feelings were only buried below the surface, and she knew they risked reemerging if she wasn't careful. She walked back underneath the pergola and out of the heat. "So, you came by to see me? I thought you were camping up at Hell Ridge?"

Parker tilted his head from side to side. "I was. I... walked back... today."

Maise's expression widened. "All the way back from Hell Ridge? To check on me?"

"And Sam." Parker explained what had happened, from the first night waiting for Sam to arrive, waiting around the next day, and finally the long walk back.

"Wow," Maise said, genuinely impressed. "You must be exhausted."

He nodded. "You're not wrong."

"Do you want to freshen up in the pool?"

Parker accepted. He removed his shoes, socks and t-shirt, then gingerly walked over to the water's edge. He sat down on the paved coping and slid in, immersing himself beneath the water, where he glided along the tiled bottom, using breast stroke to propel himself to the other edge. When he resurfaced, he stood with the water at waist height, splashing it onto his face and over his head. After a few more laps, he climbed out, dripping, and stood in the sun, letting its rays dry him off.

"Damn that feels good."

"I bet. Do you need a towel?"

Parker shook his head. "Nah. Won't take long to dry." They stood in uneasy silence for a time. Maise wondered if it would ever be comfortable between them again. She sensed Parker wanted to say more but didn't want to push too hard too early. After all, it was their first time alone in several months.

Finally, Parker asked, "you didn't say why you were at the police station?"

Maise thought about Mrs. Buckley again and sadness enveloped her. "Mrs. Buckley passed away."

"I'm sorry to hear that. What about Mr. Buckley? He gonna be okay?"

. . .

"He's keeping cool, but it's hot in there. The Police said they'd be an hour or two. They're trying to get all the part time officers in to help." Maise thought about what the woman had said at the doctor's office. "I heard the army is setting up at the show grounds. We could really use their help."

Parker's face turned to surprise. "Funny that. An army jeep passed me while I was walking here."

"The lady who mentioned it said something about the Chinese army. Stupid, ha?" Parker's face dropped. "What is it?"

"That's what I saw," Parker said. "The soldiers were all Chinese, with a Chinese flag on the doors."

"Mark joked about it being a Chinese invasion."

Parker and Maise looked at each other with the same worried expression.

"I hope he's wrong."

TWENTY-SIX

As the afternoon heat strengthened, Parker and Maise sat on slatted wooden chairs at a table under the shade of the timber-framed pergola at the rear of the house, gradually unwinding their discomfort and discussing what had transpired during the last few days. They ate the last of the grapes, some apple, and a single mango that was almost too soft. Another day and it would begin to spoil. Maise disappeared to offer some to Mark, but he turned his back on her, happy to pout in his room with Mindy curled up on the bed. Parker knew he was a professional brooder and could spend days stewing over an incident, or, if bad enough, months, which typified the current situation. Parker was just grateful he had left them alone. The initial awkwardness with Maise had mostly passed, although some of her answers were clinical and Parker didn't dare create anything more than general conversation.

The previous year on a typical summer afternoon with the temperature above thirty-three Celsius, Parker, Maise, Mark, Raven, Sam and Jas would be sitting in cushioned outdoor lounge chairs drinking beer and wine, with a few sticks of kabana and a block or two of cheese. Music would play all afternoon long and if Sam was drunk enough, he might even bring out his acoustic guitar and play some Beatles' songs. Those afternoons built the best memories, the kinds of days they all enjoyed, until this summer, when everything had changed. After Parker and Mark had their falling out, he had separated with Maise and then Raven and Mark had split. Only Jas and Sam had survived.

Parker did not raise the idea of going back up to Hell Ridge again; Mark had mentioned it during their argument and he didn't want to discuss it in detail until Sam and Jas arrived. Mark would try to influence Maise and she would always consider his point of view. Parker just had to pick his moment. Hopefully after Sam and Jas arrived, they would add weight to the idea and have a positive influence on Maise. Hell, he wasn't lying when he had asked Mark to come along; if it guaranteed Maise going too, they could make it work for as long as it took to get the power sorted out.

A little after five with still no sign of the heat receding, Jas and Sam arrived. They both had packs and bicycles. Parker and Maise helped them into the garage, where they placed their bikes vertically against one wall and brought their packs into the house. Parker was reminded of what Sam had told him earlier and made him feel good knowing how happy Jas would be when she learned of it. They took a quick dip in the pool, and enjoyed the refreshing coolness of unheated water.

Drying themselves under the pergola, Maise directed a question at Sam and Jas, raising the topic Parker had been suppressing. "So you're going up to Hell Ridge with Parker?"

"Yeah," Jas said. "And so are *you*." Parker wanted to hug Jas. Maise only smiled.

"It's getting worse out there," Sam said, as he unscrewed the top off a warm beer. "We heard shots on the way here."

"There's been a big change from last night to today," Jas added. "People are anxious. Most of the stores are closed. Even the IGA. Gilly's Meats is shut now and the fridges are bare. I can't be sure, but I think the Whittlesea Medical Clinic closed too."

"I don't think the government even knows what has happened yet," Maise said.

Sam cradled his beer. "What makes you say that?"

"The updates don't say a lot. Apparently, the army has arrived, but we haven't seen or heard from them yet. They should be telling us their plan. Step one. Step two if it doesn't work. All I've heard so far is 'we're working on the problem and hope to have the power back on soon'. It's exactly what they'd told my uncle. Same message as yesterday. That usually means they have no idea what's going on."

"You might be right," Sam said. "All the signs point to an EMP event. It's designed to fry electrical circuitry. You can't fix that easily."

Parker leaned forward. "Can it be fixed?"

"I don't think so. But I'm no expert."

"So what are you saying? All the cars are stuffed? All the phones? The TV's?"

Sam shrugged. "I've read a few books about EMP's. I guess nobody really knows, but that's what most people think. The modern world is based on electrical circuitry. Once an item has its circuitry burnt out, it doesn't work anymore. Simple."

"So anything without a chip—anything built before a certain time—

becomes very valuable," Parker added.

"Correct. If I was the government I would be trying to reboot anything old I had lying around. Sometimes they store it, sometimes its still being used. The search will be on."

"What about the Chinese military vehicle I saw coming down the mountain?" Parker asked. "And the two trucks I saw parked at the Showgrounds?"

"We saw a big army truck driving around town on the way over," Sam said.

"They haven't bloody done much," Jas scoffed.

Maise sat forward. "Exactly my point. Parker and I were talking about it earlier. There's talk of the army setting up at Yan Yean Reservoir. I heard it was the Chinese." She told them about the person she heard at the doctor's office.

"This truck was *full* of Chinese people—men and women," Sam added.

Jas bit her fingernails. "Something's definitely going on."

"It wasn't an old vehicle," Sam said. "It looked brand new. The design looked like something you see driving around nowadays."

Parked finished his bottle of water. "How do they still work when so many other's don't?"

Sam twisted his face. "The only thing I can think is that they were somehow protected from an EMP."

"You can do that?" Jas asked.

"Sure. There are ways to protect things from it."

"What will the army do? Everything is broken. It's not just the power," Maise said. "If the electricity doesn't run, the warehouses won't work, the trucks don't run, and no food or supplies get to the shops."

"Exactly. People have a little bit of food for now," Sam said, "but when it runs out, there's going to be trouble."

"Toilet paper is the big one. And other essentials like soap and toothpaste, that sort of thing," Maise said.

"Sanitary pads," Jas added.

"Brushing your teeth and having a wash are not the priorities right now," Sam joked.

"Speak for yourself," Maise said.

"Beer." Parker smiled. Maise made a face. "I'm just kidding." Once, he might have considered it the number one priority.

"It wasn't the first thing you stashed away when you left Hell Ridge?" Jas asked.

Parker laughed. "You might be surprised to know, *Jas*, that the beer I had over the last two days camping was the first I've had in weeks." He glanced at Maise and read disbelief on her face.

"Wow. I am surprised. Why the change?"

Parker sat back. "Let's just say, I've learnt a few things over the last year."

He wanted Maise to know he'd made changes to his behavior, that it wasn't the same as it had been during the last stages of their relationship, and that with heavy reflection, he now understood that drinking was a critical factor in helping unravel the relationship. But Maise was still invested in the conversation about the EMP. Sam too.

"So, what? Sam asked, looking at each of their faces. "You think they're... what, invading?" Is that what this is all about? Let's assume they let off a nuclear device above the atmosphere. We lose access to anything that allows us to retaliate."

"Anything we need to stay alive," Maise said.

"Then they sweep in and take over?" Jas asked. "Makes sense."

Parker cleared his throat and sat forward. Now was his chance, with the conversation going in this direction and having Sam and Jas there to support his argument. "This is why going back to Hell Ridge makes sense. We're off grid. Nobody will even know we're there." They were silent, but he read their faces and they all knew he was right. Parker continued. "I was thinking, maybe we leave tonight. Just pack up and run."

"In the dark?" Jas asked.

"I dunno, mate," Sam said. "The crazies come out at night."

"Yeah, I know, but it's also the coolest time of the day. And as much as the crazies come out, it gives us the best chance of getting out and not being seen."

"Seen by who?" Maise asked.

Parker shrugged. "Anyone." But he was thinking about the Chinese soldiers that had been increasingly appearing.

Jas turned to Maise. "You're coming, right Maiz?"

Maise shifted in her seat. "I don't know."

"I'm telling you," Jas said with a cheeky smile, "You don't have a choice. I'll speak to Mark if he's the problem." Maise tried a smile, but there was concern at the edges of her mouth.

"Whether we leave tonight or first thing tomorrow, I agree, we need to get out of Whittlesea," Sam said.

A little after six, Maise pulled a single burner butane cooker—similar to the one Parker had at the campsite—out of the garage and they fired it up. From the fridge, Maise used the last of their frozen meat—several rump steaks—that had defrosted, which would have been useless the next day, being sure to set aside one for Mark.

The meat tasted especially good, and went down well with the last shreds of lettuce, capsicum and cabbage. The group sat sprawled on chairs with full bellies and drank beer and wine in the fading light, using citronella candles to light the pergola area and keep the mosquitoes away.

Maise had earlier gone over to see Mr. Buckley and invited him to join them, but he wouldn't leave Mrs. Buckley's body. At a quarter past eight, there was a knock on the door. Maise answered, finding the police had arrived to take the body away. Parker offered to go with her, but she told him to stay behind with the others.

After Maise had gone and Mark was nowhere in sight, Sam said, "You think she'll come with us?"

"I hope so. She's not saying much though."

Parker knew his altercation with Mark created a bigger problem for Maise; whatever she chose to do would make the other think she was being disloyal. Her brother or her ex-boyfriend —who did she choose? He would plead his case, but in the end, he would respect her decision. Still, he'd be shattered if she chose to stay behind with Mark.

Maise returned just before nine o'clock, her eyes wet, wiping her nose with a tissue. She cried during sad movies. It was an endearing quality. Jas gave her a big hug. Parker wished he could have. She cried for Mrs. Buckley's death and Mr. Buckley's loss. Maise had asked Mr. Buckley to stay with them, but he preferred to be alone.

Maise also had an update from the police, but there was little progress. No word on the power, although they were hopeful to have more answers in the morning.

"Don't hold your breath," Sam said. "Something tells me this is going to take a lot longer than tomorrow morning."

"I asked about the army at the reservoir and the Show-grounds," Maise said. "They hadn't heard but are going to check it out. They're having some sort of community gathering at the hall later on to update people. I also heard gunshots—three or four lots. People are going off the rails."

Maise was just about to start making beds up for the guests when Mark staggered out through the sliding doors. Parker had drunk two beers, but he wasn't anywhere near drunk. He steeled himself, knowing what was coming. He'd seen it many times before but had never been on the receiving end. It seemed part two of their reunion was about to happen.

TWENTY-SEVEN

"What's goin' on?" Mark asked, leaning against Maise's chair. He suspected if he tried to stand for too long on his own legs, he'd fall over.

The grog was on him now, working its way through his blood. He'd lost count at half a dozen. He didn't care that it was warm; he just wanted more of it to quell the frustration and resentment. But the alcohol only made it worse, revealing more of both that had lived in him for the last six months.

"Go back inside, Mark," Maise said. "Please."

"Why? I can't join you?"

"We were just about to go to bed."

Mark said, "He's not stayin'." He waved a hand towards Parker. At least he was sitting on his own and not with Maise in his lap.

Mark glanced around the pergola area, trying to locate a spare seat. An old wooden chair sat against the wall, more as a decoration now, than for use. His father was the last person to sit in it; used to read books on an afternoon after work and drink cup after cup of coffee. Mark dragged it away from the wall and placed it between Sam and Jas, knocking the handle of Jas' seat.

He was still simmering from the earlier conversation with Parker, who had arrived without an invite. He'd then accused Mark of having nobody and of being afraid to be alone. That had tipped him over the edge, and he wasn't able to let it go. They had tip-toed around each other for more than six months, making sure they didn't attend the same function or sporting match, Mark leaving at the last moment if he knew Parker was visiting Maise, when they'd been together. Now, it was time to put and end to it and clear his chest.

"You stuffed up my life, man," he said to Parker.

"We back on this, are we?" Parker asked.

Mark felt blood rush to his head and he tensed.

"Mark!" Maise stood up. "Stop it now. Go back inside, will you."

"No, Maise." Parker sat forward. "Let him go. Let him say his piece. Maybe he'll feel better."

"Too right I will. I just wanna know how you live with yourself. How you live with stealing money from our business—my business, to begin with." He sat back, threw both hands up in exasperation. "How, man?"

Sam and Jasmine dropped their gazes. Maise sat back in her chair.

Parker placed his beer on the concrete pavers beside his seat. Mark was surprised he didn't take another swig.

"You know, I'm glad you asked me that, Mark. Because you haven't bothered to, yet. Six months later and you haven't even had the guts to approach me and ask why. You wrote me off—bang." He clapped his hands. "Gone, forever." He sat forward. "I made a mistake man. Plain and simple. And I'm okay to admit I've made a few of them in the last two years."

"First real thing you've said in ages. Wouldn't have taken much—"

"Let him speak, Mark," Jas said. "You asked for it." Mark pressed his lips together, then took another swallow of beer.

"I wasn't thinking, man," Parker went on. "After my mum died—"

Mark sat forward. "Uh, uh. No, you don't. You can't bring that up. My father died too and I didn't use that as an excuse."

Parker's face pinched with disbelief. "You can't compare. How my mum's death affected me is separate to how you were affected by your father's death. You know that."

"Of course I know it. I'm just saying you can't use it as an excuse for stealing the money."

"I'm not. But it was a cause for me drinking more and gambling and then stealing the money."

"So, your mum died, you drank because you were sad, you started gambling, and then you stole from me because you needed more money to gamble?"

"Yeah. Kinda."

"It's bullshit." Mark felt his words slurring, but he didn't care. "I didn't start drinking more and gambling when my dad died."

"You handled it better."

"No I didn't. I was just as upset. I just chose not to steal from my best mate. I let you into partnership with me. I trusted you. You let me down, man. You stole from me. That's the worst kind of friend."

Parker shifted in his seat. "Well, guess what? The way I see it, you let me down. You let me down because you were never there for me after my mum died. What was I supposed to do?"

"Suck it up, mate. That's what I did. I was hurting when dad died. But I didn't run around asking for help. I didn't want people to check on me everyday, I just wanted to get on with it."

"We don't all work like that, Mark. Just because you're like that you forgot about me. You never asked me how I was; never spoke to me about it. Never even said, "Mate, are you all right?" You just tried to sweep it under the carpet and forget it ever happened. Out of sight out of mind, hey?"

Mark leapt to his feet. "So its my fault? I made you steal?"

Parker jumped up too. "I didn't say that. But if you'd shown me a little more support, maybe I wouldn't have gone off the rails so much. Maise, Sam, Jas, Raven—they were all there for me, asking if I was okay, how I was feeling about it. Every time I saw you, it was work, work, work. I was struggling right before your eyes and from my point of a view, you didn't give a shit. Maybe I thought if he doesn't, why should I?"

Anger filled Mark's head like a mushroom cloud from a mini

atomic bomb. He couldn't sort through all of it and make a coherent response. He kept opening his mouth to say something, but nothing came out. He couldn't believe Parker was saying this stuff, blaming Mark for his actions.

"Sit down, guys," Sam said. "Let's cool off a bit, huh?"

But Mark was beyond cooling off. The beer fell from his hand and he leapt across the patio at Parker, fists cocked, swinging for his head. Parker saw it coming, and stepped out of the way at the last moment. Mark lost balance, fell forward and went crashing into the seat where Parker had been sitting. He tried to stand, but got his hand caught in the seat arm. When he did finally make it to his feet, Maise and Sam were standing there, blocking his way to Parker.

"Move!"

Sam was bigger and stronger than Mark. They had wrestled as kids and Mark always had trouble with Sam. He just always managed to avoid fighting. Mark might win under normal circumstances, but in his current state, he'd struggle to move Sam out of the way.

"Sorry, mate. This argument is over," Sam said, taking a handful of his shirt.

Maise put a hand on his arm. "Go to bed, Mark. Before you have nobody left."

Mark's cheeks puffed. Blood pulsed in his forehead. He started to push Sam's hand away. Sam's fist tightened around Mark's shirt. The anger began to subside just a little. He didn't have the energy to take on Sam and Parker.

He looked past Maise and Sam. "Think about this, Mr. Teflon. I ended up with a massive debt, a business that's reputation was damaged, no best mate, and no girlfriend out of all of this. You're still kicking about with not a worry in the world. And tomorrow, you'll all head back up to Hell Ridge, camp this thing out, and probably end up with the girlfriend you also betrayed. Play happy families, the lot of you." He started nodding. "I'll hold the fort back here, don't you worry. Make sure all your stuff is safe, Maise. How is any of that fair?"

Parker looked away, summing up his thoughts, then back up at

Mark, his expression defiant, his eyes glistening in the faint candle light. "I'll take responsibility for the business issues, Mark. I've paid back the money. I'll do whatever else you need me to do to fix that part of it. But when it comes to Raven, and your relationships with people, that's on you."

Mark scoffed, shook his head. There was no point. The sting had gone out of it and Parker would always play down the impact of his actions. He would never see it from Mark's point of view. "Fine. Then I guess you're the winner out of all of this."

He shrugged off Sam and Maise and walked directly towards the door, not looking back at any of them. He was on his own. No Maise, no Parker, no Raven. He would do what he had to do from now on and he would do it for himself.

TWENTY-EIGHT

Candlelight drew dancing shadows on the wall of Maise's bedroom, filled with a wooden queen-sized bed frame, a wide, modern dresser and an LED television attached to the wall. The house remained warm inside, but opening the windows had drawn in a light breeze and the temperature outside had dropped ten degrees from its daytime peak. Nothing more than a light sheet was required for sleep. Maise was grateful her room was near the back of the house, where noise from the street was muted, and on the east side, receiving softer morning sun instead of the vicious afternoon heat. Outside, beyond the confines of the property, people wandered the streets. There was frequent shouting, the occasional pop of firecrackers and even the odd gunshot. Maise had dressed in short pajamas after taking a cold shower that had been both breathtaking and invigorating. It had ended in a trickle, the water pipes beneath the house finally empty.

She had set Parker up in the lounge room on an inflatable bed, as far away from Mark as possible. After the altercation, Parker had started to bid goodbye to Jas and Sam, but Maise had felt bad for him when the rest of them were staying, and made the offer. Parker had resisted at first, but Jas had convinced him to stay. Maise had been clear about their status as friends and Parker had agreed, but she sensed his underlying disappointment.

Maise decided to check in on him once more. The confrontation with Mark had been intense. Parker lay on the single mattress in his boxer shorts and a singlet top. Maise sat on a nearby sofa chair.

"That was full on," Maise said. "You okay?"

Parker nodded. "Fine. I'm glad it happened. Mark probably won't remember much of it, he was pissed as."

"He normally remembers everything. He's certainly not a forgetful drunk."

"Even so, he didn't buy my argument. He's a bit stubborn when it comes to other people's points of view."

"A bit?" She smiled. "I thought you made a good case. Admitted responsibility for spending the money."

"What else could I do? I did wrong. I got help."

It had been awkward when Parker first arrived, but slowly, they had both loosened up, and Maise had seen things in him she hadn't witnessed in a long time, maybe ever. He hadn't drunk himself into oblivion and become the customary rowdy clown. He had admitted mistakes, spoken as if as though he wasn't the most important person in his own life, and that walk from Hell Ridge, all the way back to Whittlesea.

Parker continued. "You know I never told anyone this, Maise, but I went and spoke to someone after mum died."

"Really?" Maise was surprised.

"Only did three sessions."

"Did they help?"

"I dunno. Probably not, because we broke up."

"Have you been back?"

He shook his head. "Nah. I've made a lot of progress. But I still think about what the psychologist said."

"I can tell." He smiled at that, grateful she had noticed.

"So," Parker began, "Hell Ridge. I know you're not a big fan of camping. I—"

"Hang on. I actually *enjoy* camping. We used to go up to Whit-field with my dad when we were younger. Pack the trailer. Take our fishing rods. Have a big fire. What I didn't enjoy the one time *we* went was you sitting on your butt drinking while I cooked and kept the camp clean. You got a holiday and I didn't."

Parker made a pained face. "Yeah. Sorry about that. I know I can be a little short sighted."

"Selfish."

Parker sat up. "But it won't be like that this time, I promise. Full shares when it comes to upkeep."

"I'll be honest, Parker. I've been torn about going." She brushed a strand of dark hair from her face. "I didn't want to leave Mark alone. He's right about that, he will end up with nothing. If he had Raven, that'd be one thing, but he's got nobody. And I know he says he's fine, but most of the time, he's not. You heard him tonight. He feels like he's got nobody left."

"I get that, but that's his fault. He's brutal. Everything is his way. He's Mr. Macho all the time and sometimes you have to compromise. Imagine him in camp, anyway? That confined space? He'll go crazy."

"Probably. After his behavior tonight, I don't think he'd be able to do it. There's just too much animosity."

"I tried."

"You did."

"Look at it as a two week camping trip. I've got enough supplies up there to last us that long at least. We've got gas for lamps, burners—heaps of toilet paper." Maise smiled. "Enough food. Infinite water. It'll be good. Get away from all of this. Who knows how far it will go, anyway. And if it does end early, we can leave camp early and ride back down."

"So, what do I bring?"

"Anything you can fit into a back pack. Clothes mostly, a few personal items. I have a spare sleeping bag I always carry in the Hilux."

"Thanks," she said. She wanted to acknowledge him more. They were in a good space, but it was all still too soon. She was known for avoiding conflict and not speaking her mind—the exact opposite to Jasmine. "I know it hasn't been long, but you've changed. So far, anyway."

His brow furrowed and she could sense his deeper thought. After a long time, he said, "I know I usually put myself first. I'm... working on it. I know it was a massive reason we broke up. And the way I communicate. I'm crap at it—like Mark. But I can't very well complain about him not communicating and then do a bad job myself, can I?" She smiled. He started to say something, then stopped.

"Say it," Maise said.

He hesitated again, then seemed to relax. "I don't have high expectations, but I still care for you, Maise." He shrugged. "To be honest, I still love you. I never stopped." She started to speak and he put up a hand. "You don't have to say anything. In fact, it's better like this for now, with all of this," he waved a hand about, "going on."

She nodded. "You're right." And he was. The last thing they needed now was the additional challenge of something like that. She'd admitted to herself, this "different" Parker was more enjoyable. But she was a long way from taking him back with open arms. One day didn't make a change. She stood to leave.

"We'll get on the road early. Beat the heat." Parker lay back down on the blow up mattress. "Get your riding legs working, it's going to be a long gig. The hill going up to Kinglake is a killer."

TWENTY-NINE

Wednesday, January 25, 2023
Day 3

P arker rolled over onto his side, pulled the sheet up underneath his chin and almost rolled off the air mattress. It had been a bumpy night, with the heat and thoughts of the evening's events stealing hours of sleep. It was warm already and it couldn't have been more than six-thirty judging by the faint blades of light poking through the curtains. Morning sun. The room would be an oven by ten. He and the others would be halfway up the mountain by then, before the heat of the day zapped their bodies and scorched their skin. Though, the thought of walking a hundred meters didn't enthuse his aching muscles.

Parker still felt uneasy about leaving his Hilux and the equipment exposed to the world. Anybody could drive down the track to his camp and cart it all away. He'd never know. Even though he'd locked it all up, thieves could break the windows of his car or slash the tent and steal the camping gear—without it, they'd almost be better off staying in Whittlesea.

He used the bathroom, emptying a splash of pool water into the bowl from a bucket stored beside the toilet. He wondered if Maise was up yet. Wandering past her room, the door opened and she appeared, wearing stripy pajamas, her dark hair slightly disheveled.

"Morning."

She yawned. "You sure? It's bloody early."

"Power's still out."

Maise turned back into her room. Parker stood at the door. "Did you really think it'd be back on yet?"

"No."

"Hopefully the government and utilities companies are close to fixing the power."

The clink of ceramic mugs sounded from the kitchen. Parker heard Sam's voice. "You want coffee?"

Maise said, "Sure. Thanks. Use the gas stove."

Sam and Jas were in the kitchen, stacking non-perishable food and camping supplies they had collected from their own houses onto the laminate countertop.

"Not bad, hey? Jas asked, raising her eyebrows to Parker. He nodded in agreement. "We've got paper towel, matches, batteries, torches, and tinned food—beetroot—I love that stuff, spaghetti, baked beans, corn, tomatoes and my all time fave, baby spuds."

"It's great," Parker said. "Really good. You going to lug all of this, Jas?"

"Ha-ha, no way." She slapped Sam on the back. "That's why I've got the big guy." She put her chin on his arm. "Haven't I babe?"

"Yeah, yeah. We'll pack this in one of the rucksacks and I'll carry it on my back."

"Don't forget to pack everything," Parker said to Sam with a knowing smirk.

Sam looked at him, then punched him in the arm. "I won't, *mate.*"

"What about your families?" Parker asked.

Jas shrugged. "Both away. Mine are down the coast."

"Mine are up the bush," Sam added. "They probably won't even know this is happening.

"How long before we leave?" Jas asked.

"As soon as we have a bite to eat."

Maise appeared, dressed in light green shorts and a white polo shirt, her hair tied up in a bun. Parker felt his breath catch. Geez, she looked good. But she wasn't smiling. Her look was downcast, as though something was playing on her mind.

"You okay?"

She hesitated. "Yeah. I'll be fine."

In the past, he might have let it go, might have hurried onto whatever was occupying his mind and forgotten about Maise. And even if they weren't going out, it didn't hurt to ask. He was interested. He wanted her to be okay. "You sure?"

She adjusted her hair at the back of her head and then let her hands drop. "It's just Mark and what happened last night. He doesn't know I'm planning to go with you guys. It will gut him. And I'm worried about leaving him alone."

"He's a big boy," Parker said. "I offered for him to come along."

"It would take a miracle for that to happen."

Sam cocked his head. "He might come around."

"He's too stubborn," Jas said.

"Then he's going to have to deal with it."

Maise glanced down the hallway towards the front door. "The government has been doing letterbox drops. We should check to see if there's a new one."

"I'll check."

Parker left Maise, Jas and Sam in the kitchen discussing final checks, and walked down the hallway where he opened the front door. Bright sunlight greeted him, the dry air settling against his skin, reminding him of the sizzling terrors of the day before.

The street outside Maise's house was completely different to how he had seen it the previous afternoon. It was as though a mob had been through the place. Several cars parked along the curb had their windscreens shattered, spraying glass fragments across the road. Directly opposite, a man, woman, and two kids stood in their driveway looking inside an open garage where the contents were scattered over the ground; plastic boxes had been upturned, papers and cardboard spread about. Parker reached the letterbox. To his left, outside the next house, a handful of people hovered over a body lying in the gutter. Parker spotted tufts of grey hair. If he had to make a guess, he'd say the guy was dead. Beyond, another group of people examined the smoking, charred remnants of another vehicle. *Like something out of a futuristic movie*, Parker thought. The letterbox was empty. Nothing new from the goddamn government. What were they doing?

He took a final look at the neighborhood, not quite believing what he was seeing, and as he turned, he spotted another Jeep driving along the street perpendicular to Maise's. One soldier drove and the other sat in the passenger seat and from a distance, they appeared to be Chinese. Parker zeroed in on the door and found the red marking of the Chinese flag.

He hurried back inside, ignoring the aches and pains in his legs and ended up in the kitchen. "Good thing we're leaving. Things are getting heaps worse out there. One of your neighbor's has been burgled, there's a car on fire in the street, and what looks like a dead bloke in the gutter. And to top it off, I saw another Chinese army vehicle driving along Cressy Street."

The other three hurried away from the bench. They returned with worried looks on their faces.

"You're right," Maise said. "What do you think the army was doing?"

"I have no idea. But I think we should try and avoid them."

"What's the plan then?"

"Let's finish packing. We need to get some fuel from the servo for the motorbike I told you about last night. It will be easier if someone rides that, and we've got it in case of emergencies. Two people can always ride double and get back to Whittlesea in twenty minutes if we need to. And don't forget to look for more candles. They never go to waste."

"Good idea."

"And just do a last minute scout for anything else you think might be valuable. But remember, we need to carry it. Let's aim to leave in fifteen minutes."

"Take all the good stuff and leave Maise and me with nothing?" Mark asked from the kitchen doorway. "I should have expected that." His hair stuck out at angles; he wore a pair of bright blue football shorts and a singlet top, revealing muscular arms. His normally shaven face had a light fuzz.

"I'm going with them, Mark," Maise said. Jas stepped up beside her.

Mark's face pinched together in disbelief. "What? It's our house, Maise. You can't just bail on it."

"It's safer leaving for now. Have you seen outside? The Drake's got burgled. There's a burnt-out car in the middle of the street, an old man died in the gutter. And the Chinese army is driving around the streets. Why are they here? How long before they start making trouble?"

"I don't care about any of that. We should still wait it out here. This thing could be over by the end of the day."

"Seriously, Mark?" Jas asked.

Parker said, "We're at about sixty plus hours now, Mark. There's big problems getting the power back on, you know it and I know it." Mark glared at him.

"Come with us then," Maise said.

"I'm not gonna leave this house to be trashed. Besides," he tipped his chin towards Parker. "I'm not going with him"

"Don't be such a baby," Jas said. "This could be a matter of life and death. Put your bloody differences aside for now and just suck it up. Surely if you wanted Parker to suck it up after his mother died, you can do it now?"

Mark ground his jaw, looking from Jas, to Sam and finally Maise. "What happened, Maise?"

"To what?"

"You swore you'd never get back with this guy. You *swore*." A long, awkward silence settled over them. "Change of plan?"

Maise locked her eyes on Mark. Her bottom lip trembled and Parker read the anger in her face where her eyebrows forked down. He understood right then there had to be an element of truth in what Mark had said. "We're not back together."

"Sure looks like it."

"You know, Mark, I didn't want to leave you alone. I was feeling guilty. But stuff it, you can deal with it yourself."

"Listen," Mark said, stepping out of the doorway. The stench of alcohol was still strong and his eyes were red. Parker had seen that look in the mirror himself a hundred times. Is that what he had been like after every night out? Mark leant against the bench. An air of seriousness came over him. "I still think its better to wait it out here." He waved a hand. "Look around. At least we have the protection of the house. We can lock the doors. What have you got up there? A tent? That won't stop much." Nobody spoke. Parker looked at his old friend. There was a desperation crawling over him, in his slack mouth and his stance; he pushed off the kitchen bench and held his hands out, as if pleading.

Jas stepped in front of Maise. "It's too late, Mark." She glanced at Maise. "We're leaving now."

"You can still come," Maise said.

"Come on, man," Sam said. "It's the best thing. We're stronger together. You must know that."

Mark scowled as he found each of their stoic faces, as though he was giving them one final look. Then he turned and left the room. Parker was glad in a way. Having Mark there would only make the situation more uncomfortable. Without him, they wouldn't be walking on eggshells. He knew Maise wanted her brother around, but Parker still thought it was the best outcome.

He pushed down the thought of what Mark had said. Maise had sworn to never get back with him. It was probably true. It was like a slap in the face for him though. He knew he could be difficult —Jesus, he had been terribly selfish at times over the last fifteen months. But he wasn't done yet; wasn't giving up on the chance to get back with her. He just had to prove himself, show her he had changed enough to make it worth her while.

There were tears in Maise's eyes as she stared at the doorway through which Mark had left.

"We should leave," Sam said. Jas nodded, touched her shoulder. They disappeared into the lounge room.

Maise turned to Parker. "I said it. Just after we broke up." She diverted her gaze. " I was angry. *So* angry. Mark started saying things like 'You'll be back with him in a week.' I got so annoyed with him. He kept saying it. So, I said it. I said it and he told me to swear on it. So I did. Just to shut him up."

Parker unfolded his arms and took her gently by the shoulders. "It's fine, Maiz. You don't have to explain. I sucked. We broke up and it was tough." He looked her in the eyes, trying to summon all the honesty he could. "I was a fool. You *should* have dumped my ass. And you're right, we're not back together so you haven't broken an oath." She flinched at that. "I know how hard it is fighting against Mark and the way he insists on his way and he thinks he knows what's best for you. And even your dad was like that rest his soul, before Mark, who kind of carried it on. I'm an idiot for saying this, but maybe its best you stay here with him. Maybe he's right." He followed it up quickly with, "If that's what you want."

There was no hesitation. "No, I want to come. I do. It's the right thing. This place is getting too dangerous." He let her arms drop and turned away. "And I've noticed a change, Parker. Since you returned. You've been… different. Just keep being like that." He smiled at her. "But I want you to do one thing for me."

"Anything."

"I want you to talk to Mark, for me. Try and convince him to come with us. You know the best thing is for him to come with us. We'll be stronger. If he hears it from you, he might listen."

Parker pulled away. "I don't think so, Maiz. I've done it already. I just don't see how we can get back from last night. There's a massive divide between us. I know I've made mistakes. Hell, I admitted that, but it didn't do any good. Us two talking just won't make a difference. I think its up to Mark now to work through it in his own mind. I can't help him anymore."

THIRTY

But Maise couldn't leave it there. Couldn't give up on her brother joining the group without one final shot at it.

Mark had disappeared out the back into the shed where he began hammering nails into lengths of wood again. He didn't hear her come in and she stood there for almost a minute, watching him, attempt to get the order of words right in her mind before opening the conversation. Mindy had her head in an old pot, trying to extract another thing to chew to pieces. When she saw Maise, she wagged her tail briefly. Maise wasn't sure Mark would even listen—he might just tell her to nick off before she could plead her case, but it was time to say some things that might forge a crack in his armor and get him thinking outside the bubble in his head. For his sake *and* theirs. She knew he made them stronger. Just having him about—even with his stubborn, 'always right' personality—he added strength to their team. If anyone tried to forcefully take over them, Mark would always stand up. He had a reputation in Whittlesea as a tough nut, both for his sporting exploits and growing up, as a kid who didn't shy away from a fight.

Eventually, he sensed her standing there, and turned around to face Maise. He quickly went back to picking screws out of a small plastic drawer.

"Can you think about coming with us? Please, for me?"

"And leave this house? The one that dad built with his own hands? Have it trashed by assholes looking for batteries or food? I don't think so."

"I know it's a risk. But everyone's in the same boat. If you boarded it up, wouldn't people stay away?"

"People will find a way to get in, if that's what they really want." He hammered another nail into a length of plank. The wood split, the nail too close to the edge.

"Last night was pretty intense. You both said a lot of things."

"It's clear everyone is siding with Parker. Including you. My own sister."

"It's not like that, Mark. But there are generally two sides to every argument, and in this case, there are definitely two. You both make a point."

"So, I'm in the wrong?"

Time for him to hear a few home truths, she thought. He wasn't raging mad. He might have the capacity to listen. She lowered her voice and spoke in the clearest and calmest tone she knew.

"Clearly Parker did the wrong thing when he used the money for gambling. He shouldn't have. He's admitted that and apologized and he's shown a lot of remorse and regret." Mark said nothing. "You're both terrible communicators. That's the truth. After his mother died, he didn't cope. Maybe you were able to bottle it up and get over dad's death, but Parker wasn't. But he was closer with his mother than you were with dad. He acted out. He started drinking and gambling more. Maybe it was to take his mind off losing her. The question you need to ask yourself is how much you were there for him during that time. When he was gambling and drinking, did you call him on it? Did you call him and say, mate, I know it's hard, but I'm there for you if you need anything?" She let that last question hang. Mark adjusted the wood lengths to match. Maise hoped he was hearing her. She hoped he was pretending to be doing something so he didn't have to respond. "Parker shouldn't have taken the money. You can let that mistake ruin your friendship. Only you can decide. I know you're hurt. You feel betrayed. But I want you to give him another chance. See if he's changed." She held her breath for the next bit. He wasn't going to like it. "The same thing happened with Raven. You guys kept arguing and couldn't agree to disagree. You can't get past it. You need to accept that sometimes we don't all agree on the same thing and that's okay. Forgive a bit more. And mistakes shouldn't always mean a life sentence."

He put the hammer down, turned to her. "Is that it?" She nodded. "When are you leaving?"

"Now, but we can wait for you to pack."

Mark shook his head. "I'm not coming." Maise's mouth had gone dry from nervous talking. She searched for a response. Before she could say anything, Mark added, "And I have a question for you. Will you stay here with me, help protect our house?"

Maise shook her head. "No, Mark. I won't."

He nodded, lips pressed in a line, then brushed past her and walked out of the shed.

"Guess I'll see you when I see you then."

THIRTY-ONE

I t took another thirty minutes to get their gear in order, packs on their backs, bicycle tires checked for air pressure and do a final sweep for any items they might have missed. As Sam, Jas and Parker stood outside the garage on the driveway, Maise kept returning inside for things she had forgotten. Parker suspected she was just trying to give Mark more time to change his mind.

In the end, Mark wandered into the garage as Maise did a final useless look around. Mindy was at his heel and when she spotted Maise, she began to whimper, eager to see them as though she knew this might be the final time.

"Stay," Mark said.

Maise put her bike down and ran to Mark. They hugged, Mark stoic, Maise visibly upset. Sam wheeled his bike over and shook hands with Mark; Jas climbed off and gave him a short hug. Parker did not move, and Mark made no attempt to say goodbye to him, either.

Parker was angry at Mark's stubbornness. He'd put himself out there the previous night, admitting his faults and mistakes and had given a complete apology. It had taken him six months to do that, but it meant nothing to Mark. It validated what Parker suspected Mark thought of him. No more speculation. No more guessing games. Parker turned his back and rolled down the driveway. The others followed.

"Wait," Mark said, calling out from the garage opening.

Parker stood on the bicycle brakes and came to a stop. The others did the same.

Mark spoke to Maise. "Be careful. I didn't tell you last night, but I saw some Chinese soldiers force one of the local government councilors into an army jeep yesterday."

"Force?" Maise asked.

Mark shrugged. "On the side of the road. One of them had an automatic rifle. Pointed it at him and made him climb into the vehicle."

"When was this?" Sam asked.

"Yesterday, near the community building, on the way back from Keith Whitehead's place. I went there to pay the rest of the money for the car I was buying."

"He obviously said no."

"Wasn't even there. Place was trashed." The others looked at Mark. "That's it."

Parker led them away from the house, wondering what state it would be in when they returned. The elderly dead body had been removed from the gutter and the people across the street had cleaned up most of the rubbish from their concrete driveway and garage floor. None of the abandoned cars in the street had moved. Most had been pushed off to the side though, which allowed the group to slip through on their bicycles. He was conscious of the army jeep he'd seen, and they kept close to the edge of the road in case they had to make a quick exit into bushes or behind a car for cover.

At the top of the gentle slope near the end of the street, Parker stopped his bike and waited for the others to reach him. The empty front yards of brick houses on either side watched in unnerving silence.

Jas reached Parker first, stopping her bicycle and pointing into the distance, beyond the treetops, towards the mountains in the north-east. "What's that?"

"Smoke."

"Some idiot probably got bored and lit a match," Maise said.

"It's a long way from where we're going," Parker added. "But we need to keep an eye on it."

They could not underestimate the meaning of smoke in the Australian bush, regardless of how far away it might be. With the phones and power out, they had lost any form of communication to warn them of impending fires. They all bore the mental scars of bushfire. Anybody who was ten years old or more in 2009 knew of the catastrophic effect they had on the area, particularly in Kinglake. Across the state of Victoria on that fateful Saturday of February 7th, 173 people lost their lives. And while the heat and wind was nothing like the forty-seven degrees Celsius and blustery, scorching northerly it had been that day and in the days leading up, they didn't know what weather conditions lay ahead and only a fool would think fires were predictable.

They pedaled and glided their way through the streets, taking in the changes that had occurred in Whittlesea in the sixty-five or so hours since the blackout had occurred. It had passed though several phases, from street parties and voracious shopping in the beginning, to a more serious, concerned attitude on the second day, to one of growing frustration with the lack of progress yesterday. What would today bring? People would only stay silent for so long, would only comply with the governments orders when power, food and water were in dwindling supply. At some point, they would not accept it anymore, and the chaos already occurring would get a whole lot worse. Among the many silent houses was evidence of minor vandalism; spray-painted lampposts, empty beer bottles, old clothes and bedding strewn across the road. Parker hoped it was just silly kids taking advantage of the absence of communication and police coverage. Parker wondered what was happening inside those silent houses. Were people sleeping it off? What were kids doing without their electronic devices? Parker spotted a few lucky families packing their working vehicles with bags and bedding, hooking them up to trailers or caravans and driving for the deeper bush or large fresh-water lakes of the north. There were plenty within the area.

Despite the nine o'clock curfew, people had been out at night and there was extensive damage to property. Countless letterboxes were smashed. Further east of the town center, car windows were broken, ransacked for whatever of value had been left inside. Almost every car had its hood raised or up slightly. Parker wondered if the batteries had been stolen.

"I have to say—even though I'd trade for it in a second—it feels good not to be picking up my phone every thirty seconds to see what people are doing," Maise said.

"Yeah, but I'd give anything to be back where we were," Jas added. "I'd gladly stay off it to have things normal again."

They turned off Wyntour Street and peered down Beech, which turned into the main artery that was Plenty Road, about three hundred yards away. In the distance, a jagged line of stranded cars had been pushed off on either side of the main highway. Parker had already turned when Maise called out, spotting a line of military vehicles driving south down Plenty Road.

"Where are they going?" Jas asked.

Parker said, "or where are they coming from?"

"Yan Yean Reservoir."

"Something tells me we don't want to run into them."

They followed Beech all the way to Church Street where they turned right towards the IGA. After that, they'd aim to collect some fuel at the United Service Station and be on their way.

Before they reached the IGA store, a man with an armload of clothes staggered out of the Salvation Army store.

"He's looting?" Parker said.

Maise watched with gritted teeth. "How can people be so greedy? So inconsiderate?"

Sam said, "That's what some people are like."

Others standing outside nearby stores shouted for him to stop. Someone further along the street called for the police.

Cars that had run up over the curb and smashed through the front windows of other stores when the blackout hit, including the NewsXpress gift shop, hadn't been moved. The looting man disappeared around the corner before Parker and the others reached the retailer. When they arrived, they saw most of the items within had been cleared out. A linen shop and clothing store had suffered the same fate.

Nestled beside the empty Commonwealth Bank was Champion's IGA. Maise couldn't believe her eyes. The ransacking was at a completely new level. Despite Olsen padlocking the doors, it had not stopped the thieves. The thick steel chain and giant padlock lay discarded on the concrete pavement outside. Several people passed each other entering and exiting the store. There didn't appear to be much left though. One person had handfuls of paper plates, clear plastic cups and pink streamers. Another had three boxes of cat food.

Jas couldn't resist going closer. You're a scumbag," she said to the man carrying the cat food. "Have you got twelve cats at home?"

"Nick off," the man said.

"What about somebody else's cat?"

"What do you want me to do, let the animals starve?"

"I hope the police lock you up."

The man laughed. "The Police? Where are they? They can't keep up with the amount of stuff going on right now."

"Well just remember when this thing is over, if I see you in the street, I'm going to let everyone know what you did."

"No proof. And what about the rest of these people?"

Parker peered inside the store. Shelves had been knocked over; there were broken packets of what looked like pasta on the floor—probably the gluten free stuff.

"I can't look," Maise said.

They left the IGA in despondent silence. What they had observed confirmed to Parker that their plan to leave Whittlesea and head up to Hell Ridge was the right one.

The site at the service station was another surprise. They all used it frequently to purchase fuel and had come to know the owners quite well, an Indian family named Singh. Jaspir was the main guy and he loved to talk. He would frequently ask after his customer's family. When Parker's mother had passed, Jaspir shared his condolences with as much sympathy as someone who'd known her more closely than taking her fuel payment every week.

While the service station had lay dark and dormant for a few days, now, the Singh family had taken it back. They had barricaded the lot with temporary fencing. There were more than half a dozen of them parading with shotguns while Jaspir and his brother, Vikram, coordinated sale of the fuel supplies. A large fuel truck that had been abandoned by the driver two nights ago was the cornerstone of the operation. Vikram used a long hose to siphon fuel from the tank. A number of plastic containers that appeared to be a mix of five, ten and twenty liter drums sat on the concrete area outside the battered shop. Other family members were inside sweeping up the broken glass and the mayhem of discarded products.

Parker admired their energy to fix the mess and keep the business functioning. A queue of people was lined up, handing over cash to Jaspir, and once the transaction was complete, Vikram handed back their container full of fuel.

"How much do we need?" Sam asked.

"Just enough to get back up to camp," Parker said. "Five liters should do the job for now. It should give us at least a hundred kilometers of range. I don't know if I could carry anymore."

He lined up, cash ready. It took about ten minutes to reach the front, and as he drew closer, Parker realized why. Jaspir and Vikram greeted all their customers with genuine friendliness and a personal conversation. Eventually, Parker reached the front of the queue.

"Hello, Parker," Jaspir said with the same big smile that had greeted Parker for the last three years. There was never any keeping this guy down, Parker thought.

"Hey, Jaspir. Vikram. How goes it?"

Jaspir laid both hands out and looked around as Parker handed his container to Vikram, who headed towards the fuel tanker. "We're making the best of it, my friend. What else can we do?"

"Have to say I admire your spirit," Parker said. "Plenty of people are just waiting around for everything to get fixed."

"Not us, my man. We get twitchy if we sit for too long."

"What are people buying fuel for?"

"Motorbikes. Generators. They're even using ride-on-mowers to drive around." He chuckled.

"Hopefully you won't have to do it much longer."

Jaspir leant forward and in a whisper, said, "From what I heard, its not going to be fixed any time soon."

"Where'd you hear that?" Parker asked.

"Constable Gallagher was in here earlier buying a big container of fuel for the Police vehicles. You know they've seconded eight old vehicles from people and are using them to patrol the district?"

"No jokes. What did she say?"

"Just that the government is having trouble working out how to fix the issue."

"It's an EMP, isn't it?"

Jaspir nodded. "They say it's burnt out every electrical circuit in the country."

"We thought so," Parker said. "Did she say how they were going to fix it?"

"Apparently they're rebuilding the main utilities first. Trying to get the power back on."

"I hope they hurry." Jaspir agreed. "I see your family is well organized though." He tipped his head towards the men holding shotguns.

"It's under control, for now. Anyone gives us trouble and they'll know about it."

"What do the police say?"

Jaspir shrugged. "What can they say? Guns are registered. We're casual shooters, my friend. They might have a problem if we shoot someone, but until then…"

Parker stuck his hands into the pockets of his chino shorts, leaned forward and spoke. ""Have you guys seen any army vehicles?"

Jaspir nodded. "We did see some pass earlier, a couple of small trucks, but they didn't stop and we don't know where they went." Parker explained what he knew. "That is a concern. We'll keep an eye out."

Vikram returned with Parker's container of fuel. Parker handed Jaspir a ten-dollar note and wished them well, then walked back to where the others were parked with the bikes and packs.

"You gonna be able to ride with that?" Sam asked.

"Yeah. I've got a strap. I'll hook it to the handle bars."

Even beneath the shade of the fuel station awning, Parker sweated as he spent five minutes fighting the octopus strap and container of fuel to balance it on his handlebars. Maise and Jas waited patiently while Sam held the seat of Parker's bike.

"How long will it take us to reach Hell Ridge?" Jas asked.

"Just under two hours, I reckon," Parker said. "Climbing that hill won't be fun."

They kicked away from the service station and drove their pedals north up Plenty Road, weaving in and out of abandoned cars that had either crashed into other vehicles, run off the road into the grassy gutters, or had simply stopped mid-artery.

It was peaceful until the now unusual sound of a car engine drifted from the south. They all stopped their bikes, turned and watched as an old Holden Commodore with a packed trailer drew up to them, engine struggling. It was full of young men and they appeared to be heading out camping.

The guy sitting in the passenger seat made eye contact with Parker and nodded as the car passed. Parker's stomach dropped. It was Keith Whitehead, Maise's ex-boyfriend.

"Holy shit, that's Mark's car," Maise said. "The one he's supposed to buy off Keith."

Whitehead gave them a thumbs up, then said something to the other guys in the car, which caused him to laugh. The car drove a short distance and then made a sharp turn into Laurel Street.

Maise said, "Mark will be annoyed."

The car and trailer disappeared out of site. The easiest way out of Whittlesea was to follow Plenty Road into Beech Street and just keep on driving. Parker wondered whether they were heading out towards Kinglake—or more importantly, Hell Ridge. There were a million camping spots out there, he reminded himself.

"Hard to believe this is our town," Jas said.

They pushed off the curb and rode on.

THIRTY-TWO

The Whittlesea township's post office opened on September 1, 1853, and was originally named Plenty, before being renamed Whittlesea in 1864. In 1878, the primary school—a single stone building—opened, and stands in the same location to this day. Much of Whittlesea's early history revolved around the logging trade from timber in Kinglake provided for the greater Melbourne area. The broader township contained a mix of rural and suburban style properties; numerous sports grounds, a water park, and various establishments that serviced the pastoral require-ments of many landowners that grazed cattle, sheep or in the single case, alpacas.

As they rode along the main arterial out of the township, Maise and the others felt a definite sense that the atmosphere had changed. The small groups of people congregating in yards or on the streets, talking of their problems or imminent solutions, had vanished. Already, lawns had started to discolor, rubbish bins had been placed on nature strips—overflowing with broken bags of waste—waiting for a garbage collection that might never come.

They passed the intersection of Wallan Road—Parker reminding them to keep an eye out for army vehicles—and turned into Macmeikan Street, the beginnings of the thoroughfare that would normally see a consistent progression of vehicles leaving and entering Whittlesea from the north-east edge, leading to

Humevale, Kinglake West, Kinglake, Flowerdale and beyond. Today, there were none, but several horses approached carrying riders coming their way.

"Clever," Sam said as they watched the horses take slow, unhurried steps.

Maise had taken lessons when she was young, as most girls in Whittlesea had done. The riders gave them a nod as they passed, and then the troupe was back to pedaling along the two lane street.

To Maise's surprise, they almost ran into Raven Lee, Mark's ex-girlfriend, coming out of Walnut Street.

"Raven?" Maise said. They all stopped. "Where are you going? It's not safe to be out now."

"The veterinary clinic. Just to check on my animals."

Maise put her bike down and walked over to Raven, who stood watching, eyes narrowed with caution. They had not spoken much since the break up. When she reached Raven, Maise looped her arms around Raven's torso and squeezed gently. "It's good to see you." Maise maintained the hug; she genuinely liked the other woman. She had a calming influence on Mark and had always treated Maise like another sister. "Are you okay?"

When they ended their embrace, Raven's surprise had begun to dissolve. "I'm good, thanks," Raven said. "Hanging in there."

"I'm glad." Maise smiled, and when Raven smiled back, Maise sensed the moment was important, that she should take it to let Raven know about Mark being alone. His absence from the group and loneliness hung tight on Maise. Maybe she could still help, even if it was a long shot. "Miss seeing you around our place."

Raven's lips curled up at the edges. "Miss being there, too."

The others put their bikes down and one by one came to Raven and embraced. It hadn't been so long ago when socializing with each other was the norm. Parker and Raven held their hug a little longer, Parker still grateful for all the times Raven checked on him after his mother died.

Raven's response dared Maise to push on. "Mark really misses you." Raven's dark eyebrows lifted. Maise sensed Raven liked hearing that. "We're leaving town. This place is turning bad. I tried to convince Mark to come with us, but he won't. She glanced back towards Parker. "You know." Maise nodded. "But he's alone and he *is* sad and depressed—"

"And bloody stubborn," Jas said.

Maise and Raven both smiled. "Whether he'll admit it or not, he could do with... a friend. Someone who cares about him, even if things aren't the way they used to be."

Raven looked at Maise for a long moment. Maise caught her breath when she saw a single tear in the corner of Raven's eye. "I miss him. I've been thinking about him quite a bit. I know he's got his faults, but I still..."

Maise took Raven's hand. "It's okay. We've all been there." She thought about Parker and how he had changed. "Just go over and talk to him. He really could use your friendship right now."

Raven squeezed Maise's hand. "I think I will. Thanks."

Maise hugged Raven again, pouring her gratitude into the embrace. "No, thank you. I have a bad feeling things are going to get rougher before they improve. Just showing up will help him."

They bid goodbye to Raven with a warning about the soldiers driving around town, and rode on, soon discovering a car accident. A small blue Suzuki had run into a lamppost, destroying the front end. Parker pointed out where someone had attempted to cut the hood away and access the battery. But they had failed, the giant post landing on top of it had prevented them from retrieving the valuable item within.

Maise hung back in the group as Parker led them over the intersection with Walnut Street, where a lengthy green fenced topped by conifers now brandished pink graffiti. In all her years, Maise had never seen that happen. They followed a right bend and cycled up to a roundabout. As they rolled through the intersection, a wide green road sign greeted them, stating that YEA and KINGLAKE lay ahead on the C725. On their right sat the Royal Mail Hotel, a place they had all swallowed beers and spirits on a Friday evening after work. Many of the adult population in the township had enjoyed its service. Now, it was strangely different from the rustic, freshly painted establishment it had been four days ago. More graffiti spoiled the cream exterior. The glass windows of the open air eating area had been smashed and sprayed fragments onto the grass.

Nobody spoke.

They saw their first quasi police vehicle down Forest Street, with white sheets of paper taped over the doors and a blue Victoria police sign emblazoned on it. The car was an old HZ Holden station wagon, lime green, with a bubbling, grungy motor that promised far greater horsepower in an earlier life. The policeman and woman were talking to an elderly gentleman under the shade of an ornamental pear tree, still in his pajamas, swallowing water from a large plastic flask provided by the officer. The woman had a hand on the man's shoulder, his distress palpable; hair slick with sweat, hand shaking. Maise didn't think he was alone, and she suppressed the thought of how many people might be in the same situation. It reminded her of Mr. Buckley—she felt terrible for not waiting around to say goodbye, but she had checked his house and he wasn't there. Maise assumed he was either with a relative or worse; he might be at the hospital himself.

They passed the Rural Fence & Trade store with its bright, shiny new tractors of no use to anyone, cattle ramps, and empty water tanks that would have been worth gold if they were full. They crossed over the trickle of dirty water that was Bruce's Creek, then another slightly more full tributary that was the very upper section of the Plenty River—nothing more than a brown rivulet now—and then Parker stopped suddenly in the middle of the road.

"What is it?" Maise asked, looking ahead for a car coming their way she might have missed.

"There," Parker said in a low, cautious tone. "On the left, near the footy ground."

They had not quite reached the Whittlesea Football oval, which backed onto the Showgrounds and formed part of the massive agricultural show each November. The Showgrounds were nine hectares of old farming land, the place where the Whittlesea Show was held as an annual event that ran for three days in early November and had been running for one-hundred and sixty-two years. It began as a fair in 1859, bringing the best of country life including showcasing poultry, horses, cattle, an animal nursery, children's educational pieces, heritage, and crafts, amongst other things.

The football club had a large pavilion just beyond the entrance to the road, with clubrooms, a canteen, and a main hall where it conducted fundraising functions.

"It's the bloody Chinese army," Parker added. "Look."

Ahead, two cars and a small tip truck with an excavator in the back had been pushed off the side of the road. Maise followed Parker's initial gaze beyond the congregation and spotted two military vehicles parked at the entrance to the football oval. Four Chinese soldiers stood about. Two of them with machine guns slung over their shoulders frisked a plump, middle-aged man with thinning hair who appeared to be with his family—a lady of similar vintage and two teenage children—a lanky boy and shorter girl with long blonde hair stood nearby.

Maise began to drag her bike off the road to the right. "Get off the road," she spluttered. "Quickly."

She pushed her bicycle to the sidewalk and now, using an overhanging shrub from the front garden of a property as concealment, watched the action ahead. The others edged in beside her.

"What do you think they're doing?" Parker asked.

Sam said, "Looks like they're stopping people."

"We need to find another way around," Maise said.

Two of the military men steered the family away from the roadway towards the ground entrance. The other two soldiers remained, turning their backs on the main road momentarily as they chatted.

"Where do you think they're taking them?"

"According to Arlette Davis, they were going to start serving food and give out water, but sounds like that was crap."

"Hey!" A voice called out. Maise turned to find a fleshy man in a singlet top, shorts and bare feet step off the verandah of the property whose tree they were using to conceal themselves. "Get away from my place." He approached the street.

Maise glanced back at the Chinese soldiers. They hadn't yet noticed.

"Keep it down, mate," Parker said. "Don't you know what's going on up there?"

The man, who had a mangy beard and a mouthful of discolored teeth, glanced towards the football oval. "I don't care. You're not gonna burgle my joint. Others have already tried a few times. I got a .22 inside and I'll shoot you if ya try."

"We're not hear to steal anything," Jas sneered. "We've got bigger things to worry about than," she looked at the man's ramshackle house with corked weatherboards and flaky paint. "Your 'joint'." His dumb face remained expressionless.

"Let's go," Maise said. "We can't stay here all day and we can't go that way anymore. We'll have to backtrack and use the side streets to work our way further along the main road."

"Good idea," Sam said.

Maise led them back along the sidewalk with their bikes in tow. She glanced back over her shoulder and saw one of the soldiers moving another vehicle into the middle of the road to block potential traffic—either by foot or car. At any moment, the solider might look their way and spoil their attempts to avoid being spotted. Anything could happen then, including them being pursued. They wouldn't get far on their bicycles.

The momentary sense of relief turning the corner didn't last long, as Maise spotted two more Chinese soldiers talking to a group of three adults on the far sidewalk. She slowed her pace and the group bunched up. "They must be checking the surrounding streets."

"Bloody hell our timing is bad," Jas said.

One of the men raised his machine gun at the other group. Two of them jumped back in fear, shouting. They weren't close enough to hear but it was clear the situation was escalating.

Parker said. "Keep moving."

Maise led. "Follow me."

Heart thumping, Maise followed the bumpy, cracked sidewalk, glancing across at the action beyond the intersection. Two of the civilians in the group were on their knees, hands crossed behind their heads. Jas mumbled something and Maise recognized the alarm in her voice. Maise concentrated on the pathway; silently praying the soldiers didn't notice them.

As they reached the side street, Maise looked back to the others. "Soon as we turn the corner we ride, okay?" They all nodded.

They made the left and Maise stopped to mount her bicycle. Second in the line, Parker did the same, but he was still at the corner, watching the altercation.

Maise rode, pushing the pedals hard, desperate to get as far away as quickly as possible. She glanced back, having already increased the gap with Parker to fifteen yards. The others had over-taken him, but Parker couldn't seem to draw himself away from the altercation.

"Move, Parker," she hissed.

Maise rolled to a stop. Jas and Sam passed her. Parker started moving forward, his feet fumbling for the pedals. He finally found the right one and pushed off with his left leg, still trying to watch the incident at the intersection where a soldier and civilian were now wrestling on the ground. In the next moment, the front tire of Parker's bike found a crevasse in the concrete and came to a sudden stop, the rear tire rising off the ground. Parker, who was still trying to watch the fight, tumbled forward with the momentum and hit the concrete with a thud. As he swore, a gunshot sounded, two rapid noises like *pop-pop,* exactly as Maise had heard in the movies so many times. Fear clinched her heart and momentarily, she could not move. But Parker was still down, grappling with the bike on him. Driven by desperation, she leapt off her own bicycle, laid it down and ran to Parker. She lifted the bike from him and finally he was able to climb onto his knees and then awkwardly to his feet.

Maise handed him the bike and Parker slid his leg over the bar and jumped onto the seat, then pushed off with his left leg. Two more gunshots. This time, he made no mistake and didn't look back. Maise dared not look, running to her own bike as Parker reached Jas and Sam, then snatched it up by the handlebars and slid onto the seat perfectly. Her feet made no mistake and then she was pedaling, her heart racing, adrenaline pulsing through her.

The wheels of their bicycles took them across another intersection, running parallel to the main road and moving with more speed now. A tall line of conifers on their left shrouded them from the football ground and the military blockade. Eventually, they reached another junction—River Street—where it turned left and connected with the main arterial again. Their hope was that they would come out well ahead of the blockade.

Maise led them to the end of the street where she stopped, peering out from behind the last tree. Parker, Sam and Jas waited behind for her to give the all clear. After a minute, she pushed away on her bicycle and waved them forward.

"Let's go. Stick to the left side of the road on the shoulder."

They crossed the highway; Maise stole a glance back the way they'd come and saw the road bended around slightly, providing them enough concealment not to be seen. They might just have made it. She hardly dared believe it, but an inner voice gave her hope.

They'd made it a quarter of a mile when they heard the whirring sound of a car engine.

Parker was the first to stop, peering back over his shoulder. "Oh, shit. We've got problems."

The others did the same, and one by one, their faces dropped as they spotted one of the military vehicles speeding towards them. They had about twenty seconds to make their move.

"What do we do?" Jas asked.

Somehow, she had assumed leadership of the band. Maise glanced about. There were no side streets nearby. The road fell away on their left to a shallow, grassy gully, and beyond, thick scrub full of ankle-breaking furrows and holes. Locals knew not to walk through scrub like that, especially in high summer, where snakes were common. On their right were rows of houses, but they'd be spotted any which way they headed in that direction. The military were armed, too, and if they tried to flee, they had every chance of being shot after what they'd heard in the street moments ago. None of them moved. Maise watched Parker, whose tensed jaw and thin lips told her they would have to take their chances. A cold terror spread through Maise.

The small SUV screeched to a halt close to them, the single

passenger leaping out of the front seat with his machine gun raised before the vehicle had skidded to a stop. He barked something in Mandarin, poking the gun from one to the other. Maise glanced around, saw fear on her friend's faces, and expected hers reflected the same.

"Put the gun down, man," Parker said, his fear now battling the first signs of anger.

The other door opened and the second soldier climbed out of the driver's seat as though he had all the time in the world. He stopped, placed a cigarette in the corner of his mouth and lit it. Then he approached the group, smiling, studying them with an unpleasant grin. Maise noticed a large pistol strapped into his belt.

"I am Ju," he said in broken English. "I am the local Commander."

Maise and the others looked at each other.

"What do you want?" Maise asked. Ju smiled and shook his head as if he didn't understand. "Why have you stopped us?"

"I think the question is what are *you* doing?" Maise squinted, perplexed. "There's a curfew on in town. Why are you out on the streets?"

Jas said, "You're crazy. A curfew is for nighttime. You can't just come into our town and drive around shooting people and stopping us. You're not the police. You're a pig is what you are."

"Take it easy, Jas," Maise said.

Ju said something in Mandarin to the other soldier. He stepped towards Jas and jabbed the butt of his machine gun forward, striking her in the ribcage.

Maise cried out. "Jas!"

Jas buckled over with the sound of escaping breath. She dropped the handlebars of her bike and it clunked to the ground, then lowered herself to her knees, one hand pressed against her side.

Maise turned to the solider, fury twisting her expression. "Leave her the hell alone."

Sam was off his bike and moving, his normally passive face twisted into a snarl. It took a lot to fire him up. He was a big man, thick bodied, with hands that could hold nine eggs each and he looked menacing, striding towards the soldier. But Maise knew muscles couldn't fight bullets right now.

"No, Sam," she said, "Don't." Parker also called for him to stop.

But once Sam had gone over the edge, there was no bringing him back. The solider pointed the machine gun at Sam, and now Sam took the barrel in his left hand and turned it away. He was much taller and heavier than the slight military man. With his right hand, Sam grabbed the soldier by the scruff of the neck and shoved him backwards.

"DON'T TOUCH HER!" He screamed.

Maise hadn't seen Ju move. Suddenly he was standing beside Sam with the pistol from his belt pointed at Sam's temple. The other soldier scrambled to his feet.

"This won't end well for you," Ju said in a soft, confident voice. "But attack one of us. Go ahead. It will make it easier to justify killing you."

Sam watched the other soldier, breathing hard, as though he might be poised to make another move.

"Don't do it, Sam," Parker said. "Don't bloody move. You've got too much to lose, mate."

Sam stood with his fists clenched at his sides. In that moment, Maise couldn't tell if he was going to react or not. But her instincts told her something bad was about to happen if someone didn't diffuse the situation. She climbed off her bike and went to Sam, holding a hand up to the Chinese soldier to indicate she wasn't going to attack.

"Sam," she said, taking his hand, "calm down. Jas is okay. Nobody is badly hurt, all right? This is not the time to fight." She pulled his arm backwards. At first, he resisted, then Maise tugged again, and Sam stumbled away from the soldier. Maise lowered her voice and pushed in close to him. "We don't want to fight now, Sam. It won't end well for any of us. They're just looking for an excuse."

In the distance, a metallic hum sounded, and Maise knew instantly it was another vehicle. *More of them,* she thought with heightened terror. They all looked around at the oncoming noise and saw far ahead, towards town, a small shape driving in their direction.

"Okay," Sam said, putting both hands up as if he was being arrested. "Okay." He stepped backwards towards his bike, keeping his hands high. Jas had climbed back to her feet and now Sam put an arm around her shoulders, whispering something into her ear.

Ju lowered the pistol and turned to the oncoming vehicle. It sped up to them, and Maise watched an old Holden station wagon grow into view, lime green, with a rumbling engine and several people inside. *Relief.* It wasn't more of the Chinese military.

"They're ours!" Parker shouted.

Maise wondered how it had become them and us so quickly, but she supposed, given there were soldiers from a foreign army pulling over people and threatening them with guns, the battle context was fair.

The Holden slowed in the middle of the road and pulled up about thirty yards short. Maise spotted her uncle, the most senior ranking policeman in the area. There were two other officers in the car with him, and they all got out in unison, shotguns in hand.

The two soldiers turned to face them, standing side by side. The unnamed one spoke quietly in Mandarin. Ju grunted, shook his head. The other soldier raised his machine gun.

The police approached, weapons drawn. Uncle Jim was a large man, about six foot three, with a stomach to match, and he was so focused on the soldiers, Maise wasn't sure he had recognized her. After a few moments, he spotted her subtle wave, and made a reply for them to move away.

Maise wheeled her bike away from the Chinese soldiers, and, catching the attention of her friends, motioned them in her direction. They were standing too close if a firefight erupted.

"What's going on here?" Uncle Jim shouted. "Stand down, soldier." The soldier did not move. "NOW!"

"Turn around," Ju called out, pistol drawn. "And leave us. You no longer have authority in this area."

Uncle Jim laughed, a big bellowing laugh. "We'll see about that."

Sam had left Jas and now crept towards the two-armed

soldiers. Parker tried to wave him back, but Sam ignored it. Suddenly he darted forward and using both hands, shoved each of them in the back. They stumbled, losing balance and their line of sight. Sam scurried out of the way.

The police started firing, several booming rapports as they advanced, hunched over with their shotguns raised.

From the corner of her eye, Maise saw one of the soldiers collapse, arms flailing, his machine gun clattering to the road. Sensing he was outgunned, Ju ducked his head and dived behind the army vehicle.

The shotguns quieted.

"Surround him," Uncle Jim shouted, moving forward towards Ju's SUV. The other two policemen flanked the vehicle, weapons raised.

Maise's heart raced. It had all happened so quickly. Sam and Parker left their bikes and went to the fallen soldier. Maise noticed a large red patch spreading across his chest. Parker picked up the machine gun, while Sam kneeled at the soldier's side and felt his neck for a pulse. After a few moments, he shook his head to indicate the man was dead.

Dead. Her uncle and his men had killed a soldier. What did that mean? It was too much for Maise to process right now.

Uncle Jim and the policemen had reached the SUV. They rushed around the other side from both ends, but did not fire any shots. The cleared the rest of the space, including underneath the vehicle, then stood looking into the scrub off the side of the road and talking in low voices. After a few moments, Uncle Jim turned and walked over to Maise, while the other officers stood watching for signs of Ju.

Staring at the dead soldier, Uncle Jim said, "we've got a fight on our hands, that's for sure. All deals are off. They've already killed several civilians. We don't know exactly how many of them are in town, but we're scouting the area now trying to find out where their base of operation is located." He waved at the SUV. "This will help us be more mobile."

"How did you know we were here?" Maise asked.

"Out on patrol. Spotted this vehicle speeding off while we were talking to some civilians that had been pulled over and searched."

"What's their deal?" Parker asked.

Uncle Jim hesitated, glanced at one of the other two policemen.

"Please, uncle," Maise said. "Just tell us so we can be prepared."

"Prepared for what, Maise? You all need to get your butts up that mountain. Assume you're heading off to a campsite until this thing is under control? Good. The outcome of this situation might have been very different had we not come along. It's gonna get bad. Real bad."

"Is it an invasion?" Parker asked.

Uncle Jim sighed. "It appears so. It looks like a nuclear bomb was detonated a long way up in the sky and it caused an EMP that fried most of our cars and electrical gear. Sydney, Brisbane, Perth, Adelaide—every capital city—got 'em. And the Chinese were prepared. Equipment that's not susceptible to an EMP."

"What about the US and Europe?" Sam asked. "The news was saying they were both hit on Sunday night before the blackout here."

"Yeah. That's right. They've got their own problems. Word is that Russia is involved in the US attack, too. We don't know if they've launched a ground assault in the US or the UK, but it seems the coalition of the west, as they call it, has been blacked out entirely."

"Can it be fixed?"

He laughed without humor. "Nobody knows. Government is working on it."

"Government is working on it," Parker mocked. "Is that all they can say? It's like the response to COVID-19 all over again."

"This is a bit different," Uncle Jim said. "At least then, every-thing was still working. Now, there's nothing. We have to work out how to get around, how to communicate."

"So we just go on up the mountain?" Maise asked.

"For now. Stay put until I get you word it's safe to come back. And don't go anywhere near Yan Yean Reservoir or drink from that water supply. Looks like they've seized the place."

Maise glanced around the group. "We can do that."

"Now we have to get movin'." Uncle Jim pointed at the Chinese Army SUV and spoke to one of the men. "Throw him in the rear of that and you drive it back to town, Paul."

Maise put her bike down, walked over and gave her uncle a hug. "Take care, uncle."

"You too, darlin'. Any idea where your brother is?"

"At home. We couldn't convince him to come."

Uncle Jim nodded. "If I get time, I'll stop by and see what I can do." He turned to leave, and then spun back. "Here, take this," he said, offering a shotgun. "And I'll take that." He took the machine gun from Parker.

Maise eyed the weapon he had given them. "A shotgun?" She reached out and took it slowly. Before the blackout, she'd have resisted taking it. Now, she realized it might save their lives.

"Things are getting too dangerous now. I wanna make sure you're protected." He produced another four rounds from his pocket and handed them to Maise. "And these."

"Thanks, uncle," Maise said, but she felt uneasy.

The policemen climbed into the two vehicles. Maise and the others picked up their bikes and climbed on. She took a last look back as the old Holden and the modern SUV made a semi-circle and headed back the other way. Each member of the group climbed onto their bikes and started pedaling, overcome with contemplative silence. Maise felt edgier than ever. Their township had been invaded—no—their country had been invaded. And she'd left Mark behind. She never imagined her uncle would be handing her a police-issue shotgun to protect themselves, either. She thought the last three years of COVID had been strange, but she suspected things were about to get a whole lot crazier and more surreal.

THIRTY-THREE

Senior Captain Zhu Yao sat in his office on the Shandong aircraft carrier, picked up the grey, sleek satellite phone from his desk and dialed the number of the seventh contact on the list provided by Army Intelligence. He had worked his way down the names and numbers, receiving status updates from each person on the ground in various locations around the Australian state of Victoria, starting with his contact in the capital city of Melbourne. Now, he had reached the north-eastern town of Whittlesea, which contained within its shire an important asset critical to the mission. So far, reports had been promising and the initial stages of the invasion had gone to plan. Somehow, he had managed to meet General Yang's accelerated timeframe of eight weeks and have troops ready for D-day.

"Lieutenant Wang."

Captain Zhu identified himself. "Status report, Lieutenant."

"Sir," Chen said. "We are proceeding according to the planned timeframe of D-day plus three." Chen cleared his throat. "Local authorities have been captured and imprisoned."

"And the status of the local sleeper contacts?" Sleeper teams had completed three-year training plans as part of their recruitment and induction. The Chinese army had significant forces in position, spread throughout and around the major cities of Australia to support the ground attack.

"We have made contact with all team members in the vicinity. Lead team member Phillip Lee is coordinating their activities."

They had recruited the most patriotic Chinese nationals. These men—and women—grew up in Chinese towns and cities and spent extensive time in the military. The Chinese way had been ingrained in them since early childhood. They had been carefully selected via a precise profiling technique used by their Russian counterparts during the Cold War to select reconnoiters.

The rumble of another fighter jet sounded from the deck of the aircraft carrier. "Good," Captain Zhu said. "Good. And what are their observations of the Australians so far?"

"Feedback over the last three days supports our opinion of the last three years during Operation COVID. Greed, the inability to work together and organize, and a complete lack of empathy for each other have been evident. Factions are developing. There is a small amount of infighting, so far."

"They're hording supplies again?"

"Correct."

"And what about the impact of the heat now that they have no electricity?"

"Reports of the elderly dying are coming through."

"To be expected."

"In a few more days, the main population will be weakened, hungry and disoriented. This will help reduce the numbers further and make our job to execute the following stages of the invasion much easier."

"We don't want them all dead. They're our leverage, remember?"

"Yes, sir."

"Resistance?"

"Small pockets, nothing more. As we know, weapons in this country are much harder to come by."

"Any casualties on our end?"

"Not yet, sir."

"This is good news. All the power grids are under our control. They won't be able to fix them anytime soon. What about the water facility? It's a prime target in the area."

"We've taken it, sir. The water supply system is not functioning."

"Prisoners?

"We're keeping them in two locations—one in the central town, the others at the water facility."

"Excellent. We now have control over all the utilities. People won't survive unless we allow it."

"Can we expect any support from other countries, sir?"

"Negative. With the support of our friends in Russia, neither the Americans, the British nor other key members of NATO will be able to help these people. They'll have their own challenges to deal with. Australia will have to rely solely on their own ability to respond."

"Very good, sir."

"Operation COVID was the perfect preparation for these invasions. None of the major powers of the western world are ready for this so soon afterwards, nor will they be able to cope with a disaster on this scale."

"What's next, sir?"

"More ground troops are imminent."

"Thank you, sir."

"Kill any resistance as it happens. Keep the prisoners under control and wait for news. We expect the government will surrender in the next few days."

"What if they don't, sir?"

"That's why we're keeping people alive, Lieutenant. We'll use their lives to force the government's hand. But don't worry, they will surrender. And once they do, it will clear a path for us to begin the next phase of the plan, moving Chinese citizens into the country."

"I look forward to it, sir."

"Keep up the good work, Lieutenant."

THIRTY-FOUR

Mark drove the hammer into the last nail, securing the final board over the shed window. Everyone knew sheds contained prized items, but at least if someone climbed into the backyard and discovered boarded windows, it might deter them from trying to break in. He'd done all he could to protect the property. The hammer sank to his side as he walked across the backyard and into the house. He still couldn't believe Maise had chosen to leave. He'd tried everything to convince her not to go, but in the end, he believed it was his outburst last night that had changed her mind.

Mark's old friend had argued a good case. Mark hadn't been able to process it all because of the drink, but in the cold sobering daylight, he had tossed Parker's arguments around in his head, bouncing them from positive to negative and back to positive. Maise had also made clear and persuasive points, and at the conclusion, despite his stubborn resistance, he had to admit they may have been right.

Mark slid out a wooden kitchen chair and sat at the heavy table with a bottle of water he took from a case. The tank water was done, the thieves stealing the last precious litres. Mindy crouched by his leg, panting at the heat. The bottle crinkled in his hand as Mark unscrewed the top and emptied it into a small bowl. The dog dove into the clear liquid, tongue splashing in and out with feverish desperation. Mark scratched Mindy's head.

"You won't abandon me, will you?" Mindy looked up momentarily at him, wagged her tail, then returned to the water.

Mark took a second bottle from the bench and cracked the top, then sat back, sculling the warm liquid, considering what to do next.

Should he go after them? *No.* That would be an admission that he was wrong. After all the arguing, he couldn't just turn over, even if he thought it was a good idea—or the best idea in the circumstances. Maise had walked out on him too. Abandoned him. Despite all the things Parker had done before the blackout, she'd still chosen Parker. And they weren't even together anymore. Mark didn't understand that. He was her brother. He'd been there when Parker wasn't. Maise should have—

A banging noise sounded from the front of the house, as though something had struck the door. Maybe it was Maise or one of the others returning—they had probably forgotten something. Or it was another sucker trying to break in.

Mark snatched the golf club from the wall and crept down the hallway. With the curtains drawn, the front section of the house was dark. He checked the peephole, fingers curled around the door handle, ready to snatch it open and beat the crap out of someone if there was a repeat of Monday's water thievery.

But any feelings of threat or trepidation fled when he saw Raven standing on the porch. She was sobbing, a tissue pressed against her eyes. Mark wrenched the handle and swung the door open, then stared at her for a long moment. She stared back, still sobbing.

"Are you going to invite me in?"

Mark shook free of his shock. "Yeah. Sure. Sorry." He stepped out of the doorway and Raven entered.

He did a quick sweep of the street and spotted a group of Chinese soldiers on the curb a few houses down. One of them lay on the ground while the other three surrounded him, as though the soldier was injured. There was nobody else in view. Just before he stepped back inside and closed the door, one of the soldiers turned and saw him.

Mark closed the door. "Did the soldiers see you?"

"No. I spotted them first and was careful."

"I think one of them might have seen me."

He led Raven back down the hallway and into the kitchen, where the natural sunlight was strongest. Raven was half-Chinese, her father had emigrated to Australia in the early 1990's and married a Caucasian Australian woman, who became Raven's mother.

Mark pulled out a seat for her, then went to a cupboard, where he opened the door and removed a glass.

"Water?" She nodded. He cracked another bottle from the case and half-filled the glass. Mark's mind began to clear to the reality of having Raven sitting in his kitchen. He had a million questions. He had often wondered if that would ever happen again. He looked her over as though he hadn't seen her in a long time. It felt like it. She was a striking blend of Chinese and Caucasian; dark, narrow eyes, a slim, even nose, slight cheekbones and pleasant lips. They had been in the same class in grade one and Mark had crushed on her ever since.

"You okay?" He asked, handing her the glass and sitting down.

She shook her head. "I've just come from the veterinary clinic." She let out a small sob. "Some of the animals have died. The ones waiting for surgery. Those hooked up to devices that needed power. Could have been the heat, too. We don't know. We had to give some of them back to their owners, even though they were in no condition to go back. It's a mess."

"I'm sorry to hear that." Raven was a veterinary nurse, had studied for years to achieve the qualification, and her dedication to it was only surpassed by her love of animals. Mark had always wondered about her ability to handle the losses though. Would she become too attached? This was the question he had never answered. He hated seeing her so upset. "If you can't help, then nobody can," Mark said. "I know how much you give to those animals." She whispered the words thank you. "Where are your parents?"

"Mum's stuck at the beach house. I assume dad's been called into work for the government, to try and sort through all of this stuff. Honestly, I haven't seen him for two weeks. He's been at some special conference thing. I have no way of contacting anyone now the phones are stuffed."

"Your brother?"

She shrugged. "No idea."

"Is that normal for your dad to be away for so long?"

"Yeah, he's always working."

"So you've been on your own?"

Raven shrugged. "I'm used to it lately. The people I'm closest too…" She looked at Mark, her lips pressed into a defiant line. "It's you and Maise. Parker, Jas and Sam."

Mark leaned forward and gave her a hug. It was the first time they'd been so close in more than three weeks. It felt good, despite the gloomy circumstances.

Suddenly, Mindy was at their side, leaning into Raven. She loosened arms from around Mark and squatted down, wrapping Mindy in a tight hug.

"Oh my God, Mindy, I've missed you." The dog's tail wagged and she made soft whimpering noises. "I saw Maise, too."

Mark stiffened. "Maise?"

"Yeah." She hesitated. "To be honest, she said a few things that made me think."

"Like what?"

Raven shook her head, took his hand in hers. "The details don't matter. But she cares for you, Mark. She has a knack for saying the right thing at the right time and it just hits home."

"Tell me about it. Somewhere along the line, Maise became the older sibling, even though she's younger than me."

"We're so lucky to have her. Truth is, I've been thinking about us a lot. Maise just gave me a nudge."

"Me too," Mark said. Although, the last day or so he'd had other things on his mind. Still, the elements of annoyance retreated. Raven had a way of helping with that like nobody else.

"I'm not sure we should have broken up. Maybe we should

have tried a little harder to sort things out, you know? Did we really give it our best?"

Mark nodded vigorously, a shot of hope in his arm. "Yeah, I agree. I think we could have given it a little bit more effort." Raven smiled, took his hand. Could things take such a sudden turn for the better? Hope threatened to overwhelm him. He had to be cautious. "Are you sure?" Raven raised her eyebrows. " I mean, nothing would make me happier at this point, Raven, but I want you to be sure. I couldn't—"

She leaned forward and took both hands in his. "Yes. I am sure." They stood and embraced. Mark bent his head forward and nestled it into the side of Raven's, smelling the sweet scent of her hair. He loved that smell. It was comfort and happiness. Raven gave a final sob and hugged him tighter. It was going to be okay, Mark thought. They would stick together and make it through until this thing was over.

"So, can I say we're back together?" Mark asked hopefully.

Raven smiled. "I'd prefer to say we never broke up—we only had a break."

Mark beamed, feeling as though his face might split. "I like that." They kissed, slow and adoring, better than Mark could ever remember.

When they finally pulled away, Raven said, "Maise and the others are heading up to Hell Ridge."

Mark stepped away and walked in a circle, running both hands through his thick, wavy blonde hair. "It almost killed me, you know. Seeing her leave me here, alone."

"Why didn't you just go with them?"

"Why?" Raven stared. "I mean—"

"Did they ask you?"

Mark hesitated. Did he tell Raven the truth? They had asked him to go several times and he had refused. He'd look like—no, he couldn't mislead her straight off the bat. They were picking it all up again and there were things he wanted to do differently this time. Just small things that might make all the difference in the end. What had Maise said about him? He was one of the worst communicators she knew. That had hurt. He loved and respected his sister immensely. For her to say that... he decided he would do better, even if to prove her wrong. "No, they asked me to come, but I chose to stay."

"Why?"

He slumped down into one of the kitchen chairs. Raven had a way of digging out the details. In the past, he'd either ignored it or not been forthcoming. Maybe that was one of the reasons they'd fought. Mark sat back and brushed his hands though his hair again. "Two reasons. One, I wanted to stay and protect the house."

"Second?"

"Because I couldn't deal with Parker. We had a big fight last night. I said some things, he said some things... you know?"

Raven considered this. "Maybe it's time you and Parker buried the hatchet?"

"In his back?" Mark laughed.

Raven smiled. "Yeah. No. I mean, what did he say?"

Mark swallowed, feeling the metaphorical knife twisting in his gut. "He apologized and stuff. Said he was wrong."

"Isn't that enough?"

"I don't know. I'd had a few last night. I might not have handled it so well."

She pulled out the kitchen chair beside him. "It happens. We all make mistakes. I made one when I said we needed a break. I was too rash." She squeezed his hand. "I'll admit it."

Mark felt a small sense of vindication hearing those words. Raven was not one to admit she was wrong too often. It loosened him up; he suddenly felt even more at ease.

Raven continued. "I realized that despite the fights we had, we're better together. Stronger. When we fought, I wasn't able to let go of it. Even if it was minor. But I realized it's not the end of the world. You can't be strong if you're passive all the time. We're passionate people." She smiled. "Sometimes too passionate. You and Parker are a bit the same. Sometimes you have to let go of the resentment. Forgive people, even if they did wrong by you. What's the worst that can happen if you give him another chance?"

"He lets me down again."

"And then you'll know. You can say you gave him a chance.

And this time you're better prepared for it. Let me ask you a question." She brushed a strand of her fine black hair behind her ear. "Did he ever let you down before?" Mark shook his head. Parker had always been such a stand-up guy; that's why it hurt so much. "So he had your back a hundred times. School fights, football games, working for you when you needed help, before you had the business. That's a lot of runs on the board." Mark stared at the kitchen floor, considering Raven's words. "There are only so many good friends in the world, Mark."

"Jesus, did you do a counselor's course while we were broken up?"

"On a break, babe." She winked.

"Touché." They both chuckled. Mark continued. "You make some fair points. I need to think about it some more. But I have a question for you then. And answer it honestly."

"I've been pretty honest. I probably wouldn't have been this honest before we separated."

"You have." He smiled, and then his expression became serious. "Parker criticized me for not being there when he needed me. Said that I put too much value in just sucking it up and moving on, the way I did when my father died. What do you think of that?"

Raven pressed her lips into a thin line. Mark didn't think she was going to say anything. Then, finally, she let out a sigh and said, "you're like that with everything." His face must have changed because she put out a hand and said, "It's okay. We all know that. And most of the time it's nothing more than a bit inconsiderate, but maybe for something that big, you could have been more thoughtful towards Parker. *You* might have known how to handle the loss, but he had no idea."

"You could see that with him?"

"Of course," she scoffed. "We all spoke with him every few days. I called him twice a week just to see how he was. Just because you think you shouldn't have to be there for him doesn't mean you shouldn't." She put her arms around his neck. "My mum taught me about perception once. She said, 'Raven, when it comes to perception, it only matters what the other person thinks because they base everything on what they see from you'."

Mark thought about this. It came to him quickly. "So, you reckon the fact he thought I didn't care was all that mattered?"

She nodded. "He got off track thinking you didn't care because you never said it or showed it."

It was a profound moment for Mark and a bit of cliché on the old adage that actions speak louder than words. He recalled saying one or two things to Parker at the time but couldn't understand why he found it so difficult. Perhaps he should have been more present for him, taken him out for a drink or just sat down with him and talked it out. He'd never done that—never really considered it because when people had offered it to him after his father had died, Mark had dismissed it. He didn't want to talk about what had happened. It had *happened.* He just wanted to forget about the bad stuff and move on. He supposed not everybody looked at such a situation in the same way. He knew Maise was different from him, too.

"I get it," Mark said. "I actually think I get it now."

"Tell me."

He looked at her and hardened his expression, feeling the first smidgen of guilt he'd felt in a long time. "Bottom line is I could have done more. He needed me and I wasn't there."

"It's okay," Raven said, touching his arm. "It's in the past. The fact you get it now is the important thing. I'm so proud of you."

"Thanks," Mark said. "And thanks for coming back, too. You don't know what it means to me."

"I'm glad I did. There's been a hole in my life without you."

"Me too."

They kissed again, soft and long, and Mark felt dreamy, hoping he wouldn't wake up.

After a time, he said, "So what do we do now?"

"I don't think it's safe here, Mark. If people don't have power in the next day or two some of them will lose their shit. It won't just be robbery and looting. And the military arriving? What is that about? They're not helping that I can see. I saw three groups of soldiers in small trucks driving around the streets with machine guns. That's not helping much."

"There's something I need to tell you." Mark explained what he had seen on the side of the road with the councilor and her father.

"My father? Must be government business. Perhaps they needed his help."

"With an automatic rifle? It looked like more than that. I think something's going on."

"Maybe. Doesn't sound great, does it?" Raven contemplated this.

Mark took her hand in his. "Let's not worry about it until we find out more, okay?" She nodded.

"How long are the others planning to stay up at Hell Ridge?"

"Parker and Sam were staying for two weeks, I think."

"And they asked you to go with them?" Mark nodded. "And you said no. So what's stopping us going up there now?"

"Nothing, I guess. Other than I would have to eat a big slice of humble pie for knocking them back in the first place."

"Yeah, but I wont." Raven cracked a broad smile, the same magnetic, seductive smile that had sucked Mark in all those years ago.

"True."

"Maybe that's what you need when it comes to Parker and Maise. A little humble pie?"

"Maybe." Mark walked into the kitchen. "So, what are you suggesting?"

"Like I said, the town is imploding. People are on edge, and they are running out of food. The desperate people will start to take what they don't have. People from other towns will start to come in and look for things *they* don't have. If we stick around here, anything might happen and I'm betting it won't be good. The Police can only do so much with what they have. If this thing goes another few days then I don't really want to be here." Raven stood and came to Mark, now leaning against the kitchen sink. She bit one of the nails on her right hand, something she never did. "I was going to suggest we leave town anyway. Hell Ridge is a good option."

"I was actually going up to Eildon," Mark said. "All my stuff was packed up. I can't get there now—bloody Keith Whitehead won't sell me his old Commodore, like he promised."

"How would we get up the mountain?"

He started removing canned goods from one of the cupboards. It had been part of his allocation to keep with him at the house, but now they were leaving, he should take everything they had.

"Bikes. They—"

There was a bang on the door, an urgent *thud-thud-thud*. Mark and Raven exchanged a look of surprise.

"What if its *them*?" Raven asked.

Mark put a can of SCP peaches on the bench and started towards the hallway. Raven fell in behind him. *Thud-thud-thud.* Mark grabbed Mindy by the collar, guided her into his room, and shut the door. Then he took the golf club from its spot against the wall and crept down the dark hallway. When he reached the door, he glanced at Raven, but it was too dark to see the expression on her face. *Thud-thud-thud.* Mark tightened the golf club in his hands and leant forward against the peephole. His heart dropped.

Mark turned back to Raven, his eyes having adjusted to the dimness.

"What?" She whispered.

"It's them," Mark said. "The Chinese soldiers. And they've got machine guns."

THIRTY-FIVE

The group had made their way in an easterly direction along
the flat stretch of the Whittlesea-Kinglake Road just beyond
the township. After the incident with the Chinese soldiers and
Maise's uncle, they had ridden in silence for a time, the whine of
the crank or the squeak of the chain were the noisiest sounds.
Whilst they were in a rural setting, on a normal day, the rev or blast
of a car engine would float to them from the main town. Now, the
silence was eerie. What was there to say? The whole situation was
almost too extreme to comprehend, at least for Maise, anyway.
Each of them had looked back over their shoulders at intervals,
expecting to see an army of military vehicles chasing, but so far, the
shimmering heat over the road was all they saw. There were no
cars, no one else riding their bikes, nobody out walking in the
penetrating heat of midday, when the sun scorched everything not
in shadow. Maise pulled the peak of her cap lower, adjusted her
sunglasses and took out her water bottle. Despite the slow pace,
her mouth was dry and she had begun to sweat at the base of her
back.

Eventually, Jas dropped back and rode beside her, flashing a
somber half-smile. She was of Italian background, short in stature
but tall in feistiness and opinion. There was never any wondering
what Jas thought. Maise enjoyed her honesty, mostly to the point
and factual.

"You all right?" Jas asked.

Maise stared ahead. "Yeah. I guess so. It was a bit freaky there for a minute."

"I was the one freaked out," Jas said, her owl-eyed sunglasses glinting in the sunlight. "You were calm. Not once but *three* times. When we saw the soldiers on the road, when Parker fell over, and then when Sam almost lost his shit. I mean, you probably saved Sam's life. If he'd done something stupid…"

Maise shrugged. "I was just too focused to panic."

"You've changed, Maiz. Almost overnight."

"What do you mean?"

"You're different." Maise pursed her lips. "You're more sure of yourself now. The way you stood up to your brother and laid it out for him. I've never seen that before from you. You'd always let things go. And then when we almost got busted by those soldiers in town. You took the lead and got us out of there." She lowered her voice to an intense whisper. "Parker stacked his bike and you ran back and saved him. And then when the soldiers attacked us… you talked Sam down off the ledge and then moved us out of the way when we were standing around like stunned mullets."

Maise hadn't thought about it like that. She sensed a cool head was needed to diffuse Sam's anger, that was all.. As for her brother, Maise said what needed to be said; she was tired of him arguing his own way without good reason. She was done with his abrasive attitude towards Parker. It was partly Mark's fault Parker hadn't been able to keep it together after his mother died.

"Maybe. I guess I was just fed up with it all. Sick of taking it and not giving it back. I've spent three days bagging groceries for people. Heaps of them are super nice, but some of them are asses. I promised myself when I finished my last shift that I wouldn't take crap anymore. That I didn't deserve it."

Jas lifted her sunglasses so Maise could see her brown eyes. Nodding, she said, "Good on you, Maise. You know what I'm like. You've taken crap for too long."

Smiling, she said, "I know."

They both laughed. Jas touched her shoulder. "Not any more though. I'm glad you're finally seeing it. Your brother is one of those people who bluffs his way through life with bravado and hostility, trying to push people into doing what he wants. Yeah, he's tough, we all know that, but physically—not necessarily emotionally. Sometimes you just have to stand up to him. I've never had a problem doing that. And you did that today."

"Thanks."

"Don't under-estimate yourself. You're much stronger than you think. You're one of the smartest women I know—probably the smartest, if I'm honest." Maise turned away. "We look to you."

"Thanks, Jas."

Maise felt better after the conversation. Maybe she was changing. Maybe all the change that had enveloped her life in the past six months had made her stronger, more aware of what she wanted. Two years ago she'd have probably welcomed Parker back with open arms, but now, she was more patient and she wanted to be sure any progress between them was both justified and had the likelihood of lasting.

They rode onward, closer by the minute to the long, steep climb up the mountain and the unknown prospect of Hell Ridge. The wind had picked up, a strong northerly that brought more stinging heat, like breathing in fire, and the flies were getting worse the further they got from the township, buzzing about their faces and ears, landing, taking off, repeating the pattern incessantly. Had it been a normal end-of-January afternoon, they would have been at work, or swimming at a pool somewhere. Maise couldn't wait to get to the campsite and cool off in the creek. The water would be like ice, but she was prepared for that if it meant being clean and refreshed.

Just before they reached the start of the ascent, the distant sound of an engine sounded from ahead. It wasn't long before a vehicle came into view speeding down the hill. It was a big SUV, dark colored, dirty and noisy. There was an instant where Maise couldn't recognize if it was an older vehicle, or new, and she carried the faint, dwindling hope that it might be modern and that *something* had changed. But as the vehicle closed the gap, she saw the ancient design, like something out of an eighties television show. The vehicle slowed when it pulled near, rednecks inside yelping and hollering almost louder than the tired engine. It drove past and then circled back, fan belt clapping, until it was parallel, facing back the way it had just come. Maise heard Parker sigh. These men could either be homicidal maniacs or the salt of the earth. The mountain could deliver both. Maise sent a silent prayer for the later.

"Headed up the mountain?" The driver asked, with long raggedy hair and a face smeared with dirt. The passengers, with similar derelict appearances, all sat forward eying Maise and Jas as though they were a foreign species.

Parker nodded. "Good time to go camping."

"Why aren't you driving?" the man asked, this time his voice was softer, almost surprisingly so. "Long way to ride."

The hot wind gusted, drowning out Parker's first response. "Cars are not working," he repeated. "Modern ones with computer chips, anyway."

The man looked back at the others and said something Maise couldn't understand. "That right? We got a couple not working either. We was headed into town to find out what was happening, get some more supplies."

"Buy some choof, too" one of the men in the back seat said.

"And check on why power's out. Though, the gennie's are holdin' up."

"It's not a good place to be right now," Maise said.

The driver looked her up and down. "Why not?"

Parker added, "I hate to be the one that tells you, but some serious shit has gone down in Whittlesea."

The passengers laughed, but the driver recognized Parker's tight, solid expression and the seriousness behind his words. Maybe he wasn't a country bumpkin.

"Like what?"

"The power's down and nothing with a computer chip works anymore, sure. But..." He glanced at Maise, the turned back and said, "the army has moved in." The man's face was impassive. "But it's not our army. They're Chinese."

The men roared. The driver watched Parker. "Shut it," he said to the others. "The Chinese army. What do you mean?"

"My uncle's the senior policeman in Whittlesea," Maise said.

"Jim Findlay?" Maise nodded, wondering whether that would be a good or bad thing. "Not a bad bloke. For a copper."

"We were stopped just outside the town by two soldiers. It got... nasty. My uncle and some other officers arrived and there was a shootout." That changed the faces of the passengers. They went from loose smiles and indifference, to firm attention. "One of the Chinese soldiers got killed."

The driver rubbed one of his knuckles, looking off into the distance. "Doesn't happen every day."

"I'm telling you," Parker said. "There setting up some kind of camp at Yan Yean Reservoir and the Showgrounds."

"My uncle said there have been attacks launched all over Victoria—New South Wales and Queensland too."

With his elbow on the inside of the open window, the man chewed the tip of his thumb in thought. "The Chinese, hey? Well, if we was gonna have someone invade our country, it'd probably be the Chinese. Things haven't been good for a while, have they?"

Maise said, "It all started with COVID. Our Prime Minister asked for an investigation into its origins. They had a big sook after that and stopped importing our beef and wine and other agricultural products."

"Yeah. My old man's a fisherman down the coast. Lost his lobster business."

"Australia lost billions in exports. They stopped buying as much coal and iron ore, too, and that has cost them more."

"You're smart, kid," the driver said to Maise. "But the Chinese army attacking? That's pretty extreme."

"They probably want the iron ore."

"Or the wine." They all chuckled, but with little humour.

Parker explained what had happened coming down through Kinglake the day before, and Maise told them what Mark had witnessed on the street near the community building.

All the passengers seemed to get excited by this, bouncing around in their seats, whooping and yelling, slapping each other on the back. One of them reached into the back and removed a baseball bat, began slapping it into his palm. The SUV shook.

"All right," the driver said finally. "All right. We'll go in for a look. We owe the town that much." The others applauded.

"Be careful, man," Parker said. "They're at the Showgrounds, too. Setting up some sort of camp."

"Cool," the driver said, pulling the SUV into gear. "Hey, you guys be careful too. We almost got cleaned up by a carload of idiots with a trailer. They were driving in the middle of the road like maniacs."

Parker glanced over at Maise. "What color car?"

"An old Commodore sedan. Blue. Number plate was 1N-somthing. If I see that ass again I'll give him what for."

Maise's stomach dropped. This time, she and Parker exchanged an ominous look.

The men drove away from the gravely shoulder of the highway with a wave, making a U-turn before heading towards Whittlesea.

"I knew it," Parker hissed. "Bloody Keith's gone camping up this way."

THIRTY-SIX

"What do we do?" Raven asked. "Please don't open the door."

"I ain't opening the door," Mark said. His heart was thumping now. *What did they do?* "One of them is hurt. Maybe they just want a place for him to rest?"

Thud-thud-thud. The man outside shouted a long piece in Mandarin. "What'd he say?"

"We have to move," Raven whispered, starting down the hallway. "Now."

Mark began to follow. "They want blood, don't they?"

Raven started running. "He said we've got two minutes before he breaks the door down and if he has to do that, he'll shoot us, or hunt us down like dogs."

"Jesus," Mark said. "Are they really going to do that?"

"You want to take that risk?"

He did not. The fact the Chinese army really was moving about in Whittlesea was concern enough, but when they showed up on your door with machine guns, the chances they had come in peace were zilch. Raven was right though; Mark didn't want to find out what happened when that door opened. But were did they go? The front was blocked. They'd have to go over one of the back fences.

They reached the kitchen. Mark had all his stuff packed, but he couldn't carry all of it with him. "I've got all my gear ready."

"Take what you can. We can manage the rest later on. We just have to get out of here."

Mark estimated they had about ninety seconds before the Chinese broke down the door. He directed Raven to grab a handful of Maise's clothes; back when they all hung out, the two girls would often share clothes. Mark darted into the garage and snatched one of the backpacks from the pile in the garage that contained several pairs of shorts and t-shirts, and a small collection of personal toiletries. He filled it with bottled water and several packets of pasta, then added the clothes from Raven. She also had a small personal bag, into which she stuffed pain relief tablets, a bag of long gran rice, and some snack food. Finally, Mark took his wallet, stuffing it into the pockets of his shorts, out of habit more than imminent use.

He ran back to his bedroom, grabbed Mindy by the collar again and dragged her along with him. He opened the back door to the patio and ushered Raven through, then stopped, looking back into the house. The man on the other side of the door was shouting again. Mark slid the door closed and locked it, wondering when he would next return home. From a hook secured into the bricks beside the door, he snatched Mindy's lead.

"Which way?" Raven asked.

There were two options. Right, to the Henry's house—they weren't home so Mark and Raven could hide out there, but only in the backyard. That felt too risky. Left was the Buckley's. Mark assumed Mr. Buckley was still there. Maybe he would let them inside.

"That way," Mark said, pointing towards the boundary fence separating the Buckley property and his own. He picked Mindy up, not wanting her to run free, and carried her to the fence.

"Hold her, please," he asked Raven, passing the wriggling dog into her outstretched arms. Raven took the dog, shifting feet to manage her weight.

Mark stepped one foot onto the railing, pushed up, then swung his other leg over and landed easily on the other side. He reached back over to Raven and she passed Mindy to him. Mark lifted her over the top of the fence and placed her down, then attached her lead. Moments later, Raven landed beside him.

Several gunshots sounded, followed by breaking glass. Mark stiffened. Then a loud, metallic crash sounded from the front of the house. He and Raven both flinched.

Mark and Raven peered back over the fence. "They've broken the door down," Raven said. "What do you think they're doing?"

Mark shook his head. "Dunno. Maybe looking for a place to rest the injured soldier."

One of the military men appeared at the sliding glass doors peering out into the backyard. Mark and Raven simultaneously ducked.

"Did he see us?" Raven asked.

"I don't think so." They heard the man unlock and open the sliding door. "We have to move," Mark said.

With Mindy on the lead, he led them away from the fence and around the back of the Buckley's house. Mark's plan was to take them down the narrow sideway running alongside the dwelling and onto the street where they could make their escape. It wasn't ideal, but they had no chance of getting back into the house in the short term. He wasn't going to risk Raven or Mindy getting hurt by these people.

As they passed the small patio area with two painted iron seats underneath a table, Mark spotted someone watching the from behind the glass sliding doors. It was Mr. Buckley. He waved them over and slid one of the doors open.

"What is it?" He asked in a croaky voice. Mark explained. "You can wait in here if you like."

They slipped through the opening and crept deep inside the living room away from the windows. It was hot and stuffy—more so than in Mark's own house—and Mark wondered how the old guy dealt with it.

They needed a plan. They couldn't hide in Mr. Buckley's house forever. If the soldiers became curious, or followed through on their threat, they might start going from door to door. Mark considered their next step. "We can head to your house, Rave."

Raven brushed her hair back. "Why don't we just go with the others up to Hell Ridge?"

Maise had offered. Parker too. "I dunno."

It was as though Raven read his mind. "Based on what you told me, you've already been a fool."

He squeezed her hand. "That's scary." She smiled. "It is a long way and we don't have a car. Do you have bikes at your place?" It would take them half an hour to get across to Raven's.

"Yes. You can use my brother's."

"Where were you headed?" Mr. Buckley asked

"Towards Kinglake," Mark said. "My sister has gone up there camping." Raven squeezed his hand and smiled.

Mr. Buckley seemed to consider this. "And you're going to rides bikes?"

"Yeah. I have some at my house," Raven said.

Mr. Buckley waved a hand forward. "I have something that might help. Follow me."

Mark glanced at Raven. Did they have time for this? "Listen," Mark said. "We have to get out of here. We've—"

But Mr. Buckley was insistent. "Come on, young fella. Trust me." He turned from them and started off again.

"Let's just see what he's talking about," Raven said.

They walked through the family room and kitchen with Mindy on the lead, and Mark saw the place was as neat and clean as it had always been. Mr. Buckley stopped at a door off the passageway, placed his wrinkled hand on the handle and waited for them.

Mark resisted the urge to tell the old guy they were in a hurry again and if they didn't get out of there, the Chinese soldiers might pay *him* a visit. When they reached the door, Mr. Buckley smiled, and opened it, revealing a two-car garage and the crusty exterior of an ancient Ford sedan, half of which was covered by a plastic sheet, the remaining half full of patchwork paint duller than the thin light.

"Remember you told me to hold onto it?"

Mark felt his mouth hanging open. "I did. I forgot about this old bird."

"I know," Mr. Buckley said, stepping down into the garage. He wobbled momentarily and Mark put out a hand to steady him. "I haven't had it out very often. I've had it serviced regularly since I brought it in '95, even if I wasn't driving it. Truth is, I planned on restoring it. Just never got around to it, I suppose."

Mark dared hope. Mr. Buckley would only be showing them the car because he was letting them use it. He caught Raven's eye and saw she was thinking the same thing. It would save them an incredible amount of effort climbing the mountain to Kinglake.

Mr. Buckley smiled. "You can take it. No use to me anymore." Mark said nothing; afraid he would say the wrong thing and mess it up. "Use it to get up to see your sister in Kinglake."

Mark and Raven exchanged another glance. "Won't you need it?" Mark asked.

Mr. Buckley waved it off. "I'm not going anywhere."

Mark and Raven circled the car, removing the remainder of the plastic dustsheet. The body needed a lot of work, sections of the paint faded and cracking under the thin light of the garage's back window. But the tires had deep tread and the windscreen and windows were all in tact.

"Still runs? Mark asked.

"It did three months ago. I had it serviced last year. Done about five clicks since then. I turn it on once a month and let it run. Need to reconnect the battery though."

This was a stroke of luck, Mark thought. They had always been close with the Buckley's. The old couple had looked after Mark and Maise like they were their own.

"Just to be clear," Mark began. "We can drive the car up to Kinglake?" Mr. Buckley nodded. Mark thought about his next question. It might create more challenges for him, but it was the right thing to do. "Why don't you come with us?"

He spoke in a tired voice. "I'm not interested in leaving here. My wife just died. She might not be here physically, but she's here in spirit, and that's where I want to be."

Mark looked back at Mr. Buckley. Although he hadn't seen the old guy much lately, Mark could tell the lines on his face were deeper now, his hair a little thinner, the brown spots on his skin a little darker. Mark didn't know what it was like to lose your wife of fifty or more years, but he knew what it felt like to lose Raven after a year and that had been bad enough.

"I can't believe how hard it must be for you. Really. But are you sure?" Mr. Buckley nodded. "You can come with us for a few days until this thing settles down."

Mr. Buckley smiled, revealing gaps in a set of darkened teeth. "No, my boy. Thank you, but no."

"Do you have enough food and water?" Raven asked.

"Plenty. Found a couple of cases of bottled water in the back of the cupboard that June had stored away. I don't eat a lot anymore. And there's enough to last me a time."

"Okay," Mark said. "We'll borrow it. But we'll be back in a few days to see how you are coping."

Mr. Buckley nodded. "I look forward to it. And hopefully by then this thing is over."

THIRTY-SEVEN

P arker tried not to let the situation overwhelm him. Things were worsening. The Chinese military were threatening the town and they'd shot people dead. For what reason, he didn't know. Now, the last person he wanted anywhere near Hell Ridge or Maise had apparently escaped Whittlesea and there was a good chance he and his goon friends were headed up to Hell Ridge. Parker wondered how that might play out, but pushed the thought aside for later.

They were approaching the spot where Parker had left the motorbike, the very base of the hill that led them up the mountain into Kinglake, and beyond, to Hell Ridge. He was nervous; full of bad feelings that someone had found the bike and stolen it. *Same way you did.* Perhaps he should have pushed it into town.

Having a motorbike gave them an advantage. They could move quickly between locations. In an emergency, it might save lives. Two people could ride on it together and they could zip into town from camp in twenty-five minutes. It brought risks too, though. The longer electrical outage continued, the greater its value.

Leading the group, Parker stopped at the place where he had left the bike, having clearly marked it in his mind, being one of the few places where there was a gap in the guardrail. He peered into the trees and attempted to find the lumpy mass of loose branches and leaves, but from the road, he couldn't distinguish it in the undergrowth. Either it was gone, or he had hidden it well, which had been his aim when he had camouflaged it in the first place.

He laid his bike down along with the small fuel tank, and with an elevated heart rate, he cleared the shallow gravel ditch at the edge of the road, cut deep from run off gushing down the hill during heavy rain. Sticks and dry leaves crunched under foot as he passed through the gap in the guardrail. He moved through the opening and stepped sideways down the bank, one foot slipping on the loose earth. He ducked through the trees and dug in his footing as the ground began to slope down where a wombat had once attempted to build a burrow. Parker had heaped leaves and several sizeable tree branches over the bike. He slipped stepping around the tree, but when he saw the slightly lumpy ground, he knew the bike was still there. He did a little fist pump, then began removing the camouflage, dragging a large branch away and then tossing the leaves aside until the motorbike revealed itself. Parker leapt down below it and stood the bike up, struggling with the weight on the slope. He backed it up, then buried his head and used his shoulders and thighs to drive it up around the tree, the muscles in his arms and legs under stress.

"Need a hand?" Maise called out.

"Nah," he said, voice straining. "Nearly there."

With all his effort, Parker pushed the motorbike up above the lip and onto the flat area, over the gravel ditch and out onto the road.

"Whoa, awesome," Jas said. Maise and Sam both smiled.

"It'll make things a whole lot easier when we need get go back to town. Can you grab the fuel can for me, Sam?"

Sam unscrewed the lid of the fuel tank and handed the can to Parker. He began to empty the fuel into the bike. There as a little over a gallon, or about five liters in the metric scale. It would provide enough for several trips back to town from camp.

As the fuel emptied, flies circled their heads and landed on their bodies. Although they had passed over the flat, open outskirts of Whittlesea and reached the edge of the scrub, the heat still covered them like a warm blanket. There was no escaping it, unless they were at the—

"Today would have been a great day for the beach," Maise said, looking up at the blue sky.

"Geez you took the words out of my head," Parker said.

"Imagine us lying on the sand on our day beds, drinking ice cold soft drinks from the cooler, taking a dip every hour or so to cool off and freshen up," Maise added in thought.

"Reading a good novel," Jas said with a hand shading her eyes.

"The best," Sam smiled.

"Yeah," Parker suggested. "One day, maybe."

The fuel container was empty. Parker tipped it up a final time before placing it on the ground and screwed the cap back on.

"Maise?"

"Yeah?

"Get over here." He smiled. "You're riding the bike."

Maise stared. "What? Why me?"

"Because I said so."

"This is the time where you let the macho boys bully you into doing something," Jas laughed.

"Where's the real Parker?" Sam asked.

Parker said, "What do you mean?" Nobody spoke. Parker felt his defenses go up. "What do you mean, Sam?"

Sam shrugged. "Not long ago mate, the real Parker would have ridden the bike himself and not given a shit about anyone else."

Parker considered this. He tried to think of an example. Sam seemed to read his mind.

"The trip to Echuca? The helmet? When we went on the boat in Tasmania? Sitting on the side with the best view?"

Parker remembered. In hindsight, they had not been his best moments. He could remember a few more, too, but he wasn't going to dwell on them. "All right, all right. Maybe I've had a few epiphanies of late."

"You're changing," Maise said. She had put her bicycle down and approached the motorbike. She placed a hand on his shoulder and gave a gentle squeeze. "For the better." Her smile made Parker happy.

"Stay tuned," he chuckled. "I might have the chance to be an asshole again soon."

THIRTY-EIGHT

I t felt like such a waste. All the bags and boxes of supplies that Mark had packed in the garage for his own trip had to be left behind, but there was no chance of going back for them. All they had now were a few bags and themselves. Mr. Buckley insisted they take several items hooked on the brick walls of his garage that might assist them camping—an axe, an old chainsaw and a coiled length of bright green rope.

The forty-year old vehicle looked dull and lifeless in the cool gloom, but Mark felt optimistic it would serve their needs. Mr. Buckley stood in the doorway with a plastic grocery bag in his hand.

"You sure you won't come with us?" Mark asked, standing at the roller door in preparation. It was going to be a quick process— pull the cord on the roller door's control box—and hurry back to the driver's seat. He could have asked Raven to do it—and it wasn't about her being female—he just preferred to wear the risk himself. If the Chinese soldiers were outside, they might stat firing at them, and Mark didn't want to risk that. Mindy was sitting up safely on the backseat, excited to be going somewhere in a car again.

Mr. Buckley waved the question off. "Here." He held the plastic bag out for Mark. "A few more bits and pieces for you. Matches, a flashlight, that sort of thing."

Mark left the roller door and took the extras, stuffing them into one of the packs. He held out a hand for Mr. Buckley and they shook. "Thanks again. We'll be back to check on you." Mr. Buckley nodded.

Returning to the door, Mark tugged on the red cord, unlocking the mechanism. He took the ripples of metal between his fingers and lifted, rolling the flap upwards. It began to curl around the shaft, letting in bright sunlight. Then he hurried to the open car door with a tight squeal and slid into the sunken driver's seat, handing the bag to Raven. He turned the key, holding his breath and the five-liter carburetor engine whined at first, then rumbled to life.

"Get us out of here," Raven said, putting a hand on top of Mark's, which held the gearstick.

He accelerated gently out of the garage and the engine almost conked out. Mark let it roll halfway down the sloped driveway, stopped, and put the handbrake on. He wasn't leaving Mr. Buckley to shut the roller door. Mark glanced to the left—towards his own property—expecting to see the soldiers waiting for him, but the front steps were empty. From the corner of his eye he noticed other people in the street, watching.

He dashed to the opening, reached up and pulled the door down until it sat flush with the concrete, and then scuttled back to the Ford, the engine whining and whirring, as though waking from a long winter slumber. He hoped it wouldn't fall apart on them before they managed their escape.

Some of the people in the street had crossed the road towards them, shouting now, calling out to him, their voices loud and desperate.

"Hey man, give us a ride," one of them called.

"I'll give you five thousand bucks," another said.

Raven sneered. "Go, please."

Mark removed the handbrake and the car began rolling. He touched the accelerator and started forward, expecting it to resist, but it responded with some thrust and the edge of the hood clipped one of the people asking for a ride that didn't move aside quickly enough.

"Hey!" He shouted and slammed a fist against the Ford's heavy body. Mindy barked.

Mark had not seen the man before. As he passed others, he realized none of the people on the street were familiar to him.

It had been close. A mob could in theory overcome him and Raven and steal the car. It was valuable and this was what he had been talking about with the others. A car was a hot commodity, and people were desperate to get their hands on one. Based on what his Uncle Jim had told them, he should drive directly to the police station and hand it in, but his needs right now overtook those of the police—at least in Mark's eyes—even if his Uncle Jim was a policeman.

Accelerating onto the street, he watched the small crowd fall behind in the rearview mirror. Further along, other people strolled across their front yards, following him, and these were more familiar.

They drove with only the sound of the rumbling V8 engine and the hot wind pushing in through the gap in the windows as Mark navigated the streets; Black Road, Warner Lane, rows of middle class suburban houses, with their neat, manicured front yards, albeit with yellowing grass from the heat. He spotted an army vehicle driving in the other direction on Oakbank Boulevard and was glad they were heading the opposite way. Mindy poked her nose at the gap in the window, her pleasure sensors unable to cope with the number of scents coming at her. Now, he couldn't believe he'd scored such a relic—not only was it one of the few vehicles in town that functioned, but it was a classic, even if it needed some restoration work. Part of the reason he was after Keith Whitehead's car was because General Motors Holden had shut down production in Australia. He thought the value of these models manufactured locally would only appreciate. Even though it was in average condition, he vowed to look after it and return it to Mr. Buckley when the situation had improved.

He tightened his hands around the steering wheel; he could see a faint light at the end of a long tunnel, now, after a tumultuous last few months; fighting with Parker, losing Raven, even the mistrust and animosity between he and Maise. He understood now the previous nights events were necessary—he needed to have it out with Parker, say his piece. And the timing of Raven's return and their subsequent discussion about his behavior was perfect. Had he not heard Parker and Maise say their sermons last night, maybe he would not have been able to listen to Raven say it today? Maybe he was growing up after all.

"You okay?" Raven said, brushing a strand of black hair behind her right ear. How he had missed seeing her beside him in the passenger seat.

"Yeah. Better than I've been in a while, if I'm honest."

She squeezed his hand. "I'm glad."

Ahead, several broken down cars had been abandoned in the middle of the road, almost pushed together at their noses, leaving no obvious pathway through. Mark cursed and stomped on the brakes, bringing the car to a halt. He guided the gearstick into reverse, looking back over his shoulder, and accelerated. Taking the car backwards, he stopped where the street veered off to the right, then put the shift into drive, and accelerated slowly.

From behind stationary vehicles on both sides of the street, several men appeared. Two from one side wore fluorescent green and blue hi-visibility t-shirts—the kind anyone on a construction site or in a warehouse might wear. They were younger, with cropped dark hair and unshaven faces. Mark immediately recognized them from the service station—they had been poking around his Ute.

The two from the other side of the street were middle-aged men with tattoos covering both arms, wearing dark t-shirts and jeans. One had red hair and a red beard, the other a mop of black hair.

"Bikers," Mark said. "The cars on the road were a bloody trap."

"Go!" Raven shouted.

Mark locked eyes with one of the hi-vis men. He pointed at Mark through the open window. Mindy started barking again.

"Pull over!" One of the men shouted through the open window.

Mark would do nothing of the kind. He pushed the accelerator as all four men hurried onto the road.

Raven gripped the handhold above the passenger door. "Don't you stop."

One of the bikers lifted his baseball bat and slammed it down onto the hood of Mr. Buckley's car. The metallic crunch was deafening.

"Get out!" Another man shouted.

A second bat slammed into the side door beside Raven and she screamed.

The men fell away though as Mark sped the car on.

Not done yet, a fifth man appeared from one of the properties about thirty yards ahead. Dressed similar to the others, he stepped into the middle of the road, hair tied back in a long ponytail, dark glasses; a cigarette hanging from the corner of his mouth. He too had a baseball bat and pulled it back into a hitting position. Mark's foot hit the floor, urging the old Ford to go as fast as it dared. For a moment, Mark thought the man wasn't going to move. At the last second, he stepped aside and swung the bat, slamming it into the front right headlight. There was a dull thud and the thick crack of glass.

The man screamed at them as they passed.

Raven turned around in her seat. "Oh, sh—"

Glass shattered, the noise deafening. A baseball bat clunked off the parcel shelf and onto the back seat.

"He threw the bat at us?" Mark asked.

"Yeah. Jesus, that was close."

Mark cackled, but there was terror in his voice. "They're getting desperate. Told you this thing would become hot property."

"Stick to the main roads for now, don't you think?"

Mark guided the car in that direction, and eventually they turned onto the main drag, the most direct route to Kinglake-Whittlesea Road. Now he just had to avoid the police and the army.

They passed through the roundabout on Church Street and then alongside the battered Royal Mail Hotel on their right, but as Mark guided the big Ford sedan around a slight bend, he caught site of something in the middle of the road ahead. He yanked on the steering wheel and pulled the car right and into a side street, spilling Raven out of her seat.

"You see that?" Mark asked. "They've set up a bloody barricade."

Raven spoke in a low voice. "I saw it." She peered back over her shoulder. "Two vehicles. Both with the Chinese flags on the doors."

"What about the solider with the machine gun? You think he saw us?"

"I think so."

Mark took the thundering Ford left into another street. "We made the right choice, but it doesn't matter which way we go, we seem to run into trouble."

"I still don't understand," Raven said. "What could they be doing?"

"Has to be some sort of invasion. That's my guess. I don't see it could be anything else."

"Sounds far fetched."

Mark worked his way through the back streets, wary of anymore roadblocks and angry bikers. Raven appeared tense, watching out the side and front window with extra vigilance.

Finally, they came upon the street that hit the main highway and sped down it. Mark pressed the indicator lever as he approached the intersection and the right signal flashed. He glanced both ways with the car still rolling, not expecting to see anybody, but doing it from habit, and took off heading towards Kinglake.

Raven twisted in her seat and peered out the back window, as if expecting somebody to be following.

"It's okay," Mark said. "The bikers didn't have a car."

"What about the army?"

They reached a hundred kilometers per hour and then Mark gave it a little more fuel, testing its capacity. He didn't want to kill the old duck, but he also wanted to know that it still had the capability if he needed it. Their speed increased, a deep rumble from the engine, but there were squeaks and squeals that told him the thing might struggle going any faster.

As they wound their way out of Whittlesea past the Scrubby

Creek Reserve along the Whittlesea-Yea Road, something flashed in the rearview mirror and caught Mark's eye. Raven noticed.

"What is it?"

"Another car." He slowed down until the speed was about eighty, waiting for it to come into view.

"Don't slow down," Raven said, turning in her seat to see out the rear window. "What if it's…"

"Who? The military? Or the bikers?"

Mark thought of the same thing; what if it was the Chinese military that had just spotted them? What would they do, arrest them? Kill them? Or maybe the bikers had found another vehicle and decided they wanted Mr. Buckley's old Ford. He didn't know which party would be worse.

It didn't take long to find out. "He's hiking," Mark said, straining his eyesight against the sunlight. "Movin' real fast."

"Is it them?"

"Gimme another second. Definitely an SUV of some type."

The grill came into view, then the rest of the SUV. It was close now and the Army green color of the hood left no doubt.

"Bugger, it's the army."

"What do you think they want?"

"I don't know. And I'm gonna make sure we don't find out."

THIRTY-NINE

Parker and Sam pushed theirs and the girls' bikes the last mile along the Whittlesea-Yea Road before reaching the turn off in a slow, uncomfortable trot. They had used the shade of roadside scrub to keep out of the sun, but the temperature had to have crept above forty Celsius. And unless it was a flat or downhill ride, neither could manage to pedal uphill with their packs on while holding a second bike. There were fewer houses up here, the properties set far back from the road, hidden by thick bush, towering trees and low ground cover, making it impossible to see through, with their strong wire gates and dilapidated fences that looked like a baby cow could push over.

Maise and Jas, who rode double on the motorbike alongside the boys up the long and winding hill, were not so badly affected, using limited energy and enjoying the hot breeze when they rode. Maise was happy to share with the boys, but neither would accept the offer.

"Just so bloody hot," Sam said, wiping a hand across his slick forehead again. They had stopped half a dozen times, close to exhaustion.

The turnoff to the campsite was inconspicuous, running almost parallel to the road, covered by low hanging branches, just a hint of gap beyond as to where it might lead. Parker always said the narrow opening put off drivers, uncertain if they could sneak their vehicles through. People who used the site had deliberately avoided cutting the trees back too much so as not to make the track appealing to fisherman or campers.

Parker stood at the opening peering through. He went to one of the trees and picked out a branch. The others pulled up behind him.

"Finally," Sam said. "I've taken for granted the thirty or so minutes we'd normally take to get here by car."

"What is it?" Maise asked Parker.

"Broken branch."

Guiding the motorbike, Parker led them along the first section of flat, hardened dirt track, before it began to slope into a sharper descent. Maise took Parker's bicycle. It was impossible to see all the way to the camp through the trees and underbrush.

"Use your brakes," Parker said, guiding the motorcycle around a deep wheel rut.

They edged their way downward, kicking up dust, fighting for their footing where the ground was scuffed and rutted. As they passed another deep channel, Parker saw something on the edge of the road that made him stop. He asked Sam to hold the heavy bike and went over to it, picking up the empty Victoria Bitter beer can. He looked at it for a long time.

"What is it?" Jas asked. Parker said nothing. "Parker?"

Maise suddenly had a bad feeling in her stomach. After seeing Keith and his mates near the service station, then hearing what the Kinglake men had said, Parker had gotten progressively more edgy the closer they'd gotten to the campsite.

He turned to them. "Somebody is down there." Nobody spoke. They were all feeling it too. "When I climbed up here yesterday morning, this wasn't here."

"You think it's Whitehead?" Sam asked.

"I hope it's not, but I've got a bad feeling it is."

Parker took the bike back from Sam and recommenced down the dirt track, inspecting the thick brush to the side for more evidence. "Let's be really quiet from now on."

The heat was marginally better under the shade of the towering gums, but the air was still hot and dry and the flies had followed them.

About halfway down, the sound of laughter floated up the hill. They all stopped.

Parker pinched his lips together, then made a pained face, showing his teeth. "Bastards. I knew it." Shouting sounded, followed by the flat crack of a rifle.

"Oh shit," Jas whispered.

Parker said to Maise, "You girls have to stay here."

Maise didn't move. "What are you talking about, Parker?"

"You can't go down there."

"Because they've got a gun?"

"Whitehead is a nutter. He'll probably shoot one of us."

"That's crazy."

In a loud whisper, Parker said, "I don't care. You're not getting too close to this. It could be dangerous."

"We'll be fine," Jas said.

Still, Maise didn't move. This was Parker's natural reaction to danger. He was worried about her. He'd lapsed into a bit of his old self, trying to tell her what to do. Once, Maise would have just let it go, not spoken up and gone with whatever he was proposing. She thought about what Jas had said. She *was* different now.

"Listen, just calm down," Maise began. Parker scouted the ground at the base of a big gum. She had to ease his mind. The chances of one of them getting shot were minimal. "Parker?" He finally stopped and looked at her. "It's not just you making the decisions, okay?" She glanced at Sam and Jas who both gave her their attention. "We're going to decide this together, as a group." Parker hesitated, looked at them and then finally nodded. "So we have two options, as I see it. We sit up here and wait and see if they leave. Maybe they'll get sick of it or find what they want and nick off. But if they don't, we *will* have to confront them at some point."

"We *could* wait up here," Jas suggested. "Maybe they'll poke around a bit and then leave."

"Knowing Whitehead," Sam said, "If he finds something good, he won't leave."

"Sam's right," Maise added. "If Keith gets a sense that he can make something of it, he'll make it his own. And honestly, we've come so far. I don't want to wait around any longer."

Sam continued. "And if they can't find anything worthwhile or make a go of it they'll trash the place."

"*Or*, we go down there and kick their ass," Parker said.

Maise gave a slight smile. "Or we go down there and sort it out. You put this camp together, right? It's your stuff. Your *dad's* stuff. They can't just take it."

"Totally agree," Parker said.

Maise said, "And I'm Keith's weakness." Parker winced. "I've got that in my back pocket. I think I can convince him to leave, if it comes to that. Or maybe they're happy to coexist."

"Yeah," Jas said, her voice unsteady. "There might be room for two camps, right?"

Parker considered all of this. "Let's do it. Sorry, I wasn't thinking."

Maise smiled at him. "Sam? Jas? You're up for going down there?"

Jas nodded. "Too right," Sam said.

"And we have a gun too, don't forget. Not that we want it to come to that."

They rested their bicycles in the ground cover off the track; stumpy tussock grasses, ferns like umbrellas, ancient crumbling logs long ago consumed by bright colored moss and plants. Parker wheeled the motorbike through strips of loose bark and leant it against the back of a thick lemon gum. He unhooked the shotgun off his shoulder and took two shells out of his pack, loading them into the weapon.

"Do we need to do that yet?" Jas asked.

"It's fine," Maise added. "Better to be prepared. We don't really know who's down there."

"I've got a bad feeing," Parker said. He took three steps down the track, shotgun laid across his arm. "I hope I'm wrong, but that voice sounded a lot like Brad Moxon."

"He's not so bad," Sam said. "I used to sit next to him in biology."

"That was before he hung around with Keith. I can just see

Keith trashing the place for the fun of it. Or stealing it now that everything has become useful. He's always on edge in these situations. Be careful."

"Everyone just try to be calm, okay?" Maise said. "No macho stuff from you, Parker."

Parker feigned confusion. "Me?"

More shouting sounded. As though they might be arguing amongst themselves or maybe joking around the way blokes in their twenties did when they were out camping. The tension tightened around Maise's gut. If it were Keith and his friends, there was a fifty-fifty chance they'd have trouble.

"Like I said, be careful," Maise declared. "We leave the bikes up here. We go quietly and watch them before we make an entrance. Find out what they're up to." The others nodded in agreement. "If it looks like trouble, we turn around and leave, okay?" They all agreed.

FORTY

"Jesus Christ, drive, Mark! As fast as you can."

"I am," Mark said, tightening his hands around the wheel. "But this old girl is *old*. It's much bloody slower to take off than a new car."

"How are they driving such a new vehicle? I thought the new ones didn't work."

"Maybe they're built to withstand this whole EMP thing."

Raven let out a long sigh. "Bloody Chinese."

Mark glanced at her, gave a nervous laugh. "What would your dad say about all of this?"

She shook her head. "Don't know. He's been quiet lately."

"You feel bad about leaving him with your mum away?"

Raven shook her head. "No. Dad doesn't even know I'm there most of the time." Mark didn't know how such a beautiful girl, let alone your own child, could go unnoticed by anyone.

They were on the bottom of the long hill now, an ascent that usually took about fifteen more minutes driving at the speed limit. It climbed gradually, before sometimes rising sharply and then flattening out, full of curves and undulations. It was not the place for a race. While Mr. Buckley's Ford Fairlane was in reasonable condition for its age, it didn't have the pickup speed of modern cars. Nowadays, it was meant for a Sunday cruise around the township rather than a pursuit at top speed. Still, it could move, and they took the first turn at pace, highlighting the difference forty years made in car production. The wheel was tight; the steering rack shaking. Numerous rattles and rumbles clunked the front and rear of the chassis.

"Can you see it?" He asked.

Raven spun around. "No." She hung there for a moment.

"Okay, that's enough. I'm driving way too fast for this car and these turns."

Raven dropped back into the seat. "What about if we pull over down one of the dirt roads, or driveways? Hide and let them drive past?"

"Does that ever work?

"Only in the movies."

"Those things have no way out. We get caught and we're trapped."

A sign indicated they needed to slow down to forty kilometers an hour at the next bend. Mark touched the brakes, but the old Ford didn't slow enough, and he had to press harder. The front end vibrated. "Oh Jesus. This thing's gonna fall apart." They reached the bend, slowing to a crawl. Mark accelerated out of it and the car groaned, the engine whirring as it worked overtime to respond. "There's a long stretch up here. Can you keep en eye on them and let me know if you see them coming before the next curve?"

"How far until we get there?"

"Five minutes. Maybe eight."

Mindy whimpered on the back seat. Raven reached out and patted her head. "It's all right, girl. Hang in there. Won't be long."

Once the road had straightened, Raven turned in her seat again, adjusting the belt so it sat better across her hips and back. Mark pressed the accelerator harder, daring the vehicle to go faster. His heart thrummed against his chest, his body sizzled with adrenalin. Tree-lined scrub rushed past in a blur, dry leaves on the ground and fallen branches lazing in the hot wind. Mark wondered about the smoke they saw in the distance and the potential for fire. Was the Country Fire Authority (CFA) sill functioning? How quickly could they mobilize if the fire moved towards a town? It was just another potential hazard amongst many right now.

"There it is," Raven shouted. "It's getting closer. They're driving in the middle of the road." In a lower, more panicked voice, she added. "Hurry, Mark. They're coming fast."

"Trying, believe me."

He kicked himself for not using the middle of the road himself to avoid slowing down into the corners. Old habits, he thought. Mark did it now though, staying wide into bends and coming out early and hard against the curve, the white lines rapidly disappearing beneath the car. It helped; felt faster anyway, but each time Raven turned around she indicated they were still closing.

"How far?"

"A hundred yards."

"Shit."

It was only a minute or so later, they heard the booming voice in broken English from the vehicle behind, accentuated by a megaphone.

"Pull over immediately. I repeat, pull over immediately."

Mark glanced at Raven, her cheeks and mouth pulled into a fearful expression. Mark felt it too, but was trying not to show it.

What did he do? Pull over and risk losing the car, face arrest, or worse, be shot? *Calm down, man, you're being dramatic.* He hoped that was the case.

"What do you think?" he asked Raven. "We're only about a click or so away."

"I don't think we have a choice. No matter how close we are."

"PULL OVER OR WE WILL SHOOT!" The megaphone blared.

Raven turned again. "They're closer now. *Really close.* And they're pointing a machine gun." That struck Mark like a hot poker. "Pull over, Mark," Raven said, her voice breaking.

Mark moved his foot from the accelerator to the break. When the car had slowed, he pulled it off the road and onto the gravel shoulder, stones and rocks popping under the tires.

They were beaten. The old car had given its best, but they couldn't outrun the modern army vehicle. He turned to Raven. Whatever awaited them, they could do it together.

"Sit tight. We'll be okay." But Mark didn't feel like that, and Raven's face did not reflect it.

"Just don't talk back okay? I know what you're like, Mark. You can't help yourself in this situation. This no joke. They threatened to shoot us."

"We'll be fine," he repeated. "Put Mindy on the lead in case they ask us to get out. If she attacks, they might shoot her. And let me do the talking."

FORTY-ONE

Down they walked, creeping between old mossy logs and a plethora of broken tree branches, blackberries with their thorns, and the occasional fern sprouting luscious green fronds. The gums were shedding their bark, creating layers of the stuff on which their feet crunched, but they were grateful for the shade of the tall trees. The heat though was blustery, making breathing uncomfortable as they filled their lungs with hot air and insects by the hundred. And the flies were constant, always looking for a place to land, as though annoying them was their sole mission in life.

They were almost three-quarters of the way down when Maise froze.

"Snake," she said in a surprisingly calm voice. Everybody stopped. Sam was mid-step, and momentarily held his foot in the air.

"Where?" Parker asked, searching the tangled grass near Maise's feet.

"Just over there." She pointed about a meter and a half away near the crumbling edges of a log.

"Moving?" Maise shook her head. "Okay. Come towards me. Very slowly. Soft steps. If it turns towards you, don't move."

"Got it." Maise started moving laterally, away from the snake with high, looping steps, avoiding a knot of blackberries, placing her sneakered feet carefully down to avoid snapping twigs or worse, causing her to fall so it would alert the snake. No doubt their careful approached had probably saved them so far, but that might end at any moment. A snake attack, or worse, a bite, would alert Whitehead and his crew, and thwart any plans of a cautious arrival. Not to mention potentially killing them if they couldn't get anti-venom, which was the likely outcome.

When Maise was far enough away from the snake, they started downhill again. Parker made a sign with two fingers—pointing to his eyes and then to the ground, telling them to keep watch.

Their progress from there was uneventful, until they had almost reached the flatter grassed area, the ground became more treacherous and as the lead person, Parker found himself taking longer to pick his way over the terrain. It would have been much easier to take the road, but if anybody at the campsite went to Whitehead's car, they would have spotted Parker and the others approaching. He wanted it to be a surprise.

"Be really careful here," he said in a whisper, turning to face them. The ground was full of big ruts, as though the wheels of some giant machine had left two-foot deep trenches. "We go down here," he pointed, "and then step from that hump there to the flatter ground. The last one is a small jump, okay?"

They all understood. Parker went first, almost losing his balance on the final jump, but he nailed the landing, watching the parked vehicle at the edge of the campsite or the tree line surrounding it. At any moment, he expected to see one of White-head's crew poke their nose out and spoil the surprise. Once they crossed, they were only thirty yards from the camp and the last section would be easy to traverse.

Maise made it, then Jas took her turn. She got the first step right but her landing was awkward and the rough ground fell away. She twisted her ankle and went down crying out in pain as her knee struck a rock.

"Bugger," she said, rubbing it intensely.

Sam leapt beside her and crouched down. "You okay?"

Sam helped her up, putting less weight on the ankle she'd hurt, and then she hobbled with an arm around his waist to the flatter section of ground.

Parker was the first to notice the shouts and cries from the camp had quieted. He put a finger to his lips and met their eyes. They listened, waiting for the noises to recommence. It took about thirty seconds before one of the blokes shouted something. Maise let out an animated sigh.

They pushed on the last twenty yards, sticking to the edge of the brush and walking in single file, Parker first, shotgun ready. When they reached the thicket of trees and bushes that surrounded the actual campsite, Parker stopped to face them.

"My car is parked on the other side of this," he whispered, indicating the shrubbery. They were almost in line with Whitehead's car. He had parked it at the entrance of the campsite to block anybody who tried to get through.

"How are we going to see what they're doing?" Sam asked.

"We're going into the trees," Parker said.

With caution, they walked into the scrub, pushing sharp branches from their path, avoiding limbs and leaves from scratching their faces. Sam became stuck and had to double back. Parker listened for voices to make sure the men were still talking, but his car soon came into view and here he stopped, signaling to the others they were close enough.

Through the last line of scrub, with just enough camouflage to keep them from being seen, they could make out the campsite—the two domed tents and two Coleman gazebos; Parker's Toyota Hilux parked on the edge of the clearing. But it was evident as they watched the dappled shapes of the men move about that their interest did not lie in what Parker and the others had first thought.

"They're not just trashing the place," Sam said, "They're stealing stuff."

Even with the trees as camouflage, they could see the damage to the campsite. The Hilux's canopy had been torn off and lay discarded on the ground. The butane gas cooker and the gas lamp had been stacked near the trailer, along with several boxes of groceries. The bedding from the tent had been dragged out and strewn across the camp, along with Parker's clothes, some of which were hanging from a tree.

Parker felt a slow anger course through him. He was breathing heavier, the rage boiling. He brought the gun around, clicked the safety off, then double-checked the chamber was loaded. All it would take was to push his way through the last barrier of trees and shoot one of those bastards. He *could* do it. He felt like he wanted to do it. The thought of it all—the work that had gone into getting the group there, the money he and Sam had spent on their gear, the canopy, which his mother and father had given to him as a Christmas present the year before she died—was too much. His anger exploded in a surge. He started through the scrub.

"Wait," Maise hissed. Parker stopped, looked across and found her face etched with concern, brow furrowed. "Don't. Not yet."

But Parker couldn't hold back the rage. He pushed his way through the trees, shotgun poised. It had come down to this. He wasn't going to let those bastards ruin anymore of his stuff. It could mean their lives depended on it.

FORTY-TWO

Mark watched the army jeep pull over about fifteen yards behind where he had parked Mr. Buckley's Ford Fairlane.

"Don't say anything," he said to Raven. "That way if we get into trouble I'll be the one copping it, not you. With any luck, at least you might be able to drive away from this. And keep hold of Mindy for me, will you?"

Two soldiers climbed out of the Jeep, one of them armed with a machine gun. As they approached, Mark saw they were both Chinese and he felt uneasy, though not surprised. Mark adjusted his sunglasses and tried to relax himself in the seat.

Both soldiers reached the vehicle. The first one was medium height, with an impeccable dress; was shorter than Mark, with a thin moustache and a clean, smooth face. Mark wondered if he'd even grown any facial hair yet. When he spoke, he had a slight accent, but it was close to Australian.

"Where are you going, sir?"

Mark hadn't rehearsed anything. He glanced at Raven. "North. Up to the border."

"Where exactly?"

"Echuca. We have a caravan up there," he lied.

He turned to the other man and spoke in a different language. Mark guessed it was Mandarin. When the man had finished, he turned back to Mark, crouched lower, and looked past Mark to Raven. Again, he spoke Mandarin.

Raven put both hands out, shrugged and said with an apologetic look. "I'm sorry. I only speak English."

The man nodded. "Do you realize the Australian Defence Force is seconding all vehicles for emergency use? All citizens were asked to hand over their vehicles. Did you receive this information?"

"No," Mark lied again. "When did this happen?"

The man turned to his colleague and spoke again. "We require you to give up the vehicle now. We will take possession of it under the National Emergency Act, 1993."

"I can't give up this car," Mark said. "It's mine. I own it." He glanced at Raven. "Besides, you've got your own."

The second soldier poked the machine gun in through the window. Mark put his hands up. "Settle down, mate." The first soldier guided the machine gun away.

Mindy started barking. Raven turned around and patted her, making soothing sounds to calm her down.

The two soldiers spoke; the one holding the machine gun raising his voice, getting angrier at every response the other man gave. Eventually, the front soldier turned back to Mark.

"Out," he said. "And keep that dog quiet."

"Let's just get out, Mark. We don't want to get shot." Raven put a hand on his arm. "Please. Get out now."

Mark reluctantly opened the door and both men stepped back. He felt a mix of anger and fear. Something in Raven's voice told him to do what was being asked. He knew Raven spoke Mandarin, her father insisting she know his native language. She'd taught Mark a few words when they first started dating. Now, she understood everything the soldiers were saying, and Mark suspected it wasn't good. But Mark couldn't suppress his anger at their treatment, and he took his time, fighting to exert control.

"Hurry up."

They lined up alongside the vehicle; Raven squatting with a hand around Mindy's neck, begging her in a comforting voice to keep quiet. The first soldier ordered the second to get into the car.

"What about our stuff?" Mark asked, waving towards the trunk.

The two soldiers spoke. The second stopped at the driver's door and returned to the rear. He opened it and called Mark over. The other soldier followed. One of them handed Mark a pack. Mark passed it to Raven, and then signaled to the second pack, which the man retrieved and handed it over.

"And that stuff, "Mark said, pointing to a box of supplies, including the bag of supplies Mr. Buckley had given them.

The second solider leaned in to pick up the box, but the first barked an order and the soldier pulled back.

"No," the first soldier with the thin moustache said, putting up the palm of his hand, indicating that no more supplies were to be taken from the trunk.

Mark turned and squared up to him. He had a scar on his left cheek and his eyes bored into Mark's. There was no fear in his features, only impatience. He waved the machine gun, indicating Mark should move aside.

The second soldier closed the trunk and went back to the driver's door, then climbed in.

Mark opened and closed his fists at his thighs. He had nothing with which to fight back—no gun, no knife, not even anything that resembled a bat. There was one possibility, though it was risky. What if the soldier left in Mr. Buckley's car and the remaining soldier was alone? Would Mark risk jumping him and stealing the Jeep and weapon?

"Don't do anything," Raven said, watching him from the corner of her eye. "Just sit tight."

The first soldier waved the gun at them again, barked another order in Mandarin. Raven moved away from the edge of the road and further from the Jeep. Mark turned to face the soldier.

He could still do it, he thought. Jump the guy, take the gun, shoot him, then turn on the soldier in Mr. Buckley's car. Clearly, something wasn't right here. The soldier had used some rubbish about the Australian Defence Force but these guys were no more part of the ADF than a bag of turds. Where were the Australian soldiers?

Mark looked at Raven. Her face was stricken, pale, despite the heat. She was desperate he didn't try anything. Maybe she knew something Mark didn't; something they had said.

When he looked back, the soldier had drawn the machine gun up to Mark's face. He spoke in a low, calm, voice, but his words were strong and clipped. "Put your hands up and step away from the car."

Maybe now wasn't the time. At last, Mark put up his hands and stepped aside. But he would remember the scar on that face. He joined Raven and stood beside her.

Raven had tears in her eyes. Mark wanted to ask what was wrong but didn't want to reveal that she understood their language.

Scar Face climbed into the Jeep, turned it on and then circled around. The second soldier in Mr. Buckley's Ford did the same, and then they were speeding away back towards Whittlesea. Mindy barked with savage intensity.

"Arrggghhh!" Mark screamed. "Bastards!" He walked in a circle, watching the back of each vehicle disappear around the first corner. "What did they say?"

"Oh, Mark, he said that if you made a move, he'd shoot you in the leg and gouge out your eye. Leave you disfigured for life."

Mark's shoulder slumped. "Savage." Raven nodded. "Jesus."

"That main soldier was horrible. The other guy was not so bad, he wanted to give us the rest of our stuff but the first guy wouldn't let him. He said to let us starve like the mangy dogs we were."

"We've got to get to the campsite."

"How far?"

"Not long. Maybe ten, fifteen minutes."

"Let's get going then."

FORTY-THREE

P arker stumbled through the brush and out onto the edge of the campsite beside his Toyota Hilux Ute. Clayton Smith spotted him first and surprise registered on his face. Brad Moxon was also there, loading more of Parker's stuff onto the growing pile. Harrison Bowe, too, an African-American guy who had moved to Australia the year before on a sporting scholarship. He hung on the fringes of the group and wasn't a bad bloke; Parker was surprised to see him with the others. Harrison stood under the Coleman gazebo picking up stuff that had fallen off the table. Where was Whitehead? Parker glanced around, looking for their quasi leader, the most dangerous of all four, but he was nowhere to be seen.

Clayton stuffed his mouth with two-minute noodles from a packet, dropping them all over the ground.

"What the hell are you doing, man? Just stop," Parker said, raising the shotgun.

Clayton dropped the packet of noodles and backed away. "Whadda ya gonna do, man? Shoot us?"

Harrison's face was blank, and he wasn't moving. Moxon laughed. "One against three, mate. Where's Turner? Oh, that's right, you guys aren't mates anymore. Now if he was here, we'd be a little more concerned."

Parker took in the scene, feeling a mixture of anger and disbelief wash over him. They had unloaded most of the food and supplies from the tent and kicked it over, pulling out the pegs for fun, and now it had sunk to the ground like a deflated balloon. The canopy had been torn off the back of the Ute and kicked aside. The gas lantern was gone. Parker had spotted them loading the butane cooker into their trailer, too. If they left now with what they'd taken, Parker and the others would have nothing left with which to run a campsite.

"Why are you doing this?" Parker asked. "This is my stuff."

"Really?" Clayton said. "We didn't know."

"Our stuff," Sam said, appearing from the scrub.

Clayton's eyes narrowed. "How many more of you are there?"

Parker said nothing. A moment later, the two girls appeared through the brush and stepped into the clearing.

"Whoa, reinforcements," Clayton said. "We're done for now."

"Where's Whitehead?" Parker asked. Until he knew Whitehead's whereabouts, the risk of ambush was still high.

Brad smiled. "Around."

"Like Parker said, boys, you need to give this stuff back and piss off out of here."

"What stuff?" Brad asked.

"The stuff you've taken that's ours."

Clayton chuckled. "Not yours. Prove it?"

"Prove it?" Parker lifted the gun. "Prove that I set up this camp. That we brought half this stuff from the Henry's Camping Store in Whittlesea? Let's go ask Jake Henry himself and see what he says." Brad shrugged. Parker added. "I should shoot you in the leg for wrecking the canopy on my Ute."

"It was wrecked already," Clayton said. "A tree had fallen on it."

"Bullshit," Jas said. "You're such an ass, Clayton. Nothing changes, does it? I bet you still can't spell your name properly." Brad laughed. Clayton gave a false smile, then sneered.

"What do you think the cops are going to say when we report this?" Maise asked. "I know my uncle's not going to be happy."

Brad's expression dissolved. Clayton said, "We don't think the cops are gonna have time to worry about this. Too many other problems right now."

"But eventually," Sam said, "They're going to look into it. And you guys are going to have to answer."

"Maybe," Clayton shrugged. "That's a chance we're willing to take."

"We can't let you leave with this stuff," Parker said. "It's just not gonna happen."

"Oh, yes, it is," Clayton said, walking towards Parker. The charade of humor and joking was gone, replaced by anger which Parker realized might tip over the edge at any moment.

Parker raised the shotgun and pointed it directly at Clayton. "Keep coming."

"Oh, you got me," Clayton joked. "You're not gonna shoot me, man. You'd be more worried about the cops."

Harrison spoke for the first time in his mid-west accent. "Come on guys. This is nuts. Let's just get out of here, Clay."

"Shut up, Harry. I told you earlier, piss off if you don't want to be part of this." Harrison shoved his hands into the pockets of his jean shorts.

Parker spoke: "As you said, Clayton, the cops have got too many other things to worry about."

Clayton had walked part of the way across the camp. Now, he glanced down towards the trailer. Parker followed his gaze to a shotgun lying against its wheel.

"What's that?" Parker asked. Maise was closest. "Grab the gun, Maise."

All eyes were on the shotgun now. Brad laughed and then sprinted towards the trailer. Maise did the same, racing to get hold of it.

"She's not gonna pick that thing up" Clayton said. "She's the nicest person in the town. She'd never shoot us. Might shoot herself though."

Maise won, snatching up the weapon before Moxon could even mobilize his overweight body halfway there.

"I don't want to disappoint you, guys," Maise said. She opened the chamber and checked it was loaded.

"You're not gonna shoot us, hon," Moxon said.

"Don't call me that," Maise said, moving back towards Jas and Sam. She brought the gun up to her site. "I'm not going to shoot you? Just try me. I've got nothing to lose, either. We're stuck here for now and we want *our* stuff."

It was a tense moment. They wouldn't take on Sam and Parker. He was proud of Maise. He had no doubt she'd have picked up the weapon and thought maybe, if pushed, she would shoot at one of the guys. They now had the advantage of the situation before Keith returned.

From the other side of Parker's Hilux Ute came movement. Keith Whitehead stepped around behind Maise.

"Maise!" Parker shouted. Jas did the same.

But it was too late. Whitehead snatched the gun from her hands. Maise spun, grabbed at it, but Keith stepped back out of her reach.

"Uh-uh," he said, smiling.

"Are you serious, Keith?" Maise asked. Her tone was fearful, urgent.

"Things change. Sorry."

"You idiot. And it's a big fat no to your question about catching up for a coffee."

Keith walked across the clearing and handed the gun to Moxon, who took it with a gleeful expression. "Thank you, sir." He lifted it into position and pointed it at Parker.

Parker turned the gun towards Moxon and Whitehead. "You'll pay for this."

"Maybe," Keith said, walking towards Parker. "But what about the people that smashed up my house? Stole all the food? My family's got nothin' left. My parents had to take my little brothers away because their beds got cut up." He wiped an arm across his sweaty forehead. "Yeah. Life ain't fair, is it?"

Parker adjusted the shotgun, bringing Keith's head into sight. Would he really shoot Keith? He wanted to; wished he had the guts to pull the trigger and prevent the man from bothering anybody ever again. But Parker was too practical, and since he'd been off the booze, he had a much greater sense of responsibility and forethought. Being drunk had often limited his ability to think of consequences. Now, it was starker and more obvious than ever.

"You're not gonna shoot me, Richardson. You're too smart. You know you'd end up in jail, whenever this thing is over."

Parker willed himself to press the trigger. Even a stomach or a leg shot. He lowered the angle of the shotgun, focusing on Keith's right thigh.

His finger quivered over the trigger. *Do it.*

And then it was too late.

Keith grabbed the barrel and twisted it aside. Parker had been so focused on pulling the trigger his response was slow and then Keith had the weapon in his hand.

Keith laughed. Parker took a step back. Now they had both guns. Parker flushed with disappointment in himself. He glanced at Maise, and saw none of it on her face, only concern.

"Don't look at her," Keith said. "She can't help you." Keith tossed the shotgun aside towards Clayton Smith. "Now, I'm gonna do something I should have done years ago."

Keith lunged forward and struck at Parker's stomach. Parker tried to defend it, but he was too slow and the fist hit him in the upper abdomen, pushing the wind from his lungs. He bent over, sucking in a breath.

"Leave him alone, you ass," Maise said.

Keith put up a hand. "Stay back, Maise. This is between Richardson and me. We've had this beef for years."

Maise stopped. "Why are you doing this?"

Instinct told Parker to run. He'd never been a strong fighter and Keith was renowned for both his temper and the use of his fists. This wouldn't end well, but he refused to flee, either.

Parker struck back, throwing a right fist upwards at Keith. It glanced his shoulder as Keith twisted sideways, hitting the soft flesh beneath his collarbone. Keith's cheek twitched and Parker knew there had been some pain in the strike.

"Gotta be quicker than that," Keith said.

Keith fired a left punch, bouncing off Parker's forearm as he tried to block it, but it snuck through and struck Parker high on the cheek. His face stung and his legs buckled. Keith struck twice more, hitting Parker on the nose and the forehead with a smack of flesh. Pain erupted in his face. His vision spun and suddenly he was falling.

He hit the ground, something sharp jabbing into his back. He rolled onto all fours, his world still spinning, but he recognized Keith stepping towards him. *Get up.* From the corner of his eye, he spotted Maise running at Keith. Parker tried to stand. He crawled onto one knee as Maise pushed Keith.

"Stop it!" she screamed, her voice quaking.

Face twisted in anger, Keith turned his back on her. Not to be deterred, Maise ran around in front of him. She tried to block his way but he pushed through. Maise raise a hand and slapped him across the face. Keith froze. So did Maise. Suddenly Keith recoiled and looped a fist around, punching Maise in the cheek. She fell sideways into a bush.

Parker leapt up, screaming. He jumped at Keith, hands reaching for his throat. Keith tried to wrench him away, but Parker's momentum was too much. They collided and fell backwards onto the dirt.

Parker cocked his fist and struck, first at Keith's stomach, hitting the bones of his rib cage, once, twice, three times, Keith groaning with each punch. Parker swung again for Keith's face, but Keith managed to deflect the fist with his shoulder. He felt Keith lifting him, and then Parker began to lose his position, his weight not enough to hold Keith down.

Sensing he was about to be thrown off, Parker jabbed a hard right fist at Keith's face. Soft bone mashed under his knuckles and Keith cried out in pain.

"Bastard!"

But it unleashed Keith's fury and he shoved Parker off, then rolled so he was sitting atop Parker, one of his knees pinning Parker's arm.

Keith struck with his right fist first, then his left, elbows pumping. Parker put his arms and hands up and deflected a few shots, but every second one struck his face or head. Pain engulfed him.

Then Maise was back, shoving Keith aside. He fell, losing his advantage, and when Parker pushed him further, it allowed Parker to slither away.

"You're such an ass," Maise sobbed.

Smiling, Keith climbed to his feet and walked over towards Clayton Smith.

"Are you okay?" Maise asked. Parker nodded. She tried to smile, but there was pain and worry in it. She walked back towards where Keith had first struck her and snatched her hat up from the grass.

Breathing heavily, Parker climbed onto one knee, his face aching in several places. One eye had begun to swell shut. He tasted blood in his mouth. Through his good, eye, he saw Keith also had a cherry high on one cheek where Parker had connected. *At least that was something*, he thought.

Keith reached out for the police-issue shotgun and Clayton handed it to him. Parker had a bad feeling.

"We're taking all of this stuff," Keith said, out of breath. He checked the chamber was loaded. "And you ain't gonna do anything about it." He raised the shotgun and pointed it at Parker. "But first, I'm gonna finish this once and for all."

It came down to this then, Parker thought. Not anything close to what he had expected when he had reached Whittlesea yesterday afternoon.

A rustle in scrub sounded behind Keith. They all turned towards it; branches snapping; the crunch of dry summer leaves. Something was moving towards them. A deep, menacing growl sounded at the last moment and Parker braced himself, waiting for Keith Whitehead to shoot him dead.

FORTY-FOUR

The one consolation for Mark and Raven was that they were able to get close to Hell Ridge before the soldiers in the Jeep had caught up to them. Still, they had walked in the heat and that had been no fun, using the shade of the roadside scrub where possible, but sometimes, it crawled back from the dusty, rocky edge of the blacktop and the sun would beat down on them and there was no escaping. Mark hadn't brought a hat, his neck and ears getting more burnt by the minute. Raven had to suffer for having black hair. It hadn't taken her long to remove a t-shirt from the pack and cover her head and face.

They trudged the mile or so with Mindy falling in at their heels, feeding her water from one of the bottles in Raven's pack she had kept with her in the front seat. It also had a box of snacks, a bag of rice, and some headache tablets. Mark carried the other pack with bottled water, some toiletries and a change of clothes. Thankfully, the soldiers had allowed them to keep both.

"So pissed off," Mark said. "How can they do that?"

"You're lucky he didn't shoot you," Raven said. "The soldier with the little moustache was close."

"Scarface?"

"Yeah. He was scary. He looked like he wanted to do it."

Mark felt his anger bubbling underneath. He had to admit the soldiers had spooked him a little. He had nothing to fight back with, no control of the situation. He was used to having control. "I didn't know how far I could push them."

"I think we're lucky they let us go."

"I think you might be right."

They walked the final slope, curling around to the left, withstanding the worst of the sun, at a slow, tired pace.

"This is it," Mark said as they reached the top of the hill. It was hotter than he remembered Egypt being in September when they had sailed down the Nile just before his father had gotten sick.

Mindy whimpered as she lay down in the shade. Mark dropped the clothes bags into the dust and crouched beside his dog. Tongue rolling from her mouth, Mindy peered down the track that led to the campsite. They could afford a few minutes rest. "You all right, girl?" He scratched her neck and behind her ears. Mindy's tail wagged. She whimpered again though. It was unusual to hear her make that noise, and it usually meant something unnerved her.

"What is it? Something down there you don't like?" Mark peered down the track but it dipped and only mottled green treetops filled his view.

"Come on," Raven said. "I'm sick of standing around in the heat."

Mark stood, collected up the bags and started walking, whistling Mindy to his side. "It's only going to be a little better down there, you know. Some shade, a little bit of breeze."

"A lot of shade and a lot more breeze. And the water. Won't be the first time we've swum in the creek."

They skidded down the dusty road, sliding from one gnarled tree root to another. Mindy had no problem cutting her way in a crisscross pattern. It was just past halfway down the track that they heard the voices.

"Sounds like they're arguing already," Raven joked.

The trail curved, with the big tree on the corner blocking their view. After they rounded it, Mark felt a jolt of concern when he spotted the slotted front grill of a vehicle poking out from between thick trees at the campsite entrance.

"I know that car." His stomach dropped. It was Keith's car, the one he should have collected the previous day. "Oh, shit. Those assholes... I can't believe they came up here." He wondered if his conversation with Keith where he had mentioned that Parker was camping up near Hell Ridge, had tipped him off. Keith was the kind of guy that would stir up trouble whenever he got the chance. "If Parker's here too, there's going to be fireworks," Mark said. "Probably over Maise. Keith still likes her." Voices drifted to them again. There was a sting in the tone. "They're arguing. Something's happening."

Realization swept over Raven's face. "Let's go."

They slid down the hill, keeping to the right of the vehicle so they couldn't be spotted. Mark called Mindy to his side. "Hey girl," he said, reconnecting the leash he'd removed walking up the big hill. "You be quiet, okay? Keep close to me." It was going to be a challenge. Normally she was playful and fun, but the moment she sensed harm against someone she knew, the antagonist would face her wrath.

Reaching the bottom of the slope, they leapt over deep ruts, avoided infant blackberries and long discarded tree limbs, before finally, the scrub beckoned. Mark led them through the first wall of rough shrubs and thin, spindly trees. They had to slide their way between trunks and over sharp, prickly plants, before finding a thin gap in the hedge of brush where they observed a sketchy view of the campsite. Mark scanned the undergrowth for the heaviest length of tree branch he could find and came up with a piece about two feet long and an arm's thickness.

Raven peered through the thicket. "I can see Clayton Smith," Raven said, brushing hair away from her face. "He's just standing there. Sam and Jas too. They're all looking at something. Oh, Jesus, Brad's got a shotgun pointed at Sam."

"Where's Maise?" Mark asked.

"She's... oh wait, there she is, standing near Sam and Jas. Where's Parker?"

It was difficult to see exactly what was happening. Mark adjusted his view by shifting a tree branch, holding Mindy tight on the lead. He spotted Parker, whose bruised and bloody face looked worse than Mark had seen in their toughest of fights. "There he is. He's on one knee. Keith's got..."

"He's got a *shotgun* pointed at Parker," Raven whispered. "Oh, shit, Mark. Keith's going to shoot him."

Mark was surprised at the flare of anger he felt seeing Parker beaten and in the sights of Keith's gun. He did not expect it. He started to stand, pulling Mindy up, but the dog had spotted something and she gave a deep, angry growl. What did he do? Keith could be crazy. Maise was there too, so she was at risk. Mark wouldn't let anything happen to her.

"You've got to help."

At the very least, he would find out what was going on and make sure Maise was safe.

Mindy launched herself forward, pulling away from Mark, but his fingers tightened around her lead. She gave another desperate lurch and yanked his arm forward, then she was away, pulling him through the bushes towards the clearing.

FORTY-FIVE

Mindy, Mark's kelpie-cross appeared from a wall of scrub at the edge of the clearing. Mark followed, trying to restrain her with a lead. Raven popped out between two shrubs, and when Mark managed to halt Mindy, he handed the lead to Raven. But Mindy spotted Keith and began barking at him.

"Down, Mindy," Mark said to the dog. Raven leant back on the lead. Mark turned back to Keith. "What's going on?"

"Get out of here," Keith said, shifting from one foot to the other. He had an anxious look in his eye, adjusting the gun in his hands as though looking for a more comfortable position. Parker sensed Keith was angry and wondered if he'd been smoking something. Keith lowered the shotgun. "This is between me and Richardson."

"That so?"

Keith lifted it back into sight and his finger twitched over the trigger. Parker watched the barrel line up with his head. Jesus, he was going to do it.

"They came and messed up all our stuff," Parker said. Mark appeared to be neutral right now and Parker would try anything to sway him to their side, even if a few hours ago that had seemed impossible. "Stole some of it. Some of it *we* brought back in the day."

Mark surveyed the scene. "Gotta say I wasn't happy you

backed out on the deal for the car," Mark said. "You owe me the money I paid up front."

Keith laughed. "You're not stupid, Turner. As if I was going to give it up after everything that's happening. But I'll pay your money back." Mark ground his jaw, watching Keith.

Parker tried to stand on one knee, but he overbalanced and tumbled into a heap. He felt like a fool. His face ached; his nose, his cheek, even his ribs were sore. He pushed off both hands and made it onto his knees and when he looked up again, Mark was standing beside him. He had not felt such surprise in a very long time. Parker looked up at his old friend, but Mark was staring at Keith.

"You're not gonna shoot, him, Keith," Mark said. "I get the rivalry, sure. I even get the fight for my sister. But this ain't gonna get her back."

"Too late for that. Now I just want revenge."

"Revenge for what?" Maise asked.

Keith tipped the barrel at Parker. "He stole you from me."

"What?" Maise asked.

"He was chasing after you while we were still a couple. It wasn't long after we broke up that you two got together."

"So you're gonna shoot him for it?" Mark asked.

Keith lined up the site again. "Too right."

Mark stepped in front of Parker. "No, you're not."

"Watch me."

Keith fired and the gun cracked like a thunderclap. *We're dead,* Parker thought. Mindy yelped. They weren't dead, but Mark was sprinting at Keith and Parker wondered how that could end well.

FORTY-SIX

A rivalry that had endured for more than twenty years, through cricket and football games, in school sports, and over girls, was finally about to end. Mark knew if he didn't get the better of Keith, the bastard would shoot him. Mark would do whatever it took to save his own life or his friends for that matter, and Parker fell into that category, even if it was on the fringes.

Mark sprinted towards Keith, blocking his line of sight to Parker. It was suicidal, but he hoped Keith would be less likely to shoot him than Parker. He had to get the shotgun away from Keith —he looked apprehensive, almost as if he'd been doing drugs—it was the kind of look Mark had seen a few times before they stopped hanging out.

"Move," Keith shouted at Mark, stepping sideways to get a view of Parker.

Mark did not. He reached Keith and grabbed for the barrel, pushing it aside, and then yanked on it, attempting to snatch the shotgun away. But Keith fought back, twisting his hands and arms. Mark pulled the gun and Keith closer with his stronger right hand, then thrust his left fist over Keith's and struck him flush on the cheek. Keith's head rocked back and the gun came loose in Mark's hands.

As he brought it around into his possession, something clob-bered him in the side, knocking the breath from him, and he fell, hitting the ground with both hands and losing the shotgun. Clayton Smith had been the perpetrator, and now he dived for the free weapon. Mark had no chance of reaching it before him and Smith picked it up, eying his prize. Mark prepared himself for an attack, when Parker arrived, knocking Smith to the ground with a thundering tackle.

Keith. Pain exploded across Mark's back and he fell flat onto his stomach, dirt puffing into his eyes. He wiped at his face and jerked his head around, spotting Keith standing over him with a length of broken tree branch. He swung again as Mark pushed onto one knee and the branch cracked in two across Mark's back, bits of bark and wood exploding. This time he didn't go down, forcing himself to climb onto his feet, suppressing a groan, pain coming in waves through his body. This wasn't going to plan.

With his weapon broken, Keith returned to basics as Mark gathered his balance and turned to face his enemy. A fist crashed into Mark's jaw and he spun, pain erupting across the side of his head; he inadvertently spun around in a full circle and then Keith was at him again, swinging his fists in a blur. Mark took a step back for the first time in his life, giving himself room to parry the attack, but Keith did not let up, firing back and forth with both fists as if he recognized that this was his moment, when Mark was at his weakest and ripe for defeat. Mark regained balance, facing Keith front on, and as it had always been, Mark seemed to have an acute sense of where Keith's punches were directed. Using his forearms to block them away, Mark countered, firing two long left jabs that both missed their target, but forced Keith to step back and cease his rapid-fire attack.

Mindy darted in between them, barking at Keith, complete with her own bright red wound that must have come from an earlier shot.

"BACK, MINDY, STAY BACK!"

The dog was going to end up tripping him over. Mark stepped in front of Mindy and she finally limped away under a barrage of barking.

Another gunshot sounded. Mark snapped his head right and

saw Sam and Brad Moxon fighting over the gun, now pointed towards Maise and Raven.

At the final moment, he spotted Keith's fist en route to his face. Mark managed to duck and it glanced the side of his head. Now, Keith was in close, throwing strong uppercuts. Mark needed a killer strike. Using his elbows to defend again, Mark jabbed another long left targeting Keith's nose, and it struck the side, forcing him to stop punching. One hand went to his face, leaving him open, and Mark followed it with a right fist to his stomach. The gut shot worked, Keith exhaling in surprise and both hands dropped their guard. Mark stepped forward; slanting his hips and loading up his torso with power, then thrust his shoulder and right arm forward, focusing on the corner of Keith's chin.

The punch glanced off Keith's jaw; had it struck flush, it might have knocked his head off, Mark thought. Keith staggered forward, head down, his feet disobeying him. This was Mark's chance to close it out.

Another gunshot sounded. Was that the second or third? Mark couldn't be sure. He heard someone scream, but he couldn't stop now.

Intent on finishing, Mark went after Keith with a solid left, then a short right, connecting with both sides of his face. Keith's head rolled, his arms dropped. He looked back at Mark, his face full of surprise, and Mark threw a final right hook that connected with Keith's left eye.

His legs collapsed and Keith fell onto his back.

"JAS!" Raven screamed.

Mark turned and saw Jas lying twisted in the rough grass, Raven and Maise surrounding her. He started towards them, Sam sprinting to her inert body. It looked as though she'd been shot.

As he reached Jas, Mark turned back, realizing he had given Keith a moment. Sensing he was going to lose, Keith rolled away and scampered clear into the undergrowth.

FORTY-SEVEN

Parker had watched Mark run in front of him to prevent Keith from taking aim and shooting Parker, as he had promised. It was a brave move from Mark and had almost surprised Parker more than the situation itself.

As Keith and Mark wrestled for the gun, Parker wondered who would win in a fight between them—Keith had a furious temper and *could* fight, while Mark craved the physical nature of football and had countless times ended up punching on with someone. Parker had never seen him beaten.

Parker climbed onto his feet, looking for an opportunity to help, but Mark quickly wrestled the gun free before the fight had really begun.

Clayton Smith sprinted in from the side and tackled Mark. The blow sounded like a bag of sand hitting concrete. Mark fell, lost the gun and it spilled into the scraggy ground cover. Smith, recovering from the tackle, crawled like a spider over the ground towards the weapon.

Mark was torn, but quickly realized he wasn't going to beat Smith to the gun. Only twelve feet away, Parker raced at Smith, desperate to stop him wielding it once he took hold. As Smith seized the shotgun, Parker leapt at him, ignoring all the aches and pains in his body. Smith wasn't as volatile as Keith, but he could be stupid and careless, and he could end up shooting someone, even if it wasn't his intent.

They collided, Smith with his hands on the shotgun, Parker groping for it. They went down in a tangled ball, Smith elbowing, Parker thrusting his knees to try to dislodge the weapon from Smith's hands. Neither would relent, both fighting with white-knuckle strength, each breathing heavily; grunting and groaning as they battled. Smith had one hand at the top and one at the bottom; Parker had both hands in the middle. The barrel pointed away from them and it was going to be a case of who was strong enough to turn the end around to face their enemy.

Clayton started winning. The effect of the long ride and a long walk followed by a fight with Keith was taking a toll on Parker as his strength began to wane. He could no longer keep a strong grip on the weapon and his fingers began to slip away. Both men wore lines of tension on their faces, sweat beading on their foreheads, cheeks reddening. Slowly, the shotgun started to turn and Clayton moved his lower hand towards the trigger. Parker grunted, pushing Clayton's hand away, but it reduced his pressure on resisting the turn, and the gun moved closer towards his fate.

It was like watching the slow hand of a clock turn. The realization that Clayton Smith was going to win this battle dawned on Parker. Would Clayton shoot him? Would Parker die at the campsite he had visited since he was a little boy?

The weapon was now pointed at Parker's chest. He scratched at Clayton's fingers as they fumbled for the trigger. Panic surged. Parker was seconds from being shot. He thought about Maise and that he'd never get back together with her. He had to let go of the gun. There was no other way. He released his right hand, trying to maintain pressure against Clayton with the other, and punched at Clayton's hand with the back of this fist.

There was a loud thump and suddenly the gun came loose. Parker looked up and saw Maise standing with a length of wood. She had smashed it down onto Clayton's arm and he released the gun. She swung a second time and thumped the piece across his shoulder, knocking him away from Parker. Now Parker had the shotgun. He would throw it aside and they would fight it out with their fists. But Clayton wasn't done yet. He grabbed for the gun again, despite Maise smashing the broken tree branch onto him a third time. Parker tried to twist it away, but Clayton wouldn't have it, and again, he renewed his attempts to turn the weapon back onto Parker.

Parker realized there was only one outcome that would end with him still alive. He pushed the end of the gun into Clayton's chest. The other man's eyes widened. Parker went for the trigger. Clayton tried to close his hand over it. The gun recoiled, the sound deafening. Clayton Smith's body jumped, as though it had been shocked with electricity. Parker slumped aside, breathless.

FORTY-EIGHT

C layton Smith was dying. Parker stood over him and picked up the shotgun, watching his stomach heave in and out, his eyes wide, full of terror and knowing. A dark, bloody wound showed at the top of his chest, a wound Parker had accidentally delivered with the Stevens shotgun.

The shock of what had happened slowly pervaded Parker; he wanted to take it back now, have a different outcome to this, but Smith had tried with every ounce of his strength to kill Parker. There was nothing he could do, was there? Smith's friends were gone; Whitehead had fled and Brad Moxon had snuck away into the bushes, leaving Smith to die. Parker watched, considering what he could do. There was a first aid kit in the Ute. He might be able to— Smith's eyes stopped moving, then his chest. Parker waited for him to blink again, for him to take another breath. But it did not come. Smith was dead. A cold shiver touched the back of Parker's neck.

He turned away from Smith and limped towards the others who stood around Jasmine and Mindy, who had taken a hit too.

Sam sat hunkered over Jas, sobbing, his face pressed against her chest. It struck Parker that she was gone too. Their friend had died. Any guilt or sadness at Clayton Smith's death was replaced by the loss of Jas. It felt surreal, unreal. Her eyes stared up at the trees, forever open. He tried to speak, but his mouth wouldn't work.

There were no words. Maise sat by Jas' side, holding her hand and weeping. Parker squatted, placed a hand on Sam's shoulder and reached out the other to Maise. She took it, looking at him with tears spilling down her cheeks, and squeezed. Parker wondered how Jas had been shot. He'd seen Sam and Moxon fighting and heard several shots, so he assumed a stray bullet had struck her.

"We were supposed to get married," Sam cried. He sat up, fumbling into his pocket. A sickly feeling filled Parker's stomach remembering the previous day when Sam had told him about the imminent proposal. Sam's fingers clasped something and then he pulled out a small blue box and opened it. He took the ring from its slot, holding it out to Jas as though she might take it, hand shaking. "I was meant to propose up here." He lay the ring on her chest and his head fell into her belly, sobbing.

Parker had not felt heartache like this for someone else since he watched his father cry over this mother's death. It was too difficult to see, and he turned away.

Mark was nearby, with Mindy's head in his lap. Raven stroked the dog's neck. Mindy had also been shot and Parker suspected all the running around and barking had made the wound worse. Her chest rose and fell rapidly, and she had a bloody wound on her back flank.

"Please," Mark said to Raven. "You have to fix her."

"She need's a vet," Raven said.

"Vet?" Mark said. "What vet? There are no vets, Raven. You're the best vet we've got right now."

"How bad is it?" Parker finally managed.

"It's a flesh wound, that much is good," Raven said. "But she's in shock. We need to treat it."

"We have a first aid kit—well we did. I can check." Raven nodded.

Parker stood and went to the Hilux, glancing at Jas' body. Sam stroked her face, brushing matted hair away. Maise had her own face in her hands. Parker stopped, went to Maise, and helped her onto her feet. She fell into his arms and sobbed. Parker hugged her, unable to take his eyes from Jas. Her face was peaceful; lips perfectly symmetrical, her eyes closed, long, dark lashes beautiful against her tanned skin. He should have been crying. He had loved her as a friend. She had been honest and loyal, always the first one to give an opinion, the one to stand up for her friends in a fight. Sometimes, she could be overbearing, but Parker would have taken a lifetime of that, rather than this. Sam would take a long time to recover. They had been going out for years now and in both their minds, marriage was part of the natural course. He only wished Jas had known how soon. Despite her strong opinions, she and Sam never fought. Sam was an agreeable guy, and their personalities had worked. A knot of sadness twisted Parker's insides. Life was not fair. He rubbed Maise's back. They stood like that for almost a minute, and then she let him go and squatted down beside Jas again. Parker headed for the Hilux.

Where had it all gone so wrong?

It had started with careless people who thought they could do whatever they wanted. It wasn't meant to have gone down this way. Parker didn't think they'd meant to shoot Jas or the dog, and he certainly didn't want to shoot Clayton Smith, but Clayton would have killed Parker if he hadn't fought back. And given his intent, Clayton may well have shot others. Parker imagined Maise lying in Jas' place. As friends, he loved Jas, but if Maise had been lying on the ground, Parker wouldn't have been able to go on.

Underneath the Hilux's front seat, Parker kept a large red first aid kit. It was one of the few things Whitehead and his crew hadn't stolen from the Ute. Parker leaned in and stuck his hand under the seat, then slid it out.

There were two dozen items including gauze pads, blood clotting gel, bandages, antiseptic cream and a host of other things essential for bites, stings, cuts, grazes and sprains.

Parker took the medical supplies to Raven and squatted beside Mindy. He rubbed the white patch on her head and scratched behind her black floppy ears. Her eyes went to him and she wagged her tail. Parker thought that was a good sign.

"Is... Jas gone?" Raven asked. Parker nodded, reached out and squeezed Raven's shoulder. Tears came to her dark eyes. "Oh my God. How did this happen?"

"How does anything like this happen? Stupid people."

"Where did the others go?"

Parker shrugged. "Moxon and Bowe ran off one way. White-head the other."

"Smith?"

"Dead."

Raven sat up. "Oh, no."

Parker said, "We wrestled for the gun. He honestly tried to shoot me. He ended up getting shot in the struggle." Parker thought he might feel guilty later, but for now, Smith had brought the accident on himself. Mark watched him with a steely expression, but said nothing.

The loud, ripping sound of a motorbike broke the peace and serenity of the forest. It came from the top of the trail, where Parker had left it on their way down. He knew instantly that one of the other men—Keith most likely—had found the bike. He supposed that was karma, given he had taken it from the stranger's property in the first place. Although he couldn't help but be more annoyed, for now, they had bigger problems.

Parker returned to Maise and Sam, still lying beside Jas' body. Sam continued to stroke her hair and Maise still held her hand. The reality of the situation had not become any less surreal, for Parker. He almost expected Jas to stand up and laugh, as though she had been pretending the whole time.

Eventually, Sam stood, though he found it difficult to take his eyes from his dead girl.

"I'm sorry, mate," Parker said. "I'm so sorry."

Sam's normally serene face had turned brooding; rigid jaw, eyebrows forked, eyes narrowed. It was clear that revenge had already swallowed his heart. "Where's Moxon? We've got to hunt him down and finish this."

Parker put a hand on his shoulder. "Take it easy, mate. He'll pay for what he did, rest assured. How did it happen?"

"We were fighting," Sam said. "For the gun. He kept waving it around and it went off. Jas was…"

There was a long silence. Parker had been right. Jas had been in the wrong place at the wrong time.

Maise asked, "What do we do with Jas' body?"

"They left their car behind. We should take it into town," Mark said.

"I'll do it," Sam added. "It's my job."

"We'll come with you," Maise said, touching his arm.

"No. I need some time alone, anyway."

Nobody could argue that. But Parker wondered whether it was best he do it on his own.

Mark spoke up. "I'm coming with you, Sam. I need to get Mindy to the vet."

Sam thought about this. He glanced down at the dog and looked at Mindy for a long time. Finally, he nodded. "Okay."

Raven asked, "what about the others? What if they come back?"

"None of them have weapons," Parker said. "We've got all the guns here. They try anything, they'll end up like their mate."

"Is this really happening?" Raven asked.

Parker felt a tiny bit of guilt for not being more upset, but he had done enough of that to last him a lifetime when his mother died. He felt the pain of losing Jas' as much as either of them; he would just internalize it until time had burned away the parts he couldn't handle.

"I can't help but think it might get a whole lot worse before it gets better," Parker said.

FORTY-NINE

Mark and Parker unhitched the trailer and removed all the supplies and equipment the others had taken from the campsite. The place was still a mess, but they would piece it back together and reassemble it close to how it had originally been. Maise tried to keep hold of her emotions as Mark and Parker carried Jas' body to the back seat of the Keith Whitehead's Commodore. It was still too soon to be real. She knew grief was coming. It would hit hard, she told herself, pushing aside all the things she would never get to do again with Jas.

There was a funeral home on the far edge of the main shopping strip in the town center. They had each mumbled agreement that it was the place to take Jas' body. They had discussed what to do with Clayton Smith's and it had caused an argument. Initially, Sam had refused to move it. They had all made small, sensitive comments to persuade him. Eventually, they carried it to the trunk and clumsily loaded it in. Maise felt like a mobster out of some movie.

Cloud cover rolled in and with it a slightly cooler southerly breeze, replacing the thick heat of the northerly. Rain was in the air, and as they said their goodbyes to Sam, Mark and Mindy, the first splatters fell. Raven had patched Mindy up by cleaning the wound, using a clotting gel to stop excessive bleeding, and gauze pads to soak up the remaining blood. The dog had whimpered a little but was lying in the shade on one of the sleeping mattresses Parker had restored. Mark carried her to the car and sat in the passenger seat with Mindy on his lap. It almost looked comical. The plan was to find anti-biotic for her in case the wound became infected. They each gave the dog a scratch behind the ears and wished her good luck, while Raven and Mark said their goodbyes in a personal way.

Parker stood at the door looking at Mindy. Maise wondered if he and Mark were going to acknowledge each other. She felt certain it wouldn't be Mark to initiate the action.

"Hey, man," Parker said. Mark looked around. "Thanks for... the help. Don't know how it would have turned out if you guys hadn't arrived."

"No sweat. Look after Maise, will you?"

"You bet."

Parker turned away and headed towards Sam. She had been surprised when Mark had stepped in front of Keith as he threatened to shoot Parker. This gave her hope that all was not lost.

"Take care, mate," Parker said, giving the taller man an awkward hug. Sam nodded. His grief was far too raw for words. "I'm just so sorry about Jas."

The others hugged Sam and said their final goodbyes to Jas, who they had wrapped in a sheet. Sam got into the car with a blank expression, his tears had stopped, but there was a hint of determination on his face, as though if he got this bit done, he could face what was next.

Maise, Parker and Raven watched the rumbling Commodore climb the jagged track in fits and starts. It wasn't made for such a bumpy trail and Maise wondered if it had sustained any damage getting down to the site. When the rectangle taillights were finally out of sight, Maise and Raven hugged, sobbing into each other's shoulders.

The rain began to fall heavier, tapping the roof of the Hilux and the flattened tent in thick drops. The Coleman gazebos were still standing. They all hurried beneath one as the summer thunderstorm moved in overhead.

Parker spoke first, turning to Maise, after they had all spent several minutes watching the rain. "How's your face? I can't believe that asshole hit you." Maise touched her swollen cheek. It was sore and would bruise up if it hadn't already. She still found it hard to believe what Keith had done. He reached out and touched her arm. "Thanks for coming to my rescue. Honestly, Clayton was close to shooting me." Maise smiled. "You saved my life."

Maise had acted on instinct; Parker was in danger and she was compelled to stop it. "I just acted. I didn't even think about it. I could see he was going to shoot you. I picked up the big stick and…"

"I'm glad you did."

Raven gave a pained smile. "What about the others? It worries me that they might come back."

"Whitehead's gone. I reckon he's taken the motorbike. I don't think he'll come back." In the distance, the gentle rumble of thunder sounded. "As for the other two, Moxon will head back to Whittlesea. Bowe… not sure. He didn't even take part in the fight. Seemed like he didn't want to be there. I don't think we'll see him again, either."

"What's the plan now?" Raven asked, putting an arm around Maise's shoulders.

Maise took a deep breath and let it out in a spirited sigh. "Well, who knows what's left in Whittlesea. The Chinese military are moving about. We just lost… one of our closest friends." She took a moment then. "Sam has left. Mark and Mindy, too, but, they'll be back, I'm sure." Parker gave her a wink. "So, in light of that, we need to clean up this place." She looked around at the site. "Try and fix the tent. Set the table back up, the cooker and the gas lamp. Those idiots messed it all up but they didn't take anything and aside from the canopy on your Hilux, Parker, everything seems okay."

"Yeah it does."

"And you and Mark had the first conversation in months where one of you didn't scream at the other." Parker nodded acceptance. "One foot in front of the other, right?" Maise added.

"I'll go with that," Raven said.

"What about the police?" Parker asked. "They're going to want to talk to me. I accidentally killed Smith."

"Goddamn self-defense," Maise said. "I swear my uncle will back you all the way." Parker managed a thin, grateful smile.

Small indentations around the campsite had begun to fill with water, a welcome sight. It probably wouldn't last long, though. Summer thunderstorms at the end of a hot spell were common, but sparing. Tomorrow, it would be hot and humid again.

Through a patch in the high gums, Maise saw sheets of rain falling from sooty clouds, and below it, the vast width of Hell Ridge. Maise was looking for anything to think about other than Jas' death. She felt like she would lose herself at any moment and the tears might not stop. "Did you guys ever hear the stories about the treasure up there?" She pointed towards the bluff.

"Hell Ridge?"

"Yeah. Mrs. Wood told me about it while I was waiting with her at the medical clinic."

"Normy King lives up on the ridge. He mentioned it, too," Parker said. "There's an old mine dug into the side of the hill."

"Let's get this place cleaned up and I'll tell you what Mrs. Wood told me."

What would the next twenty-four hours bring? Maise could not even begin to imagine. But if it was anything like the last twenty-four, she didn't know how she would get through it. For the sake of those they had lost already though, they would fight on.

———

The story of Hell Ridge will continue in Invasion.

THANK YOU FOR READING BLACKOUT!

W e hope you enjoyed it as much as we enjoyed bringing it to you. We just wanted to take a moment to encourage you to review the book. Follow this link: Blackout to be directed to the book's Amazon product page to leave your review.

Every review helps further the author's reach and, ultimately, helps them continue writing fantastic books for us all to enjoy.

———

You can also join our non-spam mailing list by visiting www.subscribepage.com/AethonReadersGroup and never miss out on future releases. You'll also receive three full books completely Free as our thanks to you.

Facebook | Instagram | Twitter | Website

Want to discuss our books with other readers and even the authors? Join our Discord server today and be a part of the Aethon community.

———

ALSO IN SERIES:

Blackout
Invasion
Resistance

———

Looking for more great Post Apocalyptic books?

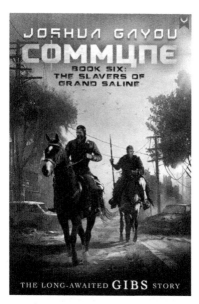

Eleven years after the fall... In the process of searching for Pinch, a long-lost mythic figure who has attained a talismanic status, Gibs has resorted to making a living doing contract work with his friend Alan, the young man who followed him out of the Wyoming commune. Hired by a family as escorts on a cross-country trip to Texas, they are ambushed by a group of raiders. The family is captured, children and all, and Gibs and Alan are left behind with only some pistols and a handful of bullets between them, and no food or water to speak of. They pursue the attackers, following the tracks left by the raiders until the trail goes cold a few days later. But evidence of further murders abounds in the region. The owner of a waystation informs them of a mining settlement out east in the fallen town of Grand Saline which operates on slave labor. Reasoning that their attackers were likely slavers, Gibs resolves to go to Grand Saline in search of the family. Settling in nearby Iron Bridge, as there is no evidence of slavery within its borders, they begin to plan. But nothing in Iron Bridge makes sense. A bizarre dual-class system is at play, its people are standoffish, and the town seems at odds with itself at every turn. Gibs and Alan are left to sound out the mysteries of this strange new place, determine what if any weaknesses Grand Saline has to exploit, and save the children from the slavers' salt mines.

Get Commune 6 now!

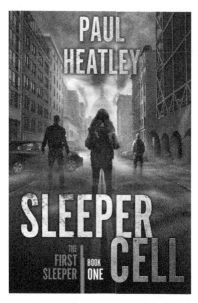

Eleven years after the fall... In the process of searching for Pinch, a long-lost mythic figure who has attained a talismanic status, Gibs has resorted to making a living doing contract work with his friend Alan, the young man who followed him out of the Wyoming commune. Hired by a family as escorts on a cross-country trip to Texas, they are ambushed by a group of raiders. The family is captured, children and all, and Gibs and Alan are left behind with only some pistols and a handful of bullets between them, and no food or water to speak of. They pursue the attackers, following the tracks left by the raiders until the trail goes cold a few days later. But evidence of further murders abounds in the region. The owner of a waystation informs them of a mining settlement out east in the fallen town of Grand Saline which operates on slave labor. Reasoning that their attackers were likely slavers, Gibs resolves to go to Grand Saline in search of the family. Settling in nearby Iron Bridge, as there is no evidence of slavery within its borders, they begin to plan. But nothing in Iron Bridge makes sense. A bizarre dual-class system is at play, its people are standoffish, and the town seems at odds with itself at every turn. Gibs and Alan are left to sound out the mysteries of this strange new place, determine what if any weaknesses Grand Saline has to exploit, and save the children from the slavers' salt mines.

Get Sleeper Cell Now!

For all our Sci-Fi books, visit our website.

AFTERWORD

Firstly, thanks for reading. I do hope you enjoyed the story. I wrote the bulk of this in the (Aussie) summer of 2021 and true to form, it sat there for most of 2021 after COVID-19 came back, left, came back, and so on. Initially, I outlined three books while we were camping at it was easy to get into the swing of what might happen sitting amongst the trees by the river drinking coffee at dawn each morning. Don't ask my why there was such a long time between writing and publishing. It's a condition. I am having therapy. If you enjoyed the first book, I hope you grab a copy of the second, because things really get going in book two where lots of loose ends will be tied up.

Once again, if you are able to leave a review on Amazon for this book (or any other of mine you've read) I'd be sincerely grateful. I can't understate the importance of reviews for an author. Often readers based their purchases solely on these.

If you haven't signed up to my mailing list, feel free to do so. It generally covers new book releases and every so often, I do a give-away of paperbacks from the series. **Click here to sign up.** Your e-mail address will never be shared and you can unsubscribe easily at any time.

Feel free to drop me a line about what you thought of the story, good or bad, or anything else. You can e-mail me at **owen.baillie@ bigpond.com.**

Thanks for reading,

Owen

Melbourne, Australia, September 2022.

Printed in Great Britain
by Amazon

27094500R00180